APRIL RENEGADE

B. G. WOLFE

Edited by
VIRGINIA TESI CAREY

Cover design by B. G. Wolfe
Editing by Virginia Tesi Cari
Proofreading by M. Richter
Beta readers: M. Richter, A. R. Rose, & Ashley Templin.

NOTE TO THE READER
WARNINGS & READER ADVISORY

Dear Reader,

Thank you for taking the time to read my debut novel. I hope you fall in love with Ash and Drew as I have. Please check the warnings below to ensure you do not run into anything that may be triggering to you. Thank you!

April Renegade is an MM romance with adult themes. It is intended for mature readers, and not recommended for readers under the age of 18. Possible triggering content includes: Sexual themes, recreational drug use, drug and alcohol abuse (mostly off-page), cheating, and mental illness (specifically Generalized Anxiety Disorder, Panic Disorder, Depression, and anxiety and panic attacks).

DEDICATIONS

To my wonderful husband, who hates reading but loves supporting me —I love you. Thank you for lifting me up in my darkest moments and for always making me laugh.

To my sweet friends Meaghan M., Shon H., and Ryn H. — thank you for always believing in me, for the long talks and life lessons, and for always staying true to who you are. I know that Meaghan is radiating her sunshine down on us each day.

Lastly, I dedicate this book to my Lele, who has given me unwavering support since the day we met, alongside lots of laughs and love. I'm super happy I met you, even if it was in a Statistics class.

CONTENTS

April Renegade   ix

Chapter 1   I
Chapter 2   3
Chapter 3   10
Chapter 4   15
Chapter 5   20
Chapter 6   31
Chapter 7   37
Chapter 8   42
Chapter 9   55
Chapter 10   65
Chapter 11   70
Chapter 12   79
Chapter 13   88
Chapter 14   98
Chapter 15   107
Chapter 16   112
Chapter 17   117
Chapter 18   123
Chapter 19   130
Chapter 20   138
Chapter 21   150
Chapter 22   157
Chapter 23   164
Chapter 24   167
Chapter 25   176
Chapter 26   189
Chapter 27   203
Chapter 28   212
Chapter 29   214
Chapter 30   225

Chapter 31   229

Chapter 32   233

Chapter 33   243

Chapter 34   249

Chapter 35   255

Three Years Later   261

Want more of Ash and Drew?   265

About the Author   267

APRIL RENEGADE

CHAPTER ONE

The only time I feel alive is under the glaring lights of the stage, music loud in my ears and bass heavy at the pit of my stomach. Even with my protective earplugs in, the thrill of the chaotic noise on all sides of me sends my pulse into a heated vibration that rolls through my body in tiny shocks.

There was a time when I was terrified to walk onto the stage. The screams from the crowd made me sweat. Back then, I was more thankful for the blinding lights that surrounded me because it made it harder to see the audience. It was always Drew; he grounded me before we stepped out from the hidden hallway and onto the stage in front of hundreds of fans. "You're doing it again," he would huff. "You're in your mind too much. Just let loose. Just be *you*."

The song picks up in tempo, heading straight for the crescendo.

"Take me in the dark, baby, take me to the moon," I sing at the top of my lungs before ending the lyrics at a high-pitched scream. Up, up, and away. *"Lift me up, baby, take me to your room...take me...take me..."*

The crowd loses their shit. They jump and mosh and go ballistic in the pit. It's almost impossible to tell with the lights in my eyes, but from what little I can see, it almost looks like a few brave souls are surfing the crowd.

I'm tempted to join them, but that would cut my very favorite part of the evening short.

"Thank you, Dallas!" I scream into the mic, voice raspy and as high as it can go.

Soon, the rest of the band joins me for a breathless, sweaty bow. Drew, my best friend and the drummer, lazily wraps a long, sticky arm around my shoulders. Brian, the lead guitarist, does the same on my other side. Sean, the bassist and my oldest friend, leaps up and joins us to stand by Brian, the same goofy smile he always has on after a show plastered on his face. Lastly, our guest musician, Trish, who has been helping us with the cello and piano this tour, comes to stand next to Drew.

Everyone knows we will be back for the encore, but still—this is my favorite part.

We rush from the stage into the backstage area. We are known for making our fans wait for their encore. First, the lights will fade until the room is pitch-black. Then, a small light show comes to life, using an instrumental mash-up of some of our more popular songs for the beat, and then gradually, one by one, we take the stage one last time and go completely ballistic.

It's what they want, after all. And I'd be lying if I said I didn't enjoy it just as much. I just have to tend to a few things before we come back on stage.

The energy from the crowd and the exhilaration from singing hypes me up and turns me on each and every show. I come the hardest in between the "last song" and the encore. It's rushed, it's sneaky, and the act is absolute perfection, even though it makes it hard to go back onto the stage sometimes afterwards.

CHAPTER TWO

10 YEARS EARLIER - APRIL 2012

I'd never really been to a concert before, unless you count a few low-key bands who played at the local bars and venues around town, as well as one orchestral concert my friend's parents dragged me and an old buddy of mine to when we were ten or so. My parents never gave a damn about my interest in music. If I played music aloud in my room, it had to be almost mute, otherwise, one of my parents (or both, in the worst-case scenarios) would bust open my door and fling my radio or my phone or whatever device I was using to play the music against the wall.

To date, I'd gone through an old iPod dock, a radio, another dingier radio, and two phones. Finally, I opted for headphones, which was usually fine, unless the music was on full volume. That would piss them off, too. For addicts who were typically passed out in the living room high or drunk, they had spectacular hearing.

Every night before bed, I curled up in my small twin-sized mattress, plugged in my headphones, got snuggled up under the scratchy quilt I'd had forever, and allowed myself to escape into dream world.

At school, I was kind of in with the cool kids, but not so popular that people flocked to me. I liked it that way. I made good grades, stayed after school to be with my friends instead of going home prematurely, and generally had a decent high school experience. I looked forward to going to school just because it meant I didn't have to be at home.

At night, I would stay up late and ponder what I'd do when school ended. I was a senior, and though I'd applied to a community college, a couple of universities, and a technical college just to see if I'd get in, each night as I listened to the music in the dark, the only thing I could picture for the future was myself on stage.

I only ever sang in private. The only people who had heard me sing were some of my friends, but that was when we were joshing around, singing at the tops of our lungs in my best friend Sean's beat up van. During those moments, I made sure my singing blended into the background of the car, terrified that even my closest friends might make fun of my voice.

Practicing my vocals while living with abusive parents who wanted nothing to do with me was a challenge to say the least. On Tuesdays and Thursdays, I stayed after school and practiced in the vacant chorus room before scarcely making it to the metro in time to catch the last ride to my parents' trailer home. It wouldn't be right to call it *my* home. It had never been mine, and they'd made sure I knew it every chance they got.

Other times, especially on the weekends when I didn't have a party to go to or a friend to hang with, I went to one of the parks either early in the morning or at dusk and practiced there. I would've gladly sung in the confines of a car if I'd been able to afford one for myself. Despite the lawn work I did, and all the cash I had saved up, my parents always seemed to sniff out my hidden stash. Of course, they'd always blow it all on booze or blow before I even realized it was gone.

I had no idea what to expect at a real-life concert, but as we rode into the city in Sean's beat up van that always reeked of stale weed and dank socks, my heart pounded harder and harder in my chest—

especially as we passed the D.C. monuments—that's when I knew we were close to the venue. We all knew parking would be an absolute bitch, but we'd manage. We were early, after all, which was a fucking miracle with how Sean drove, and how Ronnie was never on time for anything, *ever*.

I knew my friends were almost as excited as I was. Ronnie started to jump around in the van like a banshee on caffeine as we got closer and closer, and I'd lost count of how many times Sean had screamed, *"Hell yeah!"* as each new song came on over the speakers.

Blink-182. Simple Plan. All Time Low.

Fuck yeah.

The concert wasn't held at the Capital City Arena, which I was bummed about until Sean reassured me that smaller shows like the one we were headed to tended to be better. More personal. Less restricted. Sean knew his shit about music, so I trusted him. He had been playing bass for a few years and wanted to start a band of his own at some point.

For once, I could spend the weekend with my friends. More importantly, I didn't have to worry about tiptoeing around my folks all weekend. I was eighteen, and they were more than likely passed out by now, anyway. Fuck 'em. I doubted they'd even notice my absence.

The venue was called the Madder Hatter, and had been around since the early 90s. It was nestled in between a slimy dive bar and a McDonald's right in the middle of downtown. The sign for the Madder Hatter didn't have lights. Instead, the letters were burned onto a giant wooden sign.

It took us forever to find a parking spot, and the spot was sketchy at best. Ronnie and I told Sean we'd help pay if he got a parking ticket, because you just never knew in D.C.

My skin was buzzing with adrenaline by the time we made it to the line outside of the venue. We were far enough back in line for us not to be noticed, so we all took out our hidden flasks—bourbon for myself and vodka for Sean and Ronnie—clinked them together in a non-verbal toast, then downed a few sips before inching up in line.

A husky, deep throated laugh caught my attention from a few people in front of us.

The laugh was loud, but not in an obnoxious way. It was outgoing and personable—warm, even. I tilted my head a little to get a view of the person who owned that laugh. My breath caught in my throat as I took him in. Tall, and a little lanky, but in a good way. A way that told me he was probably around my age. He had a strong, defined nose that accentuated an even stronger jawline. It was hard to tell in the dark, but I thought I could make out a nose ring. Maybe even a lip ring? He wore a beanie, tight jeans that showed off lean, muscular legs, and a simple black hoodie because it was still a little chilly outside in D.C. at the beginning of April.

He was with a couple of his friends. He smacked the guy next to him on the shoulder and let off that laugh again. A small young woman, not even a total of five feet, bounced around the guys while her girlfriend who was a bit taller, stared off at nothing with a totally unamused expression on her face.

I brought my attention back to my own friends, realizing I'd zoned out for who knows how long. We were almost at the front of the line now, only a little bit behind the guy with the laugh and his buddies, who were showing their IDs to the security person. I didn't understand why this stranger's laugh affected me so much. Or why I kept trying to find him again, even as I conversed with Sean and Ronnie. Out of the corner of my eye, I kept looking around for him.

Finally, we made it inside. The line was shorter when we'd arrived, so we lucked out and got decent standing room near the front part of the pit. There wasn't a lot of room in the Madder Hatter, and I knew it would fill up quickly. In the back and on the sides of the dark-cast room were several reserved high-top tables adorned with tea lights. Above the stage and ground level, I spotted some more chairs and tables on the second floor. A couple of girls in cropped Blink-182 shirts stood against the railing with bulbous, excited eyes. I looked down at my own Blink-182 shirt, which I'd found at a fucking Goodwill of all places. There was a hole in the collar and in one of the armpits, but I didn't care. It was mine.

There were a couple of rows of people in front of us who lined up directly in front of the stage. Loud music bumped over the speakers. As the minutes ticked on, more people flooded in, chatting and jittery, and my pulse quickened with the knowledge that something *big* was going to happen.

Sean left us to smoke one of his "special cigarettes" with the other smokers on the outside patio attached to the side of the stage, though I doubted he'd need to be too discrete about it; the dank, familiar smell of marijuana rolled into the space every time the patio door opened. Ronnie was staring at his phone and tapping a foot to the music.

Meanwhile, I took in my surroundings: the stage and the equipment—a local band was opening, and their band name was proudly displayed on the drum set; the microphone deliberately placed at center stage, the vast ceiling of the venue that reached higher than I thought it would when we were outside; the smell of beer in the air and the stickiness of spilled alcohol on the linoleum under my shoes; the way people gasped and yelled at each other in a frantic, frenzied excitement that made the air around me almost addictive.

Sean came back reeking of "cigarette smoke" with pink eyes. His long, red mane was tousled and sticking up from the wind. He said something to us, but I didn't catch it–because, at that moment, I heard the laugh again.

And there he was.

He walked up right beside our group with his friends, all of them with fresh beer. I didn't think they were of legal drinking age, but that didn't mean shit.

"Dude, did you hear me?" Sean elbowed me in the rib cage playfully.

I jerked. "What? Sorry. It's hard to hear in here."

He chuckled. "Just wait. It's about to get loud as fuck."

7

"What were you saying?" I asked as I eyed the stranger who now stood next to Sean.

Sean rolled his eyes dramatically. "I swear I just met my dream girl. She took a hit, and the way she blew smoke rings, dude? Be still my *fucking heart*. Black lipstick, curvy. The whole package." He placed a hand over his heart and swooned. Literally.

I couldn't help but smile. Sean was the horniest motherfucker I'd ever met, and he seemed to find his new "dream girl" about once a week.

Sean leaned over to talk to Ronnie, but they had a hard time talking with me in the middle. I knew I wanted to stand next to the guy with the laugh and the beanie and the strong nose, and now was my chance. I nonchalantly motioned for Sean to take my place, and then I was standing next to the stranger.

The group he was with chatted about something, but he wasn't involved in their conversation, either. Now that I was closer, I peeked at him and noticed that the hoodie he was wearing said Simple Plan on the front. He smirked at his friends, and I was mesmerized in the way one side of his lips curved upward. He shook his head at them—at whatever the two girls and the other guy were bickering about—then took a long swig of beer.

I was staring, and I couldn't take my eyes away for some reason. When he felt my gaze and turned his head over to look at me, I pretended to stare at my feet. My cheeks heated instantly. I didn't even know this person. What the hell? I hadn't even noticed when the lights dimmed and flashed in preparation for the local band to come on stage.

"I like your shirt." I looked up and saw that the guy beamed at me. "They're my fave. But, alas, I don't have any of their merch yet." He looked down at his hoodie and shrugged. "I like Simple Plan, too, though. And All Time Low. Can't really complain."

My anxiety heightened as I met his gaze, but it would have been rude not to look at him while he spoke. He was only a little taller than I was, so it was easy to meet his eyes. As it turned out, he did have a nose ring. Well, two, actually. One in each nostril. He also had a tiny, gray stud in his lip. He mindlessly played with the stud with his tongue, and that made my cheeks heat even more. I made myself look away.

What was this stranger doing to me? I chalked it up to my excitement for the show. And the bourbon.

The crowd was restless. Before the band came on, I leaned into the man a little, not in a weird way, but in a way for him to hear me over the crowd and the music overhead. The music was starting to fade, signaling the opening band, but it was still noisy, and I wanted to say something to him before I lost my nerve.

"I like all the bands, too. I'm Asher, by the way." I held out a hand to him.

He placed the beer in his non-dominant hand and shook my own. His grip was warm and electric. When the first band came onto the stage, he didn't pull away immediately. In fact, his hand lingered in mine for what felt like a second too long before he retracted it.

CHAPTER THREE

I make a show of closing my dressing room door, even though I know damn well that he's stalking right behind me, ready to pounce. In the meantime, I take several large gulps of the cool water I left on one of the side tables before the show. The space is more of a closet than a dressing room—a futon shoved on one wall accompanied by two tiny tables, one floor length mirror, and rickety coatrack—not a lot of room. Nothing fancy. But I've never cared about fancy, anyway.

I'm looking at myself in the mirror when he comes in. He quickly locks the door behind him. Sweat drips from my temples, leaving my shaggy, milk chocolate hair plastered around my temples and forehead. I lift my black t-shirt up and wipe the excess.

Without a word, Ash comes up behind me. We both know there isn't time to linger.

We're almost matched in height, though Ash is a smidge shorter. Still, he has a way of making me feel small when he hugs me from behind like he is now. He delicately trails his lips, which are dry from screaming into a mic for the last hour and a half, from my earlobe down to that sweet spot right above my collarbone. I hiss and roll my neck as he snags some of my skin with his teeth and flicks my captured flesh with the tip of his tongue.

I glare at Ash playfully in the mirror as he works my belt and pants hungrily. His eyes are hooded and darker than normal. If there was more time to spare, things would be playing out much differently, and he knows this, but we have rules, and I'm not one to break them. Not unless he misbehaves, that is.

Ash's jet black, closely cropped hair scrapes across my neck as he pants, hardly able to contain the lustful monster within. I could tell by the way he exited the stage that he was anxious to get his hands on me—and I'd be lying if I said my jeans didn't rub against my cock a little tighter than they had been when we first went on stage as I felt Ash's heated gaze follow me to the room.

We don't bother taking our shirts off. There's no point, and he's wearing a plaid shirt with the sleeves rolled up, anyway–too many buttons–especially when I feel his need pressing urgently against my back.

I turn to face him and try to guide us over to the futon, but he presses my arms up and into the mirror in front of us with a curt shake of his head. The cool bite of the mirror clashes with my heated palms. He bites his plush bottom lip and meets my eyes in the reflection.

"I want you to look at me while I fuck you," he whispers.

His rough hands are at my waist, shimmying my tight jeans down to the floor. I hear them hit the carpet with a soft *thunk* from my belt. My dick breaks free of my pants immediately, standing at attention and throbbing with need. Ash removes one of his hands from the mirror to stroke me. He bites my shoulder to muffle the groan lodged in his throat, because Ash Lancing isn't just loud when he's singing on stage. I love watching him try to keep his composure in the mirror when I know that he's about to completely unravel within me.

Ash's hazel eyes meet mine in the mirror, and he gives me a cocky smirk that heats my core while he fists my cock in slow, teasing strokes.

"You'd better," I swallow roughly. "Hurry the fuck up."

We can hear the crowd cheering through the closed door. There will only be one minute, maybe two if we're lucky, before our band manager knocks on the door, or one of the guys tries to barge in to get our asses back on stage.

Of course, they don't know what we're doing back here.

Best friends since right after high school. That's all we are to them. Best friends. Bandmates. Past roommates.

Ash nibbles on my earlobe as he releases my arms so he can pull down his own jeans. A low moan erupts from him as he frees himself. I want to look behind me to see him in all of his glory, but that's for another time. He pushes me back up against the mirror, rougher this time, and I arch my head back into him.

"Like that?" he murmurs in my ear.

All I can do is nod and bite my lip.

Ash's beautiful, large hands grip my hips, then dig into each ass cheek, full of desperation for my body. He acts like we've been away from each other for months, when in actuality, it's only been a couple of weeks. Ash spreads me apart, and in a flash, one of his hands leaves me, and I faintly hear the small bottle of lube he keeps hidden somewhere pop open. Within seconds, the wet tip of his needy cock is teasing at my ass. My pulse is pounding like the beat of my drums in my ears. My head spins in delight as he moves inside of me, inch by inch.

Though he no longer secures my hands to the mirror, I keep them there, knowing exactly how he wants me. He grips my hip with his left hand, using it to steady his rampant movements. His other hand meets my mouth, and I open up for him like he's my only source of air. Ash slides three fingers into my mouth and I lick and suck. Before I know it, his coated hand is on my shaft, and he's working me in his masterful way. I look down and watch, unable to resist the temptation. I can already feel the beginning of an orgasm blossom inside of my core. As he thrusts and works me, my skin catches fire, so desperate for the release.

In the distance, the crowd grows louder. We have seconds of alone time left.

Ash moves hard and fast inside of me, but his hand that strokes me doesn't stall. I look up and meet his gaze in the mirror, consuming the way his lips are parted, the blush that's wildly apparent on his fair complexion, and spreading across arched cheekbones and the bridge of his slightly pointed nose. I twist my head to meet that delicious mouth of his.

Something about kissing Ash has always felt like coming home.

He doesn't stop, even as my tongue flicks inside of his mouth, and he doesn't stop as I nip at his bottom lip. But he does groan louder than he usually allows in these situations, completely lost in the moment.

Ash breaks our kiss and whispers, "Come."

I do. I was already on the verge, and his demand breaks whatever control I have left. I look down and watch as I spill over his long, elegant fingers, right as he crashes into me one last time with a shaky huff. His body trembles and I'm seeing stars.

Just as we pull away from one another, there's a knock on the door.

Ash grins at me wickedly, then walks over to the side table that has napkins on it and comes back to the mirror. He cleans me and his hand up, and I can't stop staring at him, totally lost in my infatuation. The eyes, the blush spreading across his cheeks and neck, the cheekbones, and the spread of beige freckles on one side of his sharp jaw. The way his lips curve into another taunting smile as he notices me checking him out like I'm seeing him for the first time.

"Alright, lads, it's go time!" Our manager, Mike, pounds on the door again.

I hastily pull on my jeans and buckle my belt after cleaning up—something that used to take much longer to accomplish, but I can now do in under a minute. I've had a lot of practice.

When I look up, Ash's pants are back on, and that beautiful flush hasn't faded from his face. People will think it's because he's over-heated from the show. Little do they know he's red, hot, bothered, and out of breath because of me.

I walk to the door hurriedly. I don't like making fans wait, even if it's on Ash's account. Before I reach the door, he tugs at my hand and whirls me around and into his chest. He places his hands on either side of my face and kisses me deeply, consuming my lips and devouring my soul before we break apart.

I kiss his forehead. "I'm getting payback later tonight."

Ash smirks at me and says, "I highly doubt that."

Then, he opens the door, and we rush right back out onto the stage with our bandmates like we didn't just fuck like horny teenagers.

My favorite part of the encore is when Ash falls into the pit. He does it at almost every show—aside from the venues that are too small—and the crowd sings the chorus with him as he's carried to the back of the room. From there, he rounds back to the stage and screams at the top of his lungs into the mic like his life depends on it.

The only sound that is sweeter is when I'm the one making him scream like that.

CHAPTER FOUR

APRIL 2012

The opening band had begun, and the small fan base they had acquired was throwing their hands in the air and screaming wildly. I'd seen the band a couple of times before, and they were pretty good, but not worth ogling over, in my opinion.

When Asher took his hand away from mine, I wanted it back for some reason. His bright hazel eyes were focused on the stage, lips parted and eyes bulging, as if he was seeing the outside world for the first time. Even if the opening band wasn't my favorite, there was nothing better than live music.

Nothing.

I leaned into him, because I hadn't given him my name, and that seemed rude. "I'm Drew," I said loudly enough for him to hear.

Asher looked back to me with a faint smile. We were almost the same height. He was a little thinner than I was, but not horribly skinny. There was something about his eyes. The hazel swirls seemingly turned darker as we occasionally made eye contact, but I figured that had to do with the stage lights that wandered over the crowd ever so often. The air felt thick as the band finished their first song.

Asher ran long fingers through his shaggy, straight hair and smirked at me. He removed a cheap flask from the waistband of his jeans and inclined his head toward mine. I couldn't help the chuckle that came from my throat.

"What is it?" I asked, close to his ear.

"Bourbon."

There was no way Asher was legal. Then again, neither was I. I had a guy in my Statistics class make me, my friend, and our girls some fake IDs for when we went out. They were hella real looking, and they'd worked well so far. I shrugged lightly and took the flask. The band rolled into their second song as I brought the flask to my lips and took a draw.

Beer was fine, but the bourbon was smooth. It warmed me from the inside out.

I passed the flask back to my new acquaintance. It looked like he was in a similar situation to me—the people we'd come with were talking to each other and not us.

I didn't really mind that. My buddy, Griffin, was just that. We hung out occasionally outside of the one class we shared, but he wasn't near and dear to me or anything. And his girlfriend, Stacy, who was always gothed up and expressionless, simply annoyed me. Sometimes I wondered if there was anything going on in Stacy's head. Even when they made out, she just kind of sat there. As for my own girl, Emma, well... we lacked chemistry, I guess. We were good friends, and sometimes I wished we'd just left it at that. Like, why'd we have to go and make it romantic? But she was so into it when we kissed for the first time, that we've been together ever since, even though my heart wasn't in it.

Two months later, and I was at a show talking with a stranger, pondering at the very back of my mind how best to break up with her. And soon. Life was too short to be with someone who didn't make every cell in my body come alive.

Asher, his friends, and my friends stared up at the stage. I suddenly felt restless. There weren't any stamps or wristbands to signal who and who was not of a certain drinking age, so I leaned into Asher and asked, "Want a beer, man? This band isn't my favorite."

He eyed the half full cup of beer in my hand but nodded. "Thanks, dude. You don't have to if you don't want."

I shrugged a single shoulder. "I'll get you one if I get another taste of that flask when I come back."

His face broke out into a wide, crooked smile where one side of his mouth lifted more than the other, and suddenly, it felt like my world was spinning. Asher nodded in assurance that there'd be more bourbon for me when I returned.

I was jittery and needed the short walk to the bar just to move around and expend some energy. In my haste, I forgot to tell Emma where I was off to. I pulled my phone out of my pocket and shot her a quick text in case she was worried. I'd probably freak out if I turned my head and she was no longer with our group.

Before I reached the busy bar, I chugged the rest of my drink. It was a strange night. I entered the Madder Hatter excited about the concert, but with a heavy feeling of dread settled low in my stomach. I'd been ignoring the feeling for days, pushing down all my worries and hoping they'd fade away.

There were too many stressors pressed against my shoulders. Ignoring everything was just making me feel sick. I didn't want to hurt Emma, but my heart wasn't in it like hers was, and the longer I put off the inevitable, the more it would crush her. On top of that, my grades were dwindling down to a percentage that was hardly passable, and I didn't even like school, so what was the point? I was only happy when I was at live shows or drumming in my parents' basement. The constant feeling of what I wanted to do versus what I should be doing was a tiresome battle.

As I made my way through the line to the bar, Asher's smile flashed in my head. For a fraction of a second, my shoulders eased back from where they'd been tensed near my ears, and my jaw unclenched. I didn't know anything about the guy, but he already seemed more interesting than Griffin and his emo girlfriend.

After I ordered a couple more beers, I made my way back to the front of the stage. It was much more crowded now, and I couldn't make out where my group was. As carefully as was possible at a punk show, I weaved myself in between the fans, trying my best not to spill the beers. I made it back to my spot beside Asher having only spilled a couple of drops on my shoes.

I handed him the beer in my right hand. "I almost got trampled by a whole hoard of women trying to get these back," I said in his ear.

He grinned. "My hero."

I chuckled and took a swig of my fresh beer. He took out his flask again, took a hearty sip, then passed it to me with a wink. Asher seemed to be coming more alive as the music crescendoed and as the anticipation escalated in the venue as we all realized the opening band only had a couple more songs. Then, Simple Plan would be on, and the night would truly begin.

I shook the flask, trying to get a feel for how much bourbon was left. There wasn't much, but I'd be more than happy to go back to the bar later for some real liquor, so long as it was in between sets. I moved the flask up and took another sip but made sure the last of it was left for him.

After I handed it back and took a swig of my beer, I felt a tug on my elbow from my other side. I looked over, expecting Griffin, but there was Emma. I had a feeling that most boyfriends and girlfriends stood together more than we did. Held hands. That kind of thing. The sinking feeling of dread returned.

I crouched a bit so she could speak in my ear. "Who's your new friend?"

Emma's beautiful, bright baby blues stared up at me. Her hair was curled for the concert, and she had put in a couple of black bows on either side. She didn't usually wear makeup, but she wore a little eyeliner and some lip gloss for the show.

"His name's Asher," I said. "He's pretty cool."

Emma walked past me and placed a hand on Asher's elbow, just as she'd done with me. I couldn't hear what she said to him over the music, but he gave her a smile and a laugh. The way he looked at her in pure delight made my chest heavy. I was overwhelmed with the need for Emma to go back to where she'd been standing with Stacy and Griffin on the other side of me. I forced my eyes down and away from them and begged my strange thoughts to disappear.

What was it about this guy?

After a moment, Emma came back to my other side and laid her head on my shoulder as best she could. I breathed a bit easier once she returned to her spot next to me. She tapped her foot a little half-heartedly as she watched the band.

Finally, curiosity got the better of me. "What did you say to him?" I teased. Or, at least I hoped it sounded teasing and not annoyed because I was more agitated than anything.

She batted her lashes. "I told him that he and his friends are welcome back at my place after the show." She shrugged. Emma lived with her parents still, like me, but they'd let her take over the in-law suite of the house because they never used it. "You seem to like him. And we need new friends. The two we came with?" Emma rolled her eyes. "They're nice and all, but..."

I nodded. I knew exactly what she meant.

"What did he say?" I cocked a brow.

The crowd erupted in applause and screams of delight, and then the opening band took their bow, said their goodnights, and exited the stage.

"He said he'd have to talk to his friends, but he wants to come hang for a bit."

My heart fluttered. The recorded music came on the surrounding speakers once more for the set change. Asher looked at me and smiled at me and Emma before taking a long drink of the beer. He leaned over to his friends and spoke.

The night was finally about to begin.

19

CHAPTER FIVE

I'm flying high off the performance when we finally exit the stage after the encore. I can still taste Drew's tongue in my mouth as I stride back to my own puny dressing room down the hall from his own.

All I want to do is go to the hotel and let him have his way with me, but we have VIP fans who paid extra to spend some time with us backstage, and as much as I want to *just* be with Drew, our fans deserve our attention, too.

It's only been two weeks.

That's what I keep repeating over and over again in my head as I walk with the rest of the band to the backstage room where we are meeting our VIP guests.

Fourteen days. That's all.

The band took a break from our third album's tour to celebrate Christmas and New Year's. After that, we had a couple of shows, then took a couple more weeks off at the end of January. It really hasn't been that long, but somehow, having Drew apart from me felt like waiting for a new day to come, only for the shitty day I had to reset all over again.

Drew almost always went back home to his hometown of Fredericksburg, Virginia to spend the holidays with his folks and sisters and their hoard of rescue pets.

His birthday was a few weeks ago, and I can't wait to give him his belated birthday present later. I would have had it ready a couple weeks ago, but shipping had taken forever, and then I felt like a dick when I saw him and didn't have a gift at the ready. Not that Drew cared—but I did.

During the break in tour, I stayed put in New York City, holed up in my loft. I can afford a bigger place, a nicer place, but I like where I live. It's where I moved to after the release of our first album, *Over Under Back and Forth,* and the space is home to me now, despite the leaking kitchen faucet and the weird noises that occasionally come from the loft above mine. Unfortunately, the paparazzi finally figured out where I lived late last year, and I spent the majority of my holiday break and the last few days of January packing my belongings, searching for a new place to call home, and thinking about how I would have much rather been with Drew.

I FaceTimed him briefly on his birthday, but we kept it short and sweet. We didn't text often for fear of someone finding us out, though admittedly, that's more of my fear than Drew's. During the last couple of weeks, Drew had agreed to be a guest drummer for a few up-and-coming bands and had been out of state, anyway. I wish I could have gone with him, or had a family of my own to visit, but my parents are drunks and don't give a fuck about me. They never have. It was better to stay in the city and focus on packing.

Drew walks in front of me next to Brian. He arches his strong arms above his head and stretches out his defined muscles, both of his drumsticks still clenched in his hands. I know that he will eventually sign both sticks off to two lucky fans tonight, because he always does. I swallow hard at the memory of his arms in that same position just minutes ago, in that tiny dressing room, underneath the weight of my body. I can already feel my blood draining south. I shake my head and force my thoughts elsewhere.

We always keep the VIP meet and greets low-key. There are only a certain number of tickets available, and once they're sold out, that's it. Too many people cause too much stress. Our band has always found pride in being close with our fan base, and if you go over twenty or so people for a meet and greet, things tend to get stressful and chaotic. We don't do the meet and greet at every show because being social after a long performance can be very taxing. We aim to host them at every other show, but if we're close to home, or in a city where we haven't toured before, we occasionally make an exception.

The guard by the door opens it for us, and we walk into a room much larger than the dressing rooms after giving him our thanks. The room is almost as big as my loft, honestly. But it's quaint and cozy with plush, cherry red couches, snacks, and drinks on a bar table off to one side of the room. Our band's merch is laid out nicely on a table at the other side if any of our guests want more swag. We make sure every VIP gets a t-shirt, poster, and stickers included in the price of the ticket. It's the least we can do. They got us to where we are now, after all.

I immediately drop down on the smaller of the two couches and lean my head back, letting a heavy sigh escape from my lungs. I'm only twenty-seven, but after all the jumping around and screaming I do on stage, sometimes I feel much older.

Trish sits on the other couch and eyes me. She's always trying to flirt with me, and if she was my type, I'd probably flirt back. She's so skinny, I wouldn't know what to hold on to, but she's got an angular face and sleek blue-black hair that looks gorgeous against her light bronze skin. Her eyes are a deep brown, but they're lost in all the eyeshadow she has on. Like the rest of us, she dresses to impress our scene, even though I know she mostly did classical concerts before signing on with us for this tour. She has ripped, high-rise, black skinny jeans on, scuffed Converse, and a crop-top cut from one of our band's original t-shirts because she's so short, and the original tee probably would have looked like an oversized dress on her.

If only Trish knew that Brian was the one who was dying to get a taste. From where he stood near the bar, his bright eyes were alert and drawn in on Trish's every move. It's so obvious, it almost hurts. But I'm rooting for him. Brian is talented, handsome, and young. He's just a little socially awkward, especially in front of the woman he worships. He's practically been head over heels for Trish since the beginning of the tour last year.

I'm about to scrounge up the strength to get my ass up and make myself a drink when Drew places two shots of what I assume is vodka on the coffee table in front of me. He sits down next to me so casually, it's no wonder we've kept our relationship a secret for so long.

Still, his knee bumps against mine ever so slightly, and my body erupts in goosebumps.

I clear my throat and try to direct my attention away from the filthy images that pop up in my mind. "Vodka?" I raise a brow. "And...no chasers?"

He smirks, takes his shot like it's water, and pats me on the back, ending his little show with a contented *ahhh*. The act makes me want to kiss him so badly that I distract myself by throwing back the shot, wincing as it goes down.

"Wimp," he murmurs.

Trish smiles devilishly. "You two are too cute."

I roll my eyes as Drew grins. Obviously, Trish doesn't understand why that comment makes me uncomfortable, but Drew does. He pats my knee and pouts. "Was the vodka too much for the baby?"

Oh, he is *so* going to pay later. Trish chuckles and opens a small bag of Fritos.

"No," I grumble. "Another?"

Drew's dark brows skyrocket, but instead of questioning me, he simply laughs and walks away. When he comes back, there are two more shots in one hand, and a Sprite in the other.

We clink the glasses together, an unspeakable toast in our eyes, and we down them. The alcohol goes down a little smoother now, but I really need warm lemon water after the show for my raspy throat. Still, the liquid feels warm and inviting.

I almost ask for a third as Sean comes into the room, finally done with his little smoke break. As the door opens, we can hear the fans eager to come in, waiting in line behind the threshold.

Our manager, Mike comes in after Sean and leaves the door cracked. "Y'all ready?" Mike is from some small town in Alabama, and he has the accent to prove it. He's a soft teddy bear unless he's super pissed, and he'd probably put his life on the line for each and every one of us. He rubs a hand over his shiny, bald head and takes in a breath, preparing for the last bit of mayhem before we can head back to the hotel.

I nod and Mike opens the door wide. The guard lets three people in, then shuts the door quietly. Two young teenage girls and their mother, from the looks of it. They're polite, charming, and everything we love about our fanbase. We take pictures, laugh, autograph their posters, and start the cycle over again as they're replaced with a couple of guys closer to our age, and so on.

I enjoy every moment, but that doesn't stop me from glancing at my watch every few minutes, begging the clock to strike eleven.

WE TAKE three more shots during the meet and greet. One more together, then two more with the rest of the crew. Even Mike joined in for one, which is highly unusual. Sometimes, I think he's incapable of fun, then he does shit like this. I don't drink a lot, and I've barely eaten today, so to say I'm a little tipsy is probably an understatement. From the looks of Drew, he's in the same boat, because his smile never falters, and his tan skin has a rosy tint that decorates his cheeks.

When we finally reach our hotel for the night, everyone is tired and buzzing. Mike goes to his suite immediately after we exit the elevator. As we walk toward the end of the hall, Trish invites all of us back to her suite for more fun. Brian and Sean quickly agree, even though they know damn well that we will have to wake up and get back on the tour bus early tomorrow morning.

Drew catches my eye, but he doesn't have to say a single syllable for me to understand.

I won't be going to Trish's room.

I fake a yawn and stretch. "Y'all have fun. I'm going to make some tea and call it a night."

"Dude. You sound like my grandma," Sean snickers.

Sean hasn't changed much since high school. He still wears his long, copper hair at his shoulders. He's still paler than pale, but there's less acne these days. I swear I've seen him wear the same shirt he wore on stage tonight a decade ago.

I roll my eyes. "Were you singing and screaming on stage tonight?"

He rolls his eyes right back. "Don't be a prima donna, Ash."

"Let me enjoy my old lady tea in peace," I counter.

Trish looks over to Drew who matches my strides as we walk behind the others. "Drew? You game?"

Drew doesn't look my way, but his hands clench and unclench. He's itching to say no but doesn't want to be obvious.

Finally, he sighs. He holds up a single finger. "One. But I'm beat, too. So, I mean it. One drink, then I'm out."

"Yay!" Trish squeals and claps.

My door is the first one we pass. Mike reserved the whole upper level for us and the rest of our crew. I stop and fish the key card out of my back pocket.

"Have a good night!" Trish yells back at me.

Drew looks back at me as he makes his way closer to Trish's room. He holds up five fingers behind his back.

Five minutes, and he's mine. That's a damn good thing, too, because if I have to wait any longer, I'll have to bust Trish's door down and haul his sweet ass back to my suite.

Once alone, I put a K-cup of tea in the Keurig and turn it on. I wasn't kidding about the tea. Or my throat feeling raw. Especially after a couple of weeks of rest. Tomorrow, I'll have to do more vocal warm-ups and drink a ton of warm water.

I move over to the king-size bed. It's been perfectly made—not a single wrinkle in the duvet. My suitcase is by the bed, but I don't bother with it yet. I kick my shoes off and slam my body down onto the mattress. I should shower, but not yet. Not when I'm waiting for him.

A faint buzz brings my attention to the phone I've been ignoring in my pocket. I take it out and see a missed FaceTime call from Lizette. I huff out a breath.

Me: Sorry, babe. I'm totally beat after the show. Raincheck?

Lizzy: Alright, babe. Just wanted to make sure you're okay. I can't wait for the show tomorrow! xoxo

Me: Same. x

The familiar wave of guilt that I've grown sickeningly accustomed to over the past couple of years creeps up from my lower back all the way up to the base of my skull. My skin and bones feel tight, like they need to be stretched out. I toss the phone onto the bedside table and rub at my tired eyes with the palms of my hands.

I've been with Lizette for a long time. She's an incredible person, and that makes my infidelity even worse. She's one of the top models in the U.S. right now, and it's not because she's skinny. She has curves for days and one of the prettiest faces—high cheekbones and a unique, angular face. Her eyes are what she's known for, though. Eyes that shine like emeralds. They're vibrant and incredibly sultry, even when she's not trying to pose.

I met Lizette at a gala when she first started in the industry. It was around the time we were gaining more attention after the release of our second album. She stood out to me because she didn't beg for the camera. Instead, Lizzy stood at the back of the massive room, body pressed against the wall, people-watching as she ate meats and soft cheeses from a small plate. I had also been leaning against the wall, because the band was invited but only Brian and I had come, and I didn't like being in spaces where I knew next to no one.

She immediately came over to me and introduced herself. She knew who I was but didn't say so. Not until later. Her laugh is almost as good as Drew's, especially when discussing her favorite B movies or when she's giggling over the newest set of memes she's stashed away for us to look at together. She's an impeccable kisser, and any other man would surely be head over heels. But every time she kisses me, or every time we do more than kiss, my mind always slips back to Drew.

I love Lizzy. I tried to force myself to fall *in* love with her, but I can't. Now, close to two years after the gala, she's head over heels for me, and I'm faking it with her and fucking my best friend on the side.

The only time I've been faithful to Lizette was when we first started dating, and Drew wanted nothing to do with me. He didn't stay away for long, and when he came back, I tried not to kiss him, not to touch him—tried not to fuck him and get fucked in return— but I couldn't hold out.

Which makes me the biggest prick on the planet, honestly.

Guilt and shame heat my face as I remember how we got together, and everything I've done to her behind her back since. I'm about to text her something more substantial when there's a faint knock at the door.

And just like that, my guilt is replaced with uncontrollable, insatiable lust.

I spring up and rush to the door. I should check the peephole, but I don't. I know who's here, and I'm not wasting a second.

Drew slides into my room and shuts the door. He leans his large, muscular frame against the door and grins at me despite his tired eyes and the tipsy tilt in his step.

I want to put my hands all over him. I want to massage his abs with my fingertips and smell his after-show scent and bite his bottom lip. But I was in control earlier. He knows that it's his turn now, so I stand there and wait impatiently for him to make his move.

He takes a step toward me. Drew still has one of his nose rings in, but the other one closed a long time ago. There's a faint scar from where his lip piercing used to be, and I miss it sometimes. Then again, it was replaced with a tongue ring, so I can't complain *too* much.

Drew's breath lands on me and I inhale an intoxicating blend of vodka, sandalwood, and sweat. My stomach rolls and my skin burns.

"Miss me?" Drew asks. His voice is low and gravelly as he closes the gap between us, centimeter by harrowing centimeter.

I lose the ability to speak as my eyes slide up to meet his. There's heat and longing in those light brown eyes, and I want to slide into each iris. Drew drags his lower lip in between his teeth and bites down a chuckle.

He kisses me so tenderly, I'm not sure if it's even a kiss at first. The touch is the opposite of how we acted together earlier. Drew leans his whole body into me, only leaning his head down a bit to meet my slightly shorter height. His calloused hands cup my jaw in soft strokes as he kisses me and kisses me, taking in my very essence. My arms circle around his waist and I tug him closer into my body. Every inch of my skin needs to feel every inch of his. I'll never be satisfied until it does.

My hand massages his tight ass, which has him moaning into my mouth in seconds. I smile against his lips. Drew deepens our kiss and slides his tongue into my mouth, grazing it delicately over my own, and then he moves to flick the roof of my mouth. I moan right back and push him into the door.

"I missed you so fucking much." My voice isn't my own and comes out in ragged breaths like I just ran a marathon.

Drew leaves a trail of wet kisses from behind my ear down to my chest, then works his way up the front of my neck with his tongue. He stops near my Adam's apple and nips at my tender skin.

"I know you did. You practically jumped me earlier," he laughs into my neck. It's that same laugh that's taken over my body and soul ever since I heard it for the first time nearly ten years ago. It makes me want to jump him all over again, but I know that Drew is aching to be in control, so I let him have the reins.

Drew comes back up and brushes his nose against mine. His full lips breathe against my own, and I've never seen a human more fucking gorgeous in my whole life. His hair is wild and sticky, and I run my hands through it to make it crazier. In the midnight shadows, his bronze skin looks violet. He kisses me again, gently, and presses me against him as much as possible.

"I have a birthday present for you," I manage to say after a few more minutes of making out and touching. It's an innocent act for us, but it shows how much we missed each other. I'd be content if I spent the whole night just like this, but no—he will have to retreat back to his room eventually.

Drew leans his head back against the door, his nose ring glittering in the little light from the room. His eyes are relaxed, his smile smug. "You do, do you?"

I walk my way over to my suitcase on the ground and rummage around in the giant bag for a while before I find it. Drew sits on the bed as I feel at the wrapped disc in my bag, making sure the paper hasn't come apart before handing him his present.

The small package is wrapped in newspaper. With a few markers, I drew hearts and music notes on it.

"You didn't need to get me anything," he murmurs.

With a halfhearted shrug, I join him on the bed. Heat settles between our bodies as we sit side by side. We aren't touching, but we're close enough to feel the electricity that pulses between us. I want to push him down on the bed and straddle him, but I resist as he tears into the present.

As soon as he sees it, he laughs so hard I think he might cry. A beautiful, wide smile and crinkling eyes decorate his face as he looks down at the dinghy CD. It's Blink-182's *Enema of the State*

—an original copy autographed by Mark, Matt, and Travis themselves.

"Dude! No way?" Drew swats at my arms and practically knocks me off the bed. He forgets his strength sometimes, especially these days because of his consistent lifting regimen. "How the hell did you get this?"

A shit ton of time on eBay. "I have my ways."

He sets the CD down on the side table and then leans over to me. He wastes no time and kisses me in a way that tells me he wants me so much that he can't stand it. I don't know why, but it's always been this way with us. Before I can catch my breath, he pushes me down onto my back, and he's on top of me.

Who needs to breathe, right?

We grind against each other for several blissful minutes, and the noises that evade his lips make me crazy. He finally lifts me and pulls off my shirt and undershirt, then trails his fingers down my chest at an achingly slow pace. Drew bends down and leaves gentle bites from my chest down to the waistband of my pants, and I truly wish he'd bite me harder, but then that would leave Lizette with questions tomorrow. I push the thoughts of her from my brain immediately. There isn't room in my head for guilt. Not right now.

Drew rubs me through my jeans and looks up at me with a wicked, lopsided grin. He licks his lips and I notice the tongue ring. I'm harder than ever when he undoes my zipper.

"Want to take a shower?" he whispers to me.

Fuck, yes.

CHAPTER SIX

APRIL 2012

Sean and Ronnie agreed to come back to the girl's house—whatever her name was, I had barely heard it. Emily? Something like that. I explained to Sean that Drew was cool, and we could go back to my new friend's girlfriend's place for an afterparty. It took no convincing at all.

Drew's eyes were locked onto the stage, and he bobbed his head to match the fast tempo of the song. Simple Plan was almost done with their set, and they were damn good. Even though the live music was hypnotic, and the bass threaded itself deep within my veins, I still felt compelled to look over at Drew every song or so. Why was that? I tried not to for fear of creeping him out, but I swore I'd seen him eye me a couple of times, too.

The air was thick from those pressed side by side in the pit. More people had arrived after Simple Plan began their set, and now Drew and I were elbow to elbow.

In between Simple Plan and All Time Low, Drew wordlessly took my empty beer cup and made his way back to the bar. Now, I stood by the blond girl he was with.

"I'm sorry," I said loud enough for her to hear, "I totally didn't hear your name before. Can you tell me again?"

Her face brightened and her round, blue eyes twinkled. "Emma! I'm Drew's girlfriend."

"Oh, I see." My face fell, and I quickly covered it up with a strained smile. The two didn't seem like they were together, but what did I know? I'd only gotten to second base once, and I'd surely never dated anyone before. "Well, it's nice to meet you, Emma. Thank you for inviting us back to your place."

She laughed and took a sip of beer. She was still on her first drink, but her cheeks were flushed, and she seemed a bit wobbly. Perhaps she had a secret flask, too.

"It'll be fun!" Emma said. She lowered her voice a tad before she murmured, "The other two we're with are kind of...boring isn't the right word, but..." she trailed off with a nonchalant shrug.

I kind of understood what she meant, even though I hadn't interacted with the other two.

"They probably won't even stay at my place long," Emma resumed. "All they do is brood and fuck."

That made me laugh.

"Do you have a girlfriend?"

I shook my head. "Nah."

Emma looked me up and down, not bothering to hide the fact that she was checking me out. "Shame. I have a few girlfriends who'd be more than happy to go out with you, I'm sure." She winked.

My gut twisted a bit. I was about to respond when Drew came back. He wiggled himself in between us, kissed Emma on top of her golden head, then handed me a drink that was definitely not beer.

"You didn't have to get me an—"

He clinked his drink against mine. "Shh. It's an old fashioned. I want a good buzz before Blink comes on."

Emma and the other girl, the broody one, disappeared. Maybe to get more drinks or visit the restroom. Either way, their absence didn't bother me. In fact, I was relieved when they left. As soon as they were gone, I leaned into Drew a bit more.

"Is Blink-182 your favorite?" I asked.

A playful, crooked smile came to life on his lips. "One of many."

I laughed. "Mine, too."

I'D NEVER EXPERIENCED anything like that before in my entire life. Simple Plan and All Time Low were fantastic. It was like each note they played and each word they sang crept into my soul and held onto my body as tightly as they could. I never wanted the feeling to stop. I couldn't live without it.

We danced and bobbed our heads. We head banged and laughed. Drew and I sang at the top of our lungs, which I felt comfortable doing because no one would hear me over the music. Sean danced with the same girl he'd met outside, and they made out through the second half of All Time Low. I couldn't help but grin. They weren't the only ones making out. Everywhere I looked, people were close together, dancing, laughing, or holding hands. Something about the live music set our souls aflame.

Before Blink-182 came on, Drew went to get us a couple more drinks. That time, I offered to come with him, despite feeling wobbly from the alcohol. He smiled and motioned for me to follow. I stood a little way back from the bar just in case the bartenders decided they wanted to ID me or question why Drew kept getting two of each beverage.

From where I stood away from the bar, my eyes were free to take in Drew without the worry that he'd get weirded out by me staring at him. It *was* kind of weird how I was so drawn to a person I'd met less than an hour ago—but no matter how hard I tried, my gaze kept wandering back to him. At the bar, he leaned against the table casually and used his elbows to prop himself up. I couldn't see his face, but the bartender looked amused, so they must have been talking about something. After a moment, Drew ran a hand over the beanie on his head, then stood up and stretched his long arms behind his back. He shot the bartender a crooked smile and placed a couple of dollars in the tip jar, then grabbed our drinks and made his way back to me.

We tapped our plastic cups together in a salute, then took a sip before we trudged back through the crowd. That was the only thing that got to be a bit much—the amount of people. It was stuffy and claustrophobic, especially with the alcohol heating me from the inside out. I did my best to focus on my feet, or Drew, or my breathing so that I didn't get caught up in the feeling of the walls closing in around me.

It was impossible to get back to the spot where we'd originally been. The people were pressed in too tight in preparation for Blink-182.

Drew stretched his neck up and scanned the crowd with wild eyes. Without a word, he nodded to the very front of the stage, to the right. There was space for maybe one person to wiggle in. Before I could protest, though, he took my free hand and led me through the sea of people. It was obvious he'd been to shows before—the way he maneuvered through the crowd, the way he knew the right time to order drinks, and how he could tell when the show was about to start.

I kept my gaze glued to my feet as I trailed behind him.

People shuffled out of our way, and I could hear a few of them scoff at us as we neared the stage. Drew paid them no mind. Finally, we came to a stop, and when I lifted my eyes up from the floor, I could touch the stage if I wanted to. It was a tight squeeze—I was pressed directly in front of Drew.

Drew's hand fell from my own, and I had half a thought to ask for it back before I remembered that I was with a person I'd just met. And a dude, too. I'd never wanted to hold onto another guy's hand before. Well, I guess I'd never really wanted to hold *anyone's* hand before.

"How's that for a view?" Drew asked in my ear. An unexpected prickling sensation tiptoed down my spine.

"It's amazing!" I called back. "Thank you."

He looked like he wanted to tell me something else, but the music faded out, and the crowd went ballistic. The redhead standing next to us started jumping up and down, up and down, and the man she was with was screaming at the top of his lungs. Behind me, Drew was yelling, too. I decided I'd do the same.

THROUGHOUT THE PERFORMANCE, the only thing I could think (when I even stopped to think) was that this was the best day of my life. I decided halfway in that it was time I attended more shows. Maybe Drew would come with me if Sean and Ronnie didn't want to.

I knew every song that Blink-182 played. Sang each verse at the top of my lungs. Sweat beaded at my forehead and fell down my face, but I forgot that I was hot, forgot that I'd been claustrophobic. A heavy weight that I'd been carrying on my shoulders seemingly since the beginning of my existence eased for the first time. I closed my eyes and let the music overwhelm my senses. I stared up at the ceiling and thanked whatever deity or goddess or whatever higher power was out there that I was at the Madder Hatter, listening to one of my favorite bands with a new friend by my side.

Maybe life wouldn't be so bad if I surrounded myself with *this*.

The lead singer crouched down and fist-bumped or high-fived everyone he could reach in the front row. Drew and I included. We looked at our hands like a god had caressed them, then we looked at each other and busted out laughing.

As they played their final song, my eyes stung and a tear fell down one of my cheeks. I wasn't ready for this concert to end. I wasn't ready to go back to my parents' hellhole, back to school, back to hiding. I wanted to live within the music forever.

When the band exited after their small encore, and the lights came on full blast, my skin vibrated, and I felt like I was floating. Drew and I finished our drinks and found our way back to our friends.

"There you are!" Emma cooed. She wrapped her arms around Drew's neck, which forced her onto her toes. "We were worried!"

I looked at Sean and Ronnie, who were the opposite of worried. Sean grinned at me with swollen lips, his goth girl for the night was wrapped around one side of his body. Ronnie looked unamused.

Emma looked back at us. "Ready to get out of here?"

I looked back at the stage and nodded even though I wanted to rewind the entire evening and watch it all play out again.

CHAPTER SEVEN

In the morning, I wake up alone. With a groan, I roll over to the side table and grab for my phone to check the time. A whopping three minutes before my alarm is set to go off. I slam a heavy pillow down on top of my face and groan again. The pillow smells of him, even through the strong scent of the hotel soap we used last night, he's right there underneath; he's always there.

I inhale deeply and feel myself harden almost instantly as flashes of last night flood my brain. Something about him always brings me to my knees. Last night had satiated my hunger for him temporarily, but I'm instantly needy all over again as the smell of him fills my nose.

After I gave Drew his gift, he gave *me* a gift in the shower. We had gotten clean as fast as possible, and then before I could wash the suds from my hair, Drew had gotten onto his knees and taken me into that fucking mouth of his, rubbing his tongue ring on the underside of my cockhead, delighting in the way he made me curse and cry out with his name on my lips.

He touched himself while he swallowed my length over and over until my eyeballs threatened to stick to the back of my head. After that, he stood up and turned me around. We'd brought my lube with us into the shower, and in no time, I was lathered up and prepped. The pleasure was blinding. He begged me not to come, but between his mouth and his cock, I came undone faster than I care to admit. He took his time with me, and I didn't mind at all. I kissed him everywhere I could reach and darted at his tongue with mine, even though my head was bent at an awful angle. When he came, he bit at my shoulder to keep himself from screaming.

I have never deserved Drew. Not ten years ago, and not now.

I force myself to take a cold shower to clear my head and make my hard on disappear. In the shower, guilt spreads over me. I don't know if I feel this way because I constantly cheat on Lizette, or if I no longer care that I constantly cheat on her and feel guilty about *feeling* that way. Somehow, I've come to rationalize the affair with Drew because we were together long before Lizzy came into the picture. Drew has always been mine; how do I give that up? All in all, it's incredibly fucked up. *I'm* incredibly fucked up. I thud my head against the shower wall and sigh. My shoulders are tight, and my breaths are shallow.

There's an engagement ring in my suitcase, and I have no idea how to prepare Drew for the inevitable. That thought alone takes me straight out of the mood. My breath hitches as I step out of the shower. My skin immediately rises with goosebumps. I refuse to look at my sorry ass in the mirror and make my way back to the bedroom.

For a moment, I stand in the middle of the room, the shame burning my chest. The sun has yet to come up, but the sky that peers into the room through a crack in the curtains is a hazy shade between gray and black, and I know the sun will rise soon enough. Water drips from what little chest hair I have, and I trail my fingers down my chest, remembering where Drew's mouth had been. Where Lizette's mouth has been. But if Lizette's kiss is like a flickering match in the wind, Drew's kiss is a raging wildfire. I turn on the Keurig for hot water and return to the bed. I sit down and check my phone as the water heats up. There are three texts.

Lizzy: Can't wait to see you tonight, babe!

Mike the Manager Man: Be on the bus in 30.

Drew: Thx for my present.

The only one I want to respond to is Drew.

He's the only one I don't respond to.

I change into my bus clothes after swiping on some deodorant—sweatpants, a ratty t-shirt, and a beanie. I fasten my Apple watch to my left wrist and put my bracelets on my right. I pack up what little I have out in the room, take my cup of hot water, and make my way out into the hallway.

At the elevator, I run into Mike. He smiles and nods at me. As we wait for the elevator to reach our floor, Trish and Brian come out of their rooms with their bags. They look like they stayed up way too late. Trish massages her temples, and she's sporting leftover eyeliner from last night's show. Brian has bags underneath his eyes that make it seem like he didn't sleep at all.

"Please tell me there's coffee on the bus." Brian yawns with exaggeration, stretching his dark brown, muscular arms above his head in a deep stretch.

Mike scoffs. "When is there ever *not* coffee on the bus?"

Brian shrugs and yawns again. I sip at my water and cringe a bit. It needs lemon, and it needs to be a few degrees cooler. But after last night, I knew I'd need my warm water regimen today.

The four of us make our way down to the ground level, a little scrunched together in the elevator with our bags. I take the sunglasses that I hung on my loose necklace off and place them on my head before the doors slide open. I hold my breath and send a silent prayer asking for there not to be any paparazzi.

"Don't worry. The hotel manager had the bus park out back where the employees park so we can fly under the radar," Mike says.

The doors open, and it's early enough that the hotel lobby is empty; the sight has me breathing easier already. I love seeing my fans, but the paparazzi can be a pain in the ass. Like a bad cold that you can't get rid of.

At the front desk, the manager, a balding man named Tom, leads us through a few doors and down a couple of long hallways until we reach the backlot.

Our tour bus, a giant red thing that we call Firecracker, barely fits. It's parked in between the actual parking spaces, backed in, and ready for its next trip. As soon as I walk up to the doors, our driver, Justin, opens the doors for us.

"Thanks, man!" I call out to Justin as I climb the three steps up with Trish and Brian behind me.

"I'm going to go wait for Sean and Drew upstairs," Mike says before walking away. "Lord knows those two will get lost immediately if left to their own devices." I snicker and Trish rolls her eyes.

The three of us enter the dining area of the bus. There's a small table that can seat six next to a small kitchen. Across from the table is a bench perfect for lounging. A pot of coffee and all of the fixings sit on the center of the table.

I move past the dining area and kitchen to claim my favorite spot at the back of the bus. It's a plush loveseat next to the bunk beds in one of the two "bedrooms." I toss my suitcase on the loveseat and make my way back to Brian and Trish. When I return, Trish is laying down on the bench and Brian is doctoring up his coffee, making it look so light it no longer resembles coffee at all.

After I slump down next to Brian, I finish off my water and pour a cup of Joe for myself. I'm really dreading today. I'm elated to be back on tour; I know that's not what's weighing me down.

It's the ring I bought for Lizette. It's the commitment that the ring symbolizes, and the heartbreak it will cause.

I should be excited to propose to Lizzy. Hell, I've spent countless hours trying to make myself feel that way. But now, I don't even understand why I bought the fucking ring.

Lizette is not Drew. No matter how many days I've spent trying to convince myself that I can live a happy life with her, I always come back to Drew.

Even though my luggage is at the back of the bus, I can feel the ring screaming at me from its tiny box, begging me not to pop the question–but the only alternative is to not propose, which would break her heart and cause more harm than good in too many ways.

I want to be the person who can come clean about their actions.

I want to be the man Drew needs me to be; has always asked me to be.

I just don't know how.

CHAPTER EIGHT

APRIL 2012

I didn't know much about Emma—or Drew, for that matter, but as Sean pulled into her parents' house, I knew one thing: Emma's parents were fucking loaded.

Emma told us before we left D.C. to park in the driveway behind Drew. Her parents were in bed and they didn't care what we did as long as we weren't devastatingly loud. It was the opposite of my house. Her parents had money and it showed. My parents spent their "disability" and "unemployment" checks on drugs. Shit, they hadn't bought me a thing since I started high school. Emma's parents didn't care if we had fun, but my parents would knock my teeth out if I brought one friend home.

Envy curled its way down my chest and settled in between my ribs. I didn't like the feeling, and begged it away as I jumped down and out of Sean's van. His one night whatever—stand? Hookup? I didn't know—came with us and was allowed to ride shotgun.

Emma and Drew got out of his dinged up black Camry and smiled back at me. Drew motioned for me to follow them, and I did. Ronnie and Sean were bickering about something, so I left them behind. Emma led us to the side of the massive, two-story colonial, down a couple of steps, and up to a side door. I could barely see anything in the dark, but I imagined Emma and Drew had done this enough that they could find their way.

I heard a faint click and Drew grabbed my elbow to guide me forward. He steered me inside of the warm house right as Emma flicked on a light.

My jaw dropped. "Whoa."

"My parents hadn't used the space in forever, so they let me take it over. I sleep in here most nights." She laughed. "I think it used to be an office or something?" Emma shrugged and made her way over to a kitchen area which held a full bar.

The room was as big as the trailer I lived in. I was envious all over again but pushed the feeling down as I took in the walls covered in band posters, the maroon drum set in the back corner, and several luxurious leather couches set up in a "C" formation around a flat screen TV. There were several Bohemian style rugs overlapped on top of each other across the floor. Emma turned on a few dim lights— one of which was a lava lamp—and then turned off the fluorescent overhead light. She reached into a drawer of a small table by the door and brought out a stick of incense. She lit it with a small box of matches, then slumped down on one of the couches right as the others made their way inside.

"Oh, shit," Goth Girl muttered as soon as she walked in. The look on her face must have been like mine.

As predicted, the other two people Drew and Emma were at the concert with had decided to go home, so it was just the six of us. Sean and Ronnie came in behind Goth Girl. Sean whistled and took off his jacket, wafting the strong scent of ganja throughout the room. Ronnie, who never said too much, even commented, "This place is cool as hell."

Drew looked at me almost as if he was embarrassed and I didn't know why. The others sat on the couches as Emma brought up her music app and turned on a playlist. Immediately, the music came on via surround sound.

"Drinks?" Drew asked the group.

"Vodka tonic, *pleeasseee?*" Emma asked with a giggle. Drew gave her a curt nod. I couldn't help but notice that he didn't smile down at her.

"Beer?" Ronnie asked.

"Yeah, I think there's some Corona in the fridge."

"I'll come help you," I said. I needed water, anyway. I still had a small buzz, and knew I needed to hydrate before I drank more.

I followed Drew into the small kitchen and bar in the corner of the room.

"Can I get a cup for water?" I asked while he rummaged through the fridge. He gave me a lopsided smirk which made my stomach tumble, then pointed to one of the cabinets. I opened it and took out a disposable Solo cup and filled it with tap water. I chugged the whole thing and filled it up again as Drew set a few beers on the granite countertop beside me.

"You mind getting out a couple more of those for me?" he asked.

I set my cup down and got two more cups. Drew went over to the bar and looked through the various liquor bottles. He came back and stood beside me with a bottle of Grey Goose. Instead of asking me to move from the sink, he simply leaned over me and poured himself a cup of water. Like me, he chugged it and then refilled it.

He smelled like bourbon mixed with aftershave and a hint of cedar. When he pulled back from me, it felt like something was missing. The strange feeling of longing was unsettling.

Drew dropped a few ice cubes in the third cup and proceeded to make his girlfriend's drink. I could have taken the beers over to the others, but I didn't want to leave him alone.

"So, um," I cleared my throat and tried to be casual. "How long have you and Emma been together?"

Drew shrugged. "A few months. We've been friends far longer than that, though." He warily looked behind us at Emma. She was laughing at something, and Sean had a shit-eating grin decorated on his face.

Drew lowered his voice. "Honestly, I liked it better when we were just friends." He shook his head as if he wished what he was saying wasn't true. "I don't know why I'm telling you this," he laughed quietly. "I barely know you, but I feel like I could tell you anything for some reason." His milk chocolate eyes met mine, and one corner of his mouth tipped up in a small smile.

I laughed awkwardly and looked away. "Yeah, I get what you mean."

Drew sighed after a drawn out moment. "Anyways—I have plans of ending things with Emma," he confided barely above a whisper.

I nodded and wanted to ask more, but figured I'd wait. "How'd you guys meet?"

"Freshman year of high school. I learned to play piano as a kid, so I joined band. Emma plays the clarinet." He paused with the drinks in his hand before we made our way over to the couches. "We kind of hated it. It was too uniform and not creative enough. After that year, we ditched band. Emma got into photography, and I taught myself how to play the drums."

"Wow," I said, astonished. A self-taught drummer. "That's impressive."

He rolled his eyes and shook his head. "Nah. I just wanted to learn. So, I did."

It was obvious that Drew wasn't aware of how big of a deal that was. I thought it was the coolest thing I'd ever heard. I wanted to ask him a lot of questions: why the drums? How did he teach himself?

Amy Winehouse's voice sounded from the speakers around us. I noticed her unique vocals immediately. I often listened to bands with male leads, but I found as I got more and more into my secret singing adventure that there was a lot to learn from leading women, and Amy had become one of my favorites.

Drew sat next to Emma on the couch she occupied. Sean and his lady were on the loveseat, cuddled up and opening their beers with red-rimmed, glossy eyes. Ronnie sat on the other loveseat, already chugging his beer down. He had his phone out, and I knew he was more than likely texting his girlfriend. Seeing as Emma and Drew were on the largest couch, I sat on Drew's other side.

Emma held up her Solo cup and beamed at us. "To great music and new friends!"

We all smiled, even Ronnie, who'd lost his energetic spirit after the concert ended. We held up our bottles and cups and clinked them together just as Amy Winehouse's song ended and was replaced with the Beastie Boys.

The music posters all over the walls impressed me. The range of music that Emma appreciated was immense, as were some of her black and white photography shots of live shows that hung framed around the front door. I knew they had to be her work because of Drew's mention, and because he was in several of the photos. My eyes skimmed her photographs before taking in the posters: Hendrix, Britney Spears, The Beatles, The Grateful Dead, Fall Out Boy, Dr. Dre, Fleetwood Mac, Creedence Clearwater Revival, Blink-182 (naturally) and so many more.

"So, where do you guys go to college?" Emma asked. She leaned forward over Drew a bit to talk.

I couldn't help but snort. "We aren't quite *in* college yet."

Emma's eyes bulged, and she reminded me of a young kid as her jaw dropped. "Oh my God! No way?" She playfully slapped my knee. "You have to at least be juniors or seniors, I hope? You don't look that young."

Drew looked amused and hid his grin underneath the rim of his cup.

"I just turned eighteen. Sean and Ronnie are a bit older." I took a swig of my drink. "We graduate next month."

Emma wiped imaginary sweat from her brow. "Whew. Good. We aren't much older, then. We both go to community college, though Drew attends down in Fredericksburg."

That caught my attention. "Yeah?" I asked him.

He nodded. "Yep. Almost halfway through with my associates. Not that I care at this point."

I wondered what he meant by that. I parted my lips to ask him about it, but Emma beat me to it. "What about you? Are you going to college?"

"Well, if I do go to college, I'll be attending with Drew." Drew stared at me inquisitively. "I live in Stafford, so we're really close. But I don't know what I'm going to do after graduation. All I know is I'm going to get the hell out of my parents' place as soon as possible."

Emma cocked a brow, but luckily got distracted by a notification on her phone.

"Stafford, eh?" Drew asked. "We're practically neighbors."

I chuckled. "You aren't kidding. What high school did you go to?"

We talked for the next twenty minutes about our high schools. He went to one closer to Fredericksburg, unsurprisingly. Drew told me about how he almost didn't graduate without Emma's help in Precalculus, and how he lucked out to have her at his school because she lived so far away. Apparently, Emma had begged her parents to let her attend elsewhere because she hated her middle school and wanted to be around different people. Then, he went on about how he used to sign up for the art electives because they were easier to skip out on. I told him about our school after that. We ended up sitting so close that our legs pressed up against each other while we talked. Emma had moved on to smoke a blunt with Sean and his girl outside. Ronnie paid no attention to us from where he sat on his separate couch, glued to his phone.

"Why did you say what you did earlier?" I asked. "About college, I mean?"

Drew looked down at the cup in his lap glumly. He smiled, but it wasn't a happy one–it was a smile that looked like he'd come to terms with something.

"I don't like it," he said, matter-of-factly. "I don't see myself becoming a lawyer, or a teacher, or a doctor, or any of that." I could feel the distress rolling off of him.

47

"Well, what do you see yourself doing?"

He looked at me. Really looked at me. Into me. His eyes trailed over my face, down my neck and Adam's apple, to my chest. They roamed over each inch of me like he was trying to figure out who I was and why I cared.

Finally, he shrugged. "A drummer. I want to be a drummer. I don't have to be in a band that makes it big or anything. Playing local shows on the weekends with a small band would suffice, but I can't tell my parents that's what I want." He blew out a breath. "At least not yet. I live with them on the condition that I stay in school."

Ah. That made sense.

"I've never really played for them. I'm still learning, but I feel like I'm really getting the hang of it now; that I might be decent. I hope with a little more practice that I can grow the balls to show them and ask them their thoughts. Then I can focus on the drums more and maybe join a band. Or form one."

My heart raced. For a split-second, I imagined Drew and me on stage. Him on the drums, me singing. I pushed the thought away immediately. No one had ever heard me sing, and there was no one to tell me whether I was any good at it. I shook my head and downed the rest of my drink to swallow up my daydreams.

"You must have good parents," I said. "If they let you stay with them, and you think that in the future you can trust them with your dream. That's not something to take for granted."

Drew was about to reply when the group returned from outside. Emma rubbed her arms with her hands and then practically jumped into *both* of our laps. Her hair was thick with smoke and an underlying hint of vanilla.

I scrunched up my nose as her long hair fell over my face. I liked the way Drew smelled more. As an excuse to get away, I got up and took mine and Drew's drinks to the bar to refill them. While I was up, I drank a bit more water, too.

My entire body was hot. I chalked it up to the alcohol combined with sitting close to others along with the long night. After taking some deep breaths and some large sips of water, I felt better.

For the next hour or so, we all talked, laughed, and listened to Emma's broad range of music. Goth Girl's name was Courtney, not that we'd ever see her again, but it was nice to know her name. Emma explained her plans of a dual-degree in business and photography as she giggled, deep in her marijuana-induced haze. Sean and Drew talked music for a while after Drew found out Sean played the bass. They talked about playing together sometime, and I couldn't help but fantasize what it would be like to be included.

Emma was the first to pass out, which Drew said was typical. He tucked her into the couch after retrieving a knitted blanket and throwing it on her shoulders, and then we sat on the ground so she could lay out fully. Next, we noticed that Ronnie had fallen asleep sitting upright with his head leaned back on the couch cushion. Sean and Courtney excused themselves to "talk" outside, which really meant they'd left to go bang in Sean's van, which was fine by me.

Drew took over the music as soon as we were alone. He immediately played "Aliens Exist" by Blink-182, and turned the volume up a notch.

"One of my favorites," I said.

"Me too."

We listened for a while in peace. We could have moved to the vacant couch at any time, but we stayed put where we were until Drew asked, "Want to go get some fresh air?"

The contentment I'd eased into while sitting next to him on the floor evaporated and was quickly replaced with anxiety and excitement, and a different feeling that I couldn't pinpoint, but had had on and off all night.

"Sure."

Drew and I made one more drink each and poured them into a couple of empty water bottles. Drew said it would be necessary so we wouldn't spill them. I didn't understand why we would spill, but I didn't question him. After that, he unhooked his phone from the cord that connected to the speakers and beckoned me outside.

The air was cooler than it had been when we'd arrived. I didn't know what time it was, and I didn't care to look, either. It was still dark, and the night wasn't over yet. I followed Drew to the back of the house, careful not to trip as I walked. Drew shoved his water bottle full of liquor into the back pocket of his jeans and motioned for me to do the same. That's when I figured out we were about to climb.

There were a few trees lining the back of the house, but one had branches that reached up to the roof. It would have been an easy climb had it not been for the lack of light.

"Climb up after me," Drew instructed. He pulled himself up and began the ascent.

I took my time and climbed in the same way he had; careful to place my feet on the same branches and knots in the trunk. It became only a little easier to see in the dark as we made our way up and my eyes adjusted. It was miraculous that I didn't slip and bust my ass.

Finally, Drew took my hand and helped me onto the sloped roof. There was something particularly intimate about taking his hand and trusting him to help me up. Like I'd known him for years rather than minutes.

"We just have to make it up this incline, then there's a spot where the roof is flat up ahead."

I nodded to him in the dark and I wondered how many times he'd done this. How many times he and Emma came up to the roof. Or, was this something he typically did alone?

Drew stopped abruptly after a few moments of silence. The roof became level underneath my feet, and I let out a breath of relief. Drew plopped down and patted the spot next to him. Before I sat down all the way, I reached in my pocket and retrieved my drink.

Drew pulled out his own drink and joined me in a silent salute to the stars.

My phone buzzed in my pocket, and the last thing I wanted to do was look at it, but my annoying sense of responsibility kicked in. No one would have texted me so late if it wasn't important.

"Sorry," I murmured to Drew as I looked down at my screen. He smiled and waved me off, then proceeded to bring out his phone. He brought up his music again, and let the silent night above transform into a concert beneath the stars.

Sean: Yo. I'm taking Courtney back to mine. And Ronnie. Where u at?

Me: I'm going to stay. Cool?

Sean: Where did u go? I'll hyu in the morning.

"Who's that?" Drew asked. I realized he was closer to my body than he had been originally. His dark, wavy locks of hair fell over his forehead, only visible in the quaint light from the stars and half-moon above us.

"Sean," I muttered. "He and Ronnie are taking off."

Drew asked, "You want to go? I know we just climbed up, but I don't mind taking you—"

I shook my head. "No. I'm where I want to be. As long as you're cool with me staying." It was cheesy, and I knew it. To my surprise, Drew's eyes warmed as they bore into mine. He leaned back and lounged on the roof tiles while Weezer's "El Scorcho" thrummed from his phone.

Before I leaned back and joined him, I made the decision to relax completely for the rest of the night. I turned my phone on silent and took another long swig from my bottle. As I got settled against the roof, I heard the flick of a lighter. I cocked my head at Drew as he lit up a cigarette that he took from a crumpled pack of Camels.

"You smoke?" I asked. I didn't want to seem like I was judging him, because I wasn't. My parents smoked, but unlike them, Drew didn't smell like nicotine and stale smoke. And he didn't smoke *inside.*

Drew inhaled deeply and held the cigarette in his fingers like a joint. He exhaled and blew the cloud out into the sky above. "I do sometimes. Mostly on nights I see shows. I like to lay back a bit." He smiled, though it seemed a little glum. Before I could ask about it, he said, "You see that pack?" He motioned to the disheveled little box by his hip. "I've had it for almost a year."

"Wow. How do you not get addicted?"

He sucked on the stick again and blew out more smoke. "Mind over matter?" he said, though it sounded like a question.

"You must not have an addictive personality," I chuckled.

He shrugged. "It depends. Don't get me wrong, I went through a whole phase where I smoked these religiously during my last two years of high school, but it was mostly out of boredom."

I'd never smoked a cigarette, but something about it in between his lips was alluring. I liked how his lips formed around the small stick; how the filter stuck to his bottom lip while he spoke.

"Can I try?" I asked. Immediately, my face felt flushed with embarrassment. Maybe I shouldn't have asked.

Drew eyed me, took one more inhale, then passed the half-smoked cigarette to me. I received it awkwardly in between my fingertips.

"Just don't get addicted, Ash," Drew said softly. "All good things in moderation." He winked at me as I lifted the cigarette to my lips.

"Deal."

I parted my lips, aware that Drew watched my every movement. I inhaled through the filter, just a little, and though I'd smoked weed before, the burn was different. On my second inhale, I was more delighted by the taste. I blew the smoke out and passed the cigarette back to Drew.

"Keep it, if you want."

I did. I smoked it slowly and didn't inhale too deeply. Still, I noticed a sense of calm and a delightful tingle spread through my chest after several puffs. After my last exhale, I looked at Drew with the leftover filter.

He chuckled and took it from me, then smashed the cherry on the bottom of his shoe before tucking the butt into his front pocket.

We laid like that on the roof in silence for a long time. We listened to the music Drew played on his phone, we drank, and we shared another cigarette.

My mind didn't race with worries. I wasn't concerned about my parents or graduation or what to do after school ended. I just was. He just was. But as calm as I felt, I still had the overwhelming urge to continue talking with Drew. I wanted to get to know him. I wanted to listen to his stories and contagious laughter. Though he was a stranger, being with Drew felt like coming home after being away for far too long.

"Can I ask something personal?" I murmured into the silence.

He chuckled. "Sure."

I paused and put the words together in my head before I continued. "Why did you like it better when you and Emma were just friends?"

I wasn't sure why I wanted to know the specifics of their relationship, but the question planted itself inside of me hours prior and grew until I was itching to ask.

"Ah," Drew said quietly. "I wish I could say it was complicated, or we'd overcome some trial that had strained our relationship or...I don't know. Something like that." He huffed out a little bit of air through his nose and took a swig of his drink. "But when it comes down to it, I don't share her feelings." He swallowed hard and then looked over at me for the first time since he started talking about Emma. "We fell into something intimate because no one else was around. Or, at least, that's how it feels to me. She's in love with me, and I can't return the favor."

I pondered his words as he looked at me with glossy eyes. A worried line formed in between his brows. I didn't know how to respond. Instead, hesitantly, I reached my arm over to him and squeezed his shoulder.

"I can't say I've ever been in a similar situation," I admitted. "I've never really been in a relationship." Usually, I felt embarrassed when I told people that. "What are you going to do?"

Drew sighed and lit another cigarette. I liked the way he blew smoke out through his nose after inhaling. "I'm going to have to end it. Sooner rather than later."

"Do you like someone else?" I pried.

He smiled crookedly and handed me the cigarette. "Nah. Not at the moment." He paused and watched me inhale the smoke. I wasn't coughing from it anymore. "Now it's my turn to ask you something."

My heart picked up its pace. I cocked a brow. "Oh?"

Drew grinned and flashed me his pearly whites in the cobalt darkness. "What do you want to do after high school?"

"Get the hell away from my parents," I said without missing a beat.

I expected him to ask about that, but he didn't. "No. I mean, what do you want to *do?* Who do you want to be?"

Drew studied me, and I focused the cigarette in between my lips before giving up and moving my eyes down to his mouth, to his lip piercing that glittered in the faint light. His broad shoulders twitched with the slight tilt of his head as his gaze enveloped me whole.

"Sing," I said honestly.

It was the first time I'd ever revealed my dreams to someone else, and surprisingly to someone I barely knew. But it felt good to say it out loud. I found that I wanted to belt it from the rooftop.

CHAPTER NINE

It's only a few hours bus ride to Austin, but with every slow minute that ticks by, my skin burns more and more as I think about Ash's skin on mine. I shove the familiar feelings of disappointment down as low as they can go each time I think about how I had to sneak out of his room before the sun rose, and ponder over how many mornings I've done so in the past.

Despite the years of hiding, the late nights spent in the dark with lust and sweat the only things on our skin, all the times we've lied to steal a minute or so alone...every time I look over at him, my aching heart swells inside of my chest.

Ash lounges in "his spot" at the back of the bus. He's always on that couch unless one of us beats him to it, typically just to mess with him. I lay on the lower bunk bed across from him, tired from making up for our two weeks apart last night.

He has his Apple AirPods in and he's bobbing his head to a familiar beat that I can hear faintly across the small room. He does this before every show, ritualistically. He listens to the songs we have on the list for that night, goes over them, and reminds himself of the beats and the lyrics as though he doesn't know them all by heart. Ash always likes to mix things up. He might draw out the last line of a song one night. He might skip that very song altogether the next. He might mash up one of our songs with a classic (though he at least warns us for those). Hell, he might be brainstorming new lyrics now for all I know.

The look plastered on his face is my favorite: his brows are knitted together in concentration, and his lips are parted ever so slightly as he sings silent words to himself. He taps a pen on his knee to the beat. Every few moments, he sits up and takes a sip of his lemon water or tea or whatever is steaming in the cup on the table.

As tired as I am, I want to go over to the couch and climb on top of him and put those lips to use on me–but no. There are people on the bus. Friends who are also coworkers, technically. It would be inappropriate, even if we were out in the open with our secrets.

Still—the thought lingers, and my cock begs for attention. I inhale a deep breath and stare at the top bunk to try and calm myself down. Right as I start to come down, though, I feel his eyes on me. I don't even have to look over to know his thoughts are similar to mine. You'd think we had been apart for far longer than a couple of weeks or that we were teenagers again.

Ash gets up from his spot and puts his phone and AirPods down on the seat. He walks out of the room, and I hear him talking to Sean down the hall, though I can't make out what he says. Then he's back. He closes and locks the door behind him, and his eyes are all heat as he stalks toward me.

"What're you doi—?"

He cuts me off by crawling on top of me and kissing me deeply. He kisses me like he'll never kiss me again, and for a split second, that scares me to my core because I almost believe it.

It's not like it's unlikely, after all. I'm not blind and there have been close calls in the past.

Ash presses his weight into me as he parts my mouth open with his tongue. I flick at his tongue with my own and moan softly into him, temporarily forgetting the others.

I pull back, already gasping for air. "What the hell did you tell them?"

Ash props himself up and runs his hands over my chest. He's always been a fan of my muscles, and I'm happy to keep going to the gym if it means he'll touch me like this.

He feels me through my jeans, and I squirm, trying not to move and trying not to lunge at him at the same time. My heart threatens to fall out of my chest as he leans forward and licks his lips. "We have work to do on a new song we're trying to write," he whispers.

It's not technically a lie. We *do* have some songs we're working on together. Our best songs come from me and Ash staying up all night and brainstorming.

"But what about the others?" I all but groan as he unbuttons my pants.

He shrugs. "Trish is asleep, Brian and Sean are watching a movie, and Mike is FaceTiming Miranda." Miranda, Mike's wife, is one of the coolest people ever, and he was constantly homesick when he was away from her. I understood the feeling all too well.

"Oh." I swallow hard. *Oh.* "Aren't you tired of me after last night?" I tease.

"I've never been tired of you, Drew," he whispers in my ear. Then, he nibbles on my lobe as he works my pants down past my ass. "And I know you want me, because I've been watching you, too."

I would have thought that by now we would have tired of one another after ten years of this, but it's the opposite. As we've grown up and turned from boys to men, we know what we like, and sneaking around has always been a turn on, despite how upset it can make me. Ash knows what gets me screaming his name in a matter of seconds. Knows how to make me see stars. Knows what to say to calm me down and support me. And vice versa.

My worries about the others on the bus fade as his lips meet mine once more. He parts from me way too soon, and I almost protest, until I feel his warm lips wrap around my crown and slowly work my length into the back of his throat inch by blissful, dizzying inch.

AUSTIN IS BEAUTIFUL. We'd stopped during our first tour, and I've always wanted to return. Especially because of Zilker Park.

It's lunchtime by the time our bus made it to the city—an hour after Ash took me in his mouth. An hour after he took me on the floor of the bus, and we spent minutes and minutes just making out like a couple of horny teenagers hiding from their parents. I guess some things never change, after all.

I want nothing more than a beer and a cigarette after what happened on the bus, and I don't even smoke that often anymore, but it's early, and we have a lot to do before the start of the show tonight. That, and there's nothing like a smoke after a mind-blowing orgasm.

Needless to say, we're starving.

Before we head to the hotel, Mike reserves us a whole ass restaurant to eat at in peace. He said it wasn't a hassle for them, that they don't open until after four anyways, and that the chef and hostess are big fans. Still, it feels pretentious to me. It always has–but the feeling fades at the taste of fresh, homemade garlic knots on my tongue. The Italian restaurant is quaint, and the chef knows his shit.

We sit at a large round table in the center of the restaurant. Sean is high as a kite after taking an edible. His red eyes almost match his hair at this point. Brian and Trish look at the menus with serious concentration while Mike taps at a game on his phone. He always orders the same thing for his Italian meals. Chicken Alfredo. He didn't even bother to look at the menu.

Underneath the table, Ash's knee bumps into mine, and a comfortable warmth spreads throughout my body. It's the same feeling as falling into bed and cuddling in a clean set of sheets.

"What're you getting?" I ask him casually. I haven't even looked at the menu yet because I've been too focused on the garlic knots. I want to go to the gym later, but after this feast, that might not happen.

"Literally everything sounds good," Ash sighs.

I open my menu and opt for their signature gnocchi immediately.

Our waitress comes up to our table. She has only been by twice to deliver us our drinks and our appetizer, but I know it's taking all of her willpower not to come over more often or ask us for a picture or an autograph. I already have plans to leave her a nice tip and whatever else. Food service isn't easy, and she's been amazing.

The girls usually crush on Ash more than me, but I have a good following, too. Sometimes they crush on both of us. We're used to it by now. It's flattering so long as they aren't into us in a creepy way.

If only they knew what I like. What *we* like.

I notice that the hostess—*Cherie*—is all eyes for me. She comes over and refills my water, even though I've only taken a couple of sips.

"Are y'all ready to order?" she asks with a wide smile.

"Can I have one more minute?" Trish asks.

"Sure thing, I'll come back in a few."

Before she leaves, I catch her lightly by the elbow. She looks down at me from where she stands, her large brown eyes wide.

"While they decide, did you want to get a picture? Only if you want to. You've been wonderful. Thank you for letting us come in early," I say.

Ash knocks his knee with mine underneath the table. He loves when I sweet talk.

She grows flustered immediately, and if I liked women, I think it would've been incredibly sexy. "I—um, I don't know if I'm allowed? I need to go ask—"

I cut her off. "It's fine. If your boss asks, we're the ones who offered, after all."

Ash smirks up at her. "We're happy to take a pic with the real fans." He winks, and her cheeks turn cherry red.

The next few minutes are spent taking pictures with Cherie, who comes out of her shy demeanor once she sees that Ash and I are just a couple of goofballs who happened to make it big in a band and became famous. We take turns posing with her alone, and then we both get a picture with her. Finally, we have the rest of the group join for one last shot. Cherie takes everyone's orders with a sunshiney glow on her face and then makes her way back into the kitchen.

"You two are generous today." Mike cocks an eyebrow at us.

If only he knew why.

Not that we aren't typically kind and generous to our fans. Quite the opposite, actually. But it was a little out of character for us to take *so* many pictures. Either way, Cherie is sweet, and she apparently came in early just to wait on us.

We cherish the delicious food once our entrees arrive, knowing that we won't be eating for a long while—not until the show is over. It's funny how all sense of need goes away when I'm on stage. If I'm thirsty or hungry or tired, well, it doesn't usually kick in until at least an hour after we've exited the stage.

Once we're done, we hop back onto the bus and almost pass out in our collective food comas. I left Cherie a two-hundred-dollar tip in cash on the table. As we drive to our hotel for the night, I wonder if she'll be at the concert. I wish I would've asked if she had tickets, but after our photo-op, I got lost in the food and in Brian and Sean's bad jokes. Ash and I might be the ones fucking, but those two act like an old married couple, and it never ceases to make me grin.

The concert tonight is at the Long Center. Our hotel is only a couple of blocks away, and it's a giant skyscraper of a thing. Sometimes I wish Mike would just rent us a cheap Airbnb for the night, but he likes the privacy of getting away from us after the concerts after long nights. I never understood why he decided to be a band manager, but he's damn good at his job for someone so introvertive.

Instead of the whole top floor, he got us a set of rooms on one side of the top level. Apparently, there are a few high-profile people staying on the other side of us, though Mike won't tell us who.

"Is it Elton John?" Sean begs as we pull up to the hotel. "Oh! Dolly Parton?" He scratches the scruff on his chin and pretends to be thinking hard. "It's the Doors, isn't it?" he gasps.

Mike huffs a sigh and rolls his eyes so hard, I think his eyeballs might fall out. "Sean, for the love of God, shut up."

Sean smirks. "I bet you it really *is* Elton John. Love that guy." Sean winks at Mike, and Mike pretends to look out of the window.

We're all sitting at the front of the bus, waiting for it to park. Well, everyone except for Ash, who must have fallen asleep on the couch.

"Remember the first time we met Elton? At that award show in, like, 2015?" Brian asks. As if any of us could ever forget. "What an awesome person."

Trish looks just about as thrilled as Mike, with her eyes glaring at Brian and Sean. The bus stops, and Mike hauls ass to go check-in for us. We know the drill. We stay on the bus until he comes back. As much as we love our fans, we still like to get checked in and ready for the show in peace. We always travel with a couple of bodyguards who accompany us almost everywhere. We only have two for now, and they're in a car behind us. Sometimes I think it's overkill until I remember the one fan who snuck behind us while we walked into a restaurant one evening several years ago and all but jumped on me, trying to get a taste of my neck before one of the guards ripped her off me.

Ash joins us and sits down on the bench seat next to Trish and Sean with a drawn-out yawn. I can tell by the slight shadows underneath his hazel eyes that he took a catnap in the back. I wish we could all take a real nap, but as soon as we put our shit in our rooms, it's go time.

Sean pats Ash on the back. "You excited for tonight, bro?" Sean wiggles his eyebrows. I can't help the crease I feel form in between my brows. Ash seems to pale a little, and I wonder what's up. Ash doesn't keep shit from me, so I'm probably overreacting.

"I'm always excited for a live show," Ash replies. But his voice is strained, and I can tell by the way he looks at Sean that he doesn't want to talk.

What is going on? I feel the hairs all over my body rise as the feeling of something heavy drops in my stomach. I hope I'm making things up, but something tells me I'm not. Something's up, and Ash hasn't told me what it is.

I stare at Ash while we exit the bus, but I don't say anything. I can't question him in front of the others. Unfortunately, I won't have him alone again for a while, either. Great. I'm going to go through this entire day with anxiety boiling in my veins.

Mike leads the way to our rooms alongside the manager of the hotel. This time, it's an elderly Black woman with a kind smile and not a single hair out of place. She beams at us in a maternal way that has me missing my own mother. I make a mental note to try and call her and Dad later.

One of our bodyguards, Jim, watches us from the side as Mike watches the front. The other guard, Evan, guards from the back. The others are joking around and getting hyped for the show, but Ash stares at his boots as we walk. He only does that when he feels bad about something. There's no way I'm making this up. But we were so normal earlier. He was even more risky than usual.

My head swims with thousands of *what-ifs* as we load onto two separate elevators up to the top floor with one guard in each. I'm in the same elevator as Jim, Sean, Trish, and Brian. Ash went with Mike, Evan, and the hotel manager.

Our elevator arrives first, and we follow Jim to the left to our set of rooms. Unable to help myself, I peek down the opposite hallway and wonder who has the other rooms. I don't think I'll ever get used to being part of the "famous" crowd, meeting celebrities and people of power frequently as we tour and go to award shows. I still feel like the nineteen-year-old misfit who lived in his parents' house and stayed up too late banging on the drums. The first time I met Billie Joe Armstrong, I almost shit myself, and the same thing happened the other two times after that—and I pissed myself a little bit when I met Tom Petty a couple of years before he passed away. Starstruck didn't even begin to cover what I'd felt.

The other elevator arrives a few seconds later. As usual, the manager sees us to our rooms and makes sure everything is in order before leaving us alone.

"Sean and Drew?" she questions. We raise our hands like we're on a third-grade field trip and we're each other's assigned buddies so we don't get lost. She smiles a perfectly glossed smile. "You two are at the end. I'll take you there. Mike, the other rooms are right after the elevators. You're sure you don't mind staying on the floor down below?" She gives Mike a gentle smile. "I'm so sorry I couldn't get you all in one place."

Mike waves her off and even smiles. "You kidding? I'm looking forward to a night away from these hooligans." He says it with his thick country accent that's heightened ever since we arrived in Texas, and winks at the manager.

The manager leads Sean and me down the hallway. The plush carpets are navy blue with a golden geometric pattern, and the beige walls are precisely decorated with chrome wall sconces. Despite the lack of decor, the hotel smells like it's thoroughly cleaned, and often, and I appreciate that.

She stops by the last two doors at the end of the hall. Our doors are across from one another, and I make the decision to ask Sean why Ash is acting weird as soon as she leaves. I don't like talking about my best friend behind his back, but I don't want to spend the day walking on eggshells, either.

"You both have the best rooms in the hotel. Just don't tell the others." The manager curves her lips into a mischievous grin. "Nothing beats the view from these rooms. Please let me know if you need anything." She passes us our keycards and then saunters off.

Sean moves to slide his card into the security lock, but I catch him by the arm before he can slide it in all the way.

"What's up, man?" Sean asks. He's still high from his edible, and he smells like he needs a shower, but that's not unusual. His eyes bug out a little bit at my hand on his arm.

I take a breath to steady myself. To make my voice sound neutral and not full of worry. "What was with Ash on the bus? Is he okay?"

We can barely see the others from where we stand. I see Trish go into her room, but no one else.

"Huh?" Sean asks, arching a bushy brow. It takes him a minute to figure out what I'm asking. "Oh, you mean about tonight?"

I give him a curt nod.

He chuckles as if it's nothing. "Lizette's meeting up with us after the show is all. I dunno why he acted weird. You'd think he'd be excited to pop the question." Sean shrugs and slides his card into the lock. "Maybe he's just nervous about it?" Sean shrugs and then enters his room and closes the door in my face without another word.

My temper rises instantly and my cheeks heat. I walk into my own room and all but slam the heavy door.

The manager was right. My corner room is surrounded by floor-to-ceiling windows which show me the gorgeous city down below. Despite the view, all I want to do is throw something heavy out of the window and scream.

I'm no fucking idiot, and Ash knows that. Which means he doesn't have the balls to tell me what's up for himself. We've fought about his and Lizette's relationship countless times.

Tonight, my worst nightmare will manifest into reality.

After ten years of living in the shadows with Ash, he's going to rip it all apart.

Everything we've built together.

Everything we've shared.

All of it.

CHAPTER TEN

JUNE 2012

After that fateful concert where I met Asher, Sean, and Ronnie, I texted Ash almost every single day. I'd only seen him in person a couple of times since then. Once was when I surprised him at his high school graduation. He was so shocked that I'd come to watch him cross the stage, and I'm glad I did despite being nervous about it, because the look on his face when he noticed I was there was well worth it. As it turned out, I was the only one in the crowd who'd shown up for him, as all his other friends were graduating with him, and his scumbag parents didn't even bother to come. Asher dodged my questions about his parents, and I let him, but I hoped he'd open up to me one day when he was ready.

The only other time I saw him was when he came to hang out at my place down in Fredericksburg. Ash didn't have a car, so I drove up to Stafford to pick him up, even though the construction paired with the awful drivers made the thirteen miles feel like three hundred.

I'd pulled up to his trailer home and understood a little bit more. The trailer wasn't one of the nice ones that you see sometimes. It looked decades old and was run-down and covered in mildew from the outside. Even from where I sat in my parked car, I could tell the home wasn't level. The roof seemed to cave in on one side, and the greenery surrounding the small patch of land it sat on was unruly. There were beer bottles and old, discarded Solo cups in the yard. No car was parked in the drive, but Ash had instructed me to park on the side of the road and he'd come out to meet me.

His face looked shameful when he opened the passenger side door and hopped in. I drove away from the trailer without saying a word about it. I wanted to comfort him somehow—after I'd realized he trusted me by showing me that side of his life—but I couldn't think of what to say or do, so I simply played one of my playlists over the car speakers.

Once we hit the highway back to Fredericksburg, he was bobbing his head along to the music, and his shoulders had eased a bit. He told me at graduation that he wanted to move out as soon as possible. He had packed a bag for the weekend to stay at my place, and we spent the two nights listening to music, playing video games, walking around my neighborhood, and eating all the food Mom made us. On the way back to his parents' home, Asher told me that they weren't good people. He didn't elaborate, and I didn't pry.

After a few hangouts and many long conversations via text, I started calling him Ash instead of Asher. I think he preferred Ash, anyway, but now that we were closer, I felt more comfortable referring to him by his nickname.

One weekend in June when Ash came over for a visit, he didn't go back home.

My mother had taken one good look at him and declared he was much too skinny as soon as she met him. The second time he visited, she insisted he bring his laundry for her to wash. I didn't tell Mom anything about his home life, but something told me he had opened up to her in a way I wasn't aware of. Mom has always been like that. She's the person you confide in, even if she's a stranger to you.

Mom had taken one whiff of the stale cigarette smoke on his clothes, looked at the holes in his t-shirts and jeans, and noticed that his clothes were a bit too small, and that was it. We were playing *Call of Duty* down in the basement where I kept my Xbox and drum set and a couple of old, ratty couches, when Mom came marching down the stairs. Usually, she knocked, but not that time.

She pointed at Ash and gave him her beautiful, well-lined smile from years of laughing and smirking, and motioned for Ash to come with her. When he came back, he looked at me with glossy, red eyes and said, "Your mom wants me to crash with you guys for a while." He looked like this was an unbelievable offer, but I knew Mom. It wasn't the first time we'd taken in someone in need. That's how we came to rescue our three dogs, four cats, and my youngest sister, Amy.

"Are you okay with that?" Ash asked.

I slapped him on the back. "Hell yeah, dude. Why not?"

My character in the video game died, but I didn't pay it any attention. I set my controller down and turned to face him.

"I-I don't know. We d-don't know each other that well, and I don't want to impose on your family and—"

I grabbed his hand in mine. It was a weirdly intimate gesture, but it didn't feel weird. He almost took his hand back, but I held it firmly. "Dude. It's fine. Amy is a junior in high school, so she's hardly ever around, and our older sister, Ellie, lives in Richmond. Mom has the space, and we love the company." I released his hand. "Does she want you to move into the guest room?"

Our house had more than enough space, and even if it didn't, I felt like Ash would have been more than happy to stay in the basement. Fortunately, Mom wasted no time when Ellie left for school. She turned her old bedroom into a guest bed so that Ellie could still stay over during her breaks, but it was also a neutral space for family and friends to come and stay, too. Mom wasn't the type to preserve her kid's childhood bedrooms. She liked a new project, and she liked to decorate. The first weekend Ellie was gone, she boxed up all her belongings in secure storage boxes and had me and Dad put them in the attic. "Everything she really needs, she has with her," Mom had said.

Ash nodded. "She wants..." he trailed off and shifted in his spot on the couch. "This is so embarrassing."

I frowned. "What? You can talk to me." Despite only hanging out with Asher—well, I'd gotten into the habit of calling him Ash by then—a few times, he'd easily become my closest friend besides Emma. I didn't want him to feel embarrassed. I wanted him to let me in through the giant walls he'd built up around him.

He refused to meet my gaze, but after a drawn-out period of silence, he said, "She wants to take me to get new clothes. She wants me to go to the grocery store with you and pick out food that *I* like. And..." he huffed but told me about the last part in a rushed sentence, "she wants me, you, and your Dad to get the rest of my stuff from my parents' place tomorrow. She said she'd come to help, but she's pissed at my parents, and she doesn't know if she can 'keep cool.'"

I couldn't help but grin. Good ole Mom. I could see how all her demands would be overwhelming, though. Especially since he was used to absent, unobservant parents.

"Anything you don't want to do, you just tell her," I said.

Ash looked up at me for the first time. "I don't want to take advantage of your parents. New clothes and food? That's expensive."

I shrugged my shoulders. We weren't rich by any means, but we were comfortable. Ellie had gotten into university on a full scholarship, and I paid for my community college classes out of my own pocket, though Mom bought my textbooks. Dad was a pretty well-known and highly respected attorney at a private family law firm, and Mom was a substitute Spanish teacher for several of the local schools. Buying Ash a new wardrobe and some food wouldn't break us.

"I know it's a bit uncomfortable to have their help, but Ash, believe me when I tell you that my mom wants to do this for you. And my dad will too." Ash had yet to meet my father, but I wasn't worried about them getting along. "And if you really want, once you get a job, you can try and repay Mom, but I'm telling you right now that she won't take a penny."

He gave me a half-hearted smile and shook his head.

"There's no way in hell that I'm letting Mom take you shopping, though." I took a sip of my Mountain Dew that rested on the coffee table in front of us, then leaned back on the couch and picked up my controller. "Mom doesn't think black should be in the majority of a person's wardrobe, and she'll try and get you to wear Polo shirts and khakis. I'll take you."

He beamed at me, then he eased back into the couch beside me after picking up his controller and taking a deep breath. "That sounds good. But let's come home with *one* Polo shirt. I'll wear it for her." He turned to me and wagged a finger. "But only on very special occasions."

CHAPTER ELEVEN

JULY 2012

All of us sat at the dinner table for once, because Dad got off work early, and Mom made her famous chicken fricassee, which Ash begged for almost daily. He'd been living with us for about a month, and he fit in with our family dynamic in a natural way, and got along well with Dad and my sister. My sister formed a crush on him almost immediately, which was a bit annoying, but still. Either way, it was nice having him around.

Dad undid his tie at the table and tossed it on the sixth, vacant chair. Dad doesn't look remotely like me or Ellie with his pale skin and bright blue eyes. Ellie and I got our dark hair and olive skin from Mom, whose Puerto Rican features are on the darker side. She has dark brown eyes, had almost black hair before it started turning silver, and beautiful, bronze skin. And then there's Amy, who has been in our family from the time she was four. We don't know a lot about her background, but we know that her biological mother was Latina and her biological father was Black. She was sent to foster care at the age of three, and that was the time Mom wanted to foster. Instead, we ended up fostering to adopt, because when Mom brings you home, you're home for good. We're a blended family, and I love that about us.

Amy ogled Ash from where she sat next to him. I made a point to roll my eyes at her. She winked at me and then took the bowl of chicken and spooned a few heaping piles on top of her rice.

Ever since Ash moved in, he's put on some weight, looks more rested, and wears his new clothes with pride. He wore a light blue V-neck shirt and dark wash jeans and looked good with his new haircut. It was cut a lot shorter than mine, but it suited his sharp cheekbones.

"Your mom said it would bring out my eyes more," Ash commented when he came home with Mom earlier. She'd been right–his hair no longer hung in his eyes, and he looked older.

I caught *myself* staring and ripped my eyes away from him. I'd been doing that more often. Staring at him. Feeling my body turning toward him whenever he was nearby without even thinking about it.

"Well," I sighed as I took the bowl from Mom and began to spoon the chicken into my bowl. "I did it. I broke up with Emma today."

"Aww, *hijo.* How did she take it?" Mom asked. She patted me on the arm and gave me her big eyes of concern. Everyone in the house knew I had plans to break it off, but even with their support, it hadn't been an easy thing to do.

I sighed and mixed up the chicken with the rice. "Not well."

There was no need to elaborate. Emma had taken it *worse* than I thought she would. It was apparent now that she was much more invested in our relationship than I was. When I mentioned trying to stay friends, she said she didn't know if it would be possible. Watching Emma sob all over herself and all over me, and then pleading with me before I left to give "us" another chance—well, that's not something I ever wanted to experience again. She even texted me a few times after I got back from her house, pleading with me more. In a moment of weakness, I almost gave in, but it wouldn't be fair to her. Not in the long run. Emma was an absolute catch, and

I knew without a doubt that she'd fall in love with a more deserving man one of these days. I just wasn't that man.

Mom leaned over and pecked me on the cheek, then Dad told me to keep my chin up or something cliché like that. When I looked up at Ash, his expression was unreadable. He didn't comment on it. He obviously knew my feelings about Emma, but still. It felt like there was something secretive behind his gaze.

"So." Dad cleared his throat and took a sip of his whisky before turning to Ash. "Have you thought more about my offer, son?"

Dad had offered Ash a clerical position at his law firm. It would pay quite well, especially for a recent high school graduate with no prior work experience except for some lawn management. Ash hadn't mentioned it much to me, but I had a feeling he felt like working at my father's firm would be just another favor from my folks, and he didn't want to take advantage of them. Still, he'd been searching for jobs all over and hadn't had any luck.

Ash gulped down a bite of chicken and nodded. "Yes, sir. I think I'd like to take you up on the offer if you're still willing."

Dad grinned. "Of course, Ash! I think it'll be a great start for you."

Ash had made the decision not to pursue higher education. At least, not yet. I wished I'd been able to make that decision a year before when I was in his place, but it had been expected of me to jump right into college. My parents had done so much for me and my sisters that I didn't want to question their vision for my future. I never felt like I had a choice when it came to higher education. I was envious that Ash had that freedom. Still, I was happy knowing he wouldn't be in the position I was in.

"Thank you so much, sir," Ash said. He smiled, but it didn't reach his eyes.

"How about I take you with me on Monday? I can show you around the place and we can get a schedule and all the other paperwork settled." Dad paused. "Do you have your social security card, son? Driver's license?"

Ash nodded, though a slight flush crept up into his face. Dad asked a valid question, but I felt that if I were in Ash's position, I might be embarrassed or even offended by the question. Dad didn't mean it like that. He was always one to talk first and question his words later. I knew he wanted to ensure that Ash would be settled when they went into the office, but by the looks of Mom's glare, I knew she didn't like how he asked about it.

"I don't have a license, but I have a valid identification card. And my social. I, uh, couldn't find my birth certificate," Ash murmured into his food.

Mom sent a glare across the table to Dad which wordlessly demanded that he shut his trap, and he obeyed.

Then, Mom turned her attention to Ash and smiled brightly. "We'll get you a replacement. It's no biggie, *nene.*"

Ash eased up and we ate the rest of our meal without bringing up anything serious. Amy talked about what courses she was looking forward to taking for her senior year and Mom talked about the garden space she was adding to the backyard. Dad didn't comment too much but made sure to listen and stay engaged.

When dinner was done, Ash gave me a pleading look. I knew he wanted to go and hang in the basement for a while, to get away from my family for a bit. He was so thankful to us, to my parents, but that didn't mean they weren't overwhelming sometimes. I understood that more than anyone, especially being the one brother with two sisters.

"Amy, you mind clearing the table tonight?" I asked as I stood up from the table. Before she could open her mouth in protest, I added, "We've cleared it all week, *and* washed the dishes." I winked.

Amy rolled her eyes but nodded. Mom blew me and Ash kisses before we retreated.

"Do you mind if I practice on the drums for a bit?"

Since Ash moved in, I hadn't been practicing all that much. I worked at the local gas station from early in the morning until mid-afternoon on most days, and when I got home, we typically hung out and did chores around the house when necessary. I enjoyed the freedom that the summer gave us, but I missed my drums. I felt comfortable enough with Ash now that I wouldn't mind practicing with him around.

To my surprise, Ash's face lit up beside me on the basement couch.

"Dude, yeah. Of course. This is your house, and I've wanted to hear you play since you told me you're self-taught." His face stretched into a lopsided smile, and a weird flutter motioned in my stomach.

"Are you ever going to let me hear you sing?" I arched an eyebrow at him.

Even at the mention of singing, he paled, and his boyish grin dissipated into something closed off. He shook his head. "Not yet. Maybe sometime soon?"

I squeezed his shoulder. "Whenever you're ready."

Over the next hour and a half, I beat on the drums, and damn, it felt good to release the tension that had gathered in between my shoulder blades over the last month. Not because of Ash, but because of the impending break up, school, my shitty ass job—it all added up after a while. I was a little rusty after not playing for a few weeks, so I warmed up with some simple beats first. Then, I moved on to an easier song that I always enjoyed playing, "Another One Bites the Dust" by Queen. After I felt nice and warm, and the drumsticks felt like an extended part of my own body, I played some of my own beats. I experimented with pieces of my own creation. Many times, I had to stop and start over or tweak a few things, then start over again.

Ash watched me from where he sat perched on the edge of the couch's arm the entire time.

After a long burst of non-stop drumming, I was drenched in

sweat, and my arms throbbed. I stood up and stretched my arms above my head, then walked over to Ash as I wiped at my brow and ripped off my t-shirt. I felt like I'd spent way too long in a sauna, and the basement had shitty AC, which didn't help.

I chugged an entire bottle of water and then slumped down on the couch next to him.

There was an intensity to the way his hazel eyes took me in, and that made me squirm a little. "What? You okay?" I asked. My heart was beating hard from the energy I exerted, but now my nerves made it worse. Did Ash think I sucked?

"You're amazing," Ash stated, matter-of-fact. "You taught yourself all of that?"

I wasn't expecting a compliment. My breath caught in the back of my throat, and my stupid heart picked up even more. All I could do was nod.

"You're fucking brilliant," Ash said. His face broke out in the most gorgeous smile. Probably the most genuine I'd seen on his face since the night we'd met.

"You think so?" Ash's comment tugged at something deep inside of me, hidden somewhere in my core.

He nodded viciously. "Are you going to play more?"

I shrugged and tried to remain cool, like his comment didn't send my stomach into a nervous tidal wave.

"I'm a little wiped from not practicing in a while," I said.

"Well, you should definitely practice more. A lot more. Were those last few beats your own?"

His perception of me and my music was almost unbelievable. I nodded again. "Just a few things I'm playing around with right now."

Ash shook his head. "It's more than just playing around with a drumset. You're talented, Drew."

I didn't comment, but I didn't look away from him, either. He leaned into me a little, and I couldn't help but stare at the long, lush lashes that lined his eyes.

"You make me want to sing," he said with the sound of slight embarrassment in his voice. "That's such a cheesy thing to say. Jesus." Ash ran a hand through his cropped hair and licked his lips. "I just mean—you give me hope, you know? You could easily be on stage, Drew. Easily."

I couldn't breathe. My mind whirled at his words. "I bet you could be, too," I said quietly. "Have you written any songs?"

He pulled back from where we were huddled together. His gaze dropped from mine to his hands in his lap. Then, he nodded.

"I've written songs. But they don't have a tune, you know? I don't play any instruments." Ash laughed a little coldly. "So, they're almost like poems."

I shrugged. "That's a good place to start, don't you think?"

We sat in silence for so long that I thought the conversation was over, that he'd retreat back into himself like I was used to him doing.

And then, the most beautiful fucking thing happened.

I was about to get up to go to the bathroom, just to have something to do other than sit with him in the awkward silence because I was worried he would hear the loud rhythm of my heart pounding through the still air. But Ash opened his mouth and began to sing.

The beginning of Everclear's song "Portland Rain" was so quiet, I could barely hear him, but as he continued to sing, he gained confidence with each passing word of the lyrics. Ash kept his eyes locked down at his hands as he sang but didn't stop. Eventually, he looked up.

He sang the song from start to finish without missing a single word, but that wasn't what was impressive. Everclear's lead singer, Art Alexakis is known for many things, and one of those things is his unique voice. Somehow, Ash outdid him. Somehow, with his unique, high-pitched voice, he made a song that he didn't write his own. Not only that but the range of his vocal cords...Christ, I'd never heard a voice like that before. It hit me somewhere deep inside of me, and my body was overtaken by chills. Suddenly, I understood why my drumming made him want to sing because his voice made me want to hop back onto the drums all over again.

Ash finished the song and looked up at me sheepishly with those light eyes of his ablaze.

My breathing became ragged and uneven, and my whole body burned. And I knew that it was for *him*. I couldn't ignore it anymore—ever since he moved in, my body gravitated toward him, and I wanted to be around him every time he wasn't home. Several mornings, I'd woken up hard as a rock after having very particular dreams about Ash, and though I dug those dreams into a hole and covered them up as best I could, I knew it was no use.

Before I could overanalyze my reaction any further, I leaned forward, cupped his face in my hands, and inched closer to him. I gave him a moment to retreat from me, but he didn't. He opened his mouth as if to say something, then closed it. He looked at my lips, and as I leaned in to brush my lips against his own, his eyes fluttered closed.

It was barely a kiss, just a gentle sweep of my lips on his.

Yet, my whole body came to life, a fire ignited within me that I didn't know had been dormant, and every inch of my skin vibrated with need. It was the reaction I'd been searching for with Emma and my girlfriend before her. I deepened the kiss, and he moaned into my lips, losing some of whatever reserve he'd had. It wasn't just me—Ash felt this, too. The undeniable attraction. Perhaps even from that first night we'd met. I'd tried to ignore it, but the moment I saw him at the show, something changed inside of me.

Ash tugged on my hair, deepening the kiss, and pulling me into him. I all but growled into his mouth as he ran his tongue over my lip ring. I'd never gotten so hard so fucking fast. His hands traveled and explored down the planes of my chest as my own hands massaged the back of his neck.

The next thing I knew, Ash was straddling me, and the hard length of him was grinding against my stomach. With that confidence, I moved to grab his ass right as he slid his tongue into my mouth. I almost came from that alone.

Gripping his hips, I explored his mouth with my tongue. He smelled like sandalwood and something smokey, and he tasted like spearmint from the gum he'd been chewing earlier. It was intoxicating.

I immediately needed more.

Ash moved his lips along my jaw and traced the hard edges with the tip of his warm tongue. He sucked on my neck and pressed into me.

"Ash," I gasped. He laughed into my neck, and his voice was gravelly and thick with undeniable lust.

He moved his hands down my chest to the edge of my pants, but as we finally made eye contact at the simple touch, he broke away from me abruptly. He stood up and stared at me with a flushed face and swollen lips.

"I—" he started. "I'm going to go to bed. Goodnight."

And with that, he all but ran away from where he left me panting on the couch.

CHAPTER TWELVE

At the Long Center, our stage has been set up on the H-E-B Terrace and Hartman Concert Lawn, which allows the audience to view the gorgeous city as they lounge in the grass or stand near the open stage. There are two local bands setting up to open for us, and I look forward to seeing the sun slowly retreat down into the earth in a couple of hours, where it will hide below the skyscrapers until tomorrow morning.

By the time we hit the stage, the sun will have fully set, and the stars will be replaced by the lit windows of the tall buildings on all sides of us.

A section of the lawn and stage is taped off so that we can all get set up, even though it's nearly impossible to keep onlookers from getting close. Luckily, no one has tried anything drastic; just a few excited shouts and words of love from those walking along with their dogs or partners from afar.

The last few hours after we checked into the hotel and immediately drove over to the Long Center, this time in sedans via private drivers, we worked with our stage crew and Mike extensively on when to enter, the setlist, the lighting, and all the nitty gritty details that are worked out and set up before the audience arrives. Without our crew members who accomplish all the behind the scenes and sound work, we wouldn't live up to our full potential.

Sean and I sit on the lawn, soaking in the last of the sun's bright rays before heading backstage. The audience will start arriving soon, and we want to relax as much as possible beforehand.

Sean sucks on a joint and offers it to me. I pass with a small shake of my head, knowing how just one puff would agitate my throat and turn me into more of a wreck than I already am with the impending engagement. I sip on more warm water as we stare up into the sky. I'd love to take a puff of the weed to calm my nerves, but it's out of the question.

My heart aches in my chest as I think of the best way to tell Drew. He won't understand. Hell, I don't even understand myself most of the time. But I can't be with Drew. Not wholly—not how he needs me to be. The strain of something like that on the band would be calamitous, and it would break Lizette along with it. It's not like I haven't run the different scenarios in my mind daily for the past few years. I let out a rough exhale into the sky and twirl a piece of grass that I plucked from the earth in between my fingers.

Drew has been distant since we got to the hotel, and I have no idea why. I wonder if he knows about my plans for tonight; but how would he? Did he see the ring in my bag? That didn't make sense. He would've brought it up last night. Still, I can't help but be overly aware that he's avoided me ever since we arrived at the venue. He, Brian, and Trish are currently hanging out backstage with the local bands.

I wish he was the one laying with me in the grass.

The rose gold, flashy diamond ring I chose for Lizette sits in my pocket like an anchor. I've had it for two months and have been putting it off. Everyone around the world expects me to propose to my beautiful, down to earth, girlfriend. If I was a different man, I know I'd be looking forward to proposing to her—but I'm not.

As if I summoned her, I hear Lizette before I see her. I raise my body up on my elbows and see her walking up to us on the lawn.

Lizette *is* gorgeous. Her natural golden hair flows around her, perfected into flawless waves that surround her upper body as she walks closer. Her skin is smooth. It shimmers in the sun, and I can see the sparkle of her emerald eyes from yards away. She wears black skinny jeans that hug her curves paired with one of our older band tees.

Aside from Drew and Sean, Lizzy is my closest friend. I fake my best smile as hatred for who I am rolls through my body. The guilt comes back tenfold. While I smile up at her, I see Drew's body underneath mine from the night before.

She beams down at me and then sits alongside us in the grass.

"You're early," I say.

She winks. "I wanted to give you a good luck kiss before the show." She looks around the venue. "And I wanted to get a good seat." I chuckle because we both know she will be watching from the sidelines next to our bodyguards.

Lizzy leans over and presses her plump, glossy lips against my mouth. I feel nothing. Yet, I kiss her back, falling deeper into my own facade.

Sean leans over me after we break apart, and he and Lizette fist bump. He stands up to take his leave but doesn't do so without looking back at my soon-to-be fiancée to say, "Lookin' smokin' as always, Lizzy."

She rolls her eyes but grins as he walks away.

As soon as he's out of earshot, she turns her body to me and leans in. She covers me in a deeper kiss that tells me she's longing for my body. I try not to tense, but it can't be helped. She pulls back.

"What's wrong, babe? You seem off."

Damn her for being able to read me so well. I shrug. "Just didn't get much sleep last night." It wasn't a total lie.

Mike calls to us from the bottom of the hill. "They're letting people in! Get your ass backstage, Lancing!"

We stand. "Mama bear is a bit grumpy today," Lizette jokes.

"He's homesick. You know how he gets when he's away from Miranda for more than a few days."

We make our way down to the stage and come to a stop. Lizzy grabs my hands in hers and even though she's taller than most women, she still has to reach up to meet my lips on her tiptoes. She kisses me softly and runs her hand gently over my jaw. But her lips and hand are too smooth; too delicate. They aren't rough like I need them to be. The smell of her floral perfume is too sweet when all I crave is the sweet smell of Drew's leftover aftershave intertwined with his sweat.

"I'll come meet you in the dressing room before the show?"

I nod and squeeze her hand, then retreat backstage.

I'M HOLED up in the dressing room that I share with Sean. I sit on the couch, sipping on tea and honey, and I stare down at the velvet ring box in my hands.

Lizette hasn't been by, Sean is watching the opening band with the others, and Drew hasn't said a word to me, not even when we had our band meeting before the show.

My mind is dizzy, and my limbs are jittery. I feel lightheaded, so I force a deep breath through my nose and take my time exhaling.

I decide to change to keep myself busy. I slip the box back into my pocket and begin to get ready. At every show, I wear several layers that I gradually take off throughout our set. Tonight, I put on a ripped black tank top underneath a t-shirt covered in old spatter paint. Over that, I wear a formal, black button-down shirt. I put my usual ashen gray beanie in my back pocket and trade my Chucks for my black combat boots. In the mirror next to the vanity that sits in one corner of the room, I stare back at myself and the circles underneath my eyes. My face looks peaked; my complexion is pale. With a shake of my head, I tap at my cheeks with my hands and demand myself to snap out of it.

I've just taken my place back on the couch when there's a rap on the door. Two quick knocks and three slow. It's Drew.

"Come in."

Drew comes in with fury written all over his painfully beautiful face. He's freshly shaven. His wavy locks fall in his eyes and shadow them. He comes into the room and closes the door behind him. Locks it. Drew leans against the door clad in ripped-up light-wash jeans and a muscle tank that I know he will rip off once his body gets too hot during the show. He crosses his arms defensively; his biceps threaten to pop.

"You know." There's no way to go back in time and tell him first before he found out. "How?" My voice is barely above a whisper as I grow the courage to meet his heated eyes.

"Sean."

Of course. I told Sean after the holidays about my plans, and he wouldn't have known not to tell my other best friend. Why would he keep that from Drew? He probably assumed Drew knew–was the first to know. I run a shaky hand through my hair just to focus on something other than the conversation. I drop my eyes from his and feel shame and disdain for who I've allowed myself to become coarse through my veins.

"You're really going to go through with it?" he asks, voice coated in poison.

When I look back up at him, it's not fury I see. It's pain. I feel like I've gutted him when all he's ever done is raise me up, love me, and support me.

I sigh and hold my head in my hands. "I—I can wait. It doesn't have to—"

Drew laughs coldly. "'Doesn't have to be now,'" he quotes. "But you're going to do it. Right? No matter how long you wait?"

I stay silent.

"You're living a lie, Asher," he says. I know he's upset by the sound of my full name on his lips. "No one can help you but you. You keep ignoring who you really are, and if you want to keep on with that, so fucking be it." He unlocks the door and places a hand on the handle. "But you're going to do a lot more harm than good."

Without registering what I'm doing, I race toward him and invade his space. I snake an arm around him and lock the door again.

"You think this is easy for me?" I scoff. "You think this is what I *want?*"

Drew's eyes cloud with more rage. "Isn't it? If you didn't want it, why the hell are you *doing* it?"

We're nose to nose, fuming at each other. Drew's nostrils flare with fury. I don't know how to make this better. I don't know the reason behind my actions. I've spent years trying to come to terms with my past and who I've become, only to make everything around me worse.

"I don't want this," I breathe into him. "I've never wanted *this.*"

I don't know how to make him understand—don't know how to wrap my head around it all—my deeply rooted fears, the terror, the horrible heartache I would cause by coming out.

"You have a funny way of *not* wanting it."

We're so close that I can feel his nose brush up against mine.

"Do you want her pussy wrapped around your cock, too? Or do you have to think about me inside of you to get off?" Drew growls.

His warm breath washes over me and I snap my eyes shut at the sting. When I look at him again, his hand flies back to the door handle, and I lunge. I grip his wrist and keep him there, not holding back any strength. He grunts in contempt, shooting daggers at me from where I've trapped him.

My lips slam into his. He tries to resist by turning his face away, but he can't move. After a couple of seconds, his lips part, and his tongue slides along my bottom lip. Then, he bites down. Hard. I moan into him while he demolishes me, releasing his wrist as I do. He realizes he's free and immediately comes back to his senses. He pushes me back and storms out of the room.

I'm left there panting. I lean forward and press my head against the door. "I'm *always* thinking of you, Drew," I whisper as hot tears fall down my cheeks.

After a moment, I slowly make my way back to the couch and retrieve the ring from my pocket. I want to chuck it across the room. Instead, I clench the box tightly and curse at it.

I've decided to put the ring away and rethink the proposal because of Drew—because he's right. About everything.

As I stand up with the ring in my hand, Lizette walks in. Her eyes immediately drop down to what I'm holding.

THROUGHOUT THE ENTIRE SHOW, I feel like I'm using whatever energy reserve I have left in my body just to move my lips. I want to perform and light their souls on fire. But after Lizette walked in on me and saw the ring, there wasn't much else I could do. She rushed over to me on the couch with giddiness. I asked her the question I didn't want to ask. She cried and slipped the ring on her finger, and the rose gold accented her skin perfectly.

It took every ounce of my willpower not to fall apart.

We agreed not to announce anything until after the show, but as I sing our chilling lyrics out into the city of Austin, there's a boulder in my stomach and a tear in my heart. I typically dance around Drew for one of the songs, and he usually gets up and sings with me into the mic as he stands, still playing his instrument for the crowd.

I can't bring myself to do those things tonight. I can feel his broken gaze on my back as I sing, and I want nothing more than to go back to last night. I could've changed everything. As much as I want to change it all now, what would I have done? Broken things off with Lizzy and abruptly told the whole world that I've been hiding who I am the whole time—lying to myself and to my girlfriend?

I'm a fucking coward. Always have been. Probably always will be.

Once Lizzy posts about our engagement on her heavily followed social media accounts, there's no going back. News will travel fast. People who fantasize about us will be jealous. Fans will be ecstatic. Talk show hosts will reach out for exclusive interviews. Pictures will be scheduled and taken.

I only want Drew.

"It's on the roof that I saw you, saw you for the first time, and it's there I'll stay, I'll stay there in my mind..." I rage into the microphone as I relive the night Drew took me up to Emma's rooftop and we smoked and drank and talked and listened to music. A tear rolls down my face as the song comes to a close. I wipe the tear away and hope no one noticed it.

After our last song, Drew doesn't greet me in my dressing room. I know better than to try and knock on his door. What would be the point? Our long-established in between songs love session won't happen tonight. Maybe it won't ever happen again. A knot forms in my throat at the thought.

Lizette walks in, flushed from singing and dancing on the sidelines.

"Can we take a picture?" she asks as she points to her new ring, already sitting on her finger with a promise of permanence.

I nod and take a long swig of water. She comes over and sits beside me.

"It's so beautiful, Ash. You have great taste." She kisses my cheek, grooms my sweaty, messy hair, and we pose for a photo of us with her hand held up high and proud. This is the picture she will post. I can't give the camera a genuine smile, so I lean in and kiss her cheek for our pose.

She squeals in delight and looks at the photos she's taken. "Thanks, baby. I love you. See you after?"

I nod again. "I love you too." She leaves me alone in haunting solitude.

After the show, Lizette posts our photo on Instagram and Twitter, then shares a video from our show and the engagement photo on TikTok. The whole world knows before I've even gotten a drink. I regret doing a meet and greet in Austin, and it has nothing to do with the fans.

Sean, Brian, and Trish laze about in total bliss, unaware of the storm brewing between me and Drew. I sip on a strong vodka soda and watch as Drew takes a shot at the table with the liquor.

"I hear congrats are in order?" Brian asks cheesily. Trish smiles, but it's insincere.

"Yeah, man. Congrats," Trish says out of obligation and nothing else. "You're a lucky man."

A cough comes from where Drew stands, but he doesn't say anything. He takes another shot. I try my best to ignore him and look at my phone instead.

Except my phone is the worst place to look and scrolling through the thousands of comments on Lizette's post has my throat closing up and my vision blurring.

Took him long enough! Such a lovely couple, xoxo.

Not fair! Not fair at all. Ash was supposed to be MY future husband!

Omg please have babies. They'll be gorgeous.

!!!!!!!!!

When's the wedding?!!

I exit out of my apps and lock my phone as I hear the slam of another shot on the table.

CHAPTER THIRTEEN

JULY 2012

I felt on top of the world after I sang for Drew. Like maybe I was decent, or I could sing professionally one day.

But that was nothing in comparison to how it felt when he kissed me. When I kissed back.

The months leading up to that kiss—that make-out session—had been littered with thoughts about him. Thoughts I'd never had about anyone other than him, really. I would have tried denying it, but it was impossible to do. From the first time I heard his laugh, I was captivated. From the first time I saw him and talked to him, I was under his spell.

Our long nights playing video games in the dark basement where our knees gradually touched, with his laughter filling the room had me rubbing myself raw before I went to bed most nights. And though I tried lying to myself over and over like a mantra, I knew he was the reason I went to bed rock hard every night, because it was his face that I came to.

I kissed Drew back, hungrily. I was so worked up after months of watching him do yard work half naked, walking in on him in just a towel in the bathroom we shared—from his scent that lingered in the basement, even when he left it, and from the way his eyes crinkled as he laughed and lit up my whole fucking world.

Our kiss escalated so quickly, it unnerved me. His power over me frightened me. It had all felt so natural, but when he said my name and looked into my eyes, mere centimeters away from where our lips hovered near each other, reality snapped back into place, and I ran back to the bedroom that had been loaned to me.

I locked myself in there and panted heavily against the closed door. I brought my knees up to my chest and hugged myself tightly as I wondered if we'd just destroyed our friendship. So many emotions flooded through me, that I didn't know which to pay attention to first. I was proud I'd sang for him. I was ecstatic he thought I was good. Watching him play the drums had made my heart swell. I was exhilarated and paranoid. I was starving for him. I wasn't in a relationship, yet guilt still rolled through me as I struggled to understand why I felt dirty. Like I'd done something wrong.

My body wasn't listening, though, because my cock still strained as it pressed against my jeans. I replayed the feel of his lips, the look in his eyes, and the feel of him against me as I untucked myself and started stroking.

AUGUST 2012

Neither one of us brought up the kiss after that night, which made things easier and so much harder.

The morning after, I'd found whatever courage I could muster and went downstairs as I usually did, and we ate cereal and watched a rerun of *Fast and Furious*. We commented on the movie, laughed, and made bad jokes, and by the time the credits were rolling, we were back to how we'd been before the kiss, which was great and horrible at the same time. I was relieved that things weren't insanely awkward like I'd thought they'd be, but almost more than that, I was begging to feel him underneath me again.

Whatever happened between us later that night, it was obvious that neither one of us was up for *that* kind of discussion. At least, not yet.

A week and a half after that night, I began working for Drew's father at the firm. Drew dropped me off each morning, and in the afternoons, he would pick me up, or if he was working at the gas station, I'd ride home with his dad.

The firm was simple. The people there were older than me, and they were cozy in their roles. They welcomed me with open arms, and they were patient with me as I learned my new duties.

I was bored out of my mind.

Most of my days were spent on mail runs, purchasing supplies for the office online, taking notes in meetings, making the coffee, keeping the office pristine, and answering phones. I felt bad for not loving the job that had been handed to me, but I didn't let Drew's dad know how bored I was. It was a job I could do, and I made sure to do it well. It was the least I could do for him.

On Fridays, the office was typically vacant except for the select few who had to come in, like me. A lot of the lawyers had meetings that they took at their home on those days, or they would go out for extended "work lunches" and not return until the following Monday.

Fridays were my favorite days because of the silence. The silence gave birth to my creativity, and though I knew next to nothing about writing songs, one day I just sat down and wrote. And then I wrote some more. Then, I edited and tried to hum a tune for the strings of sentences that had spiraled from my mind.

At the end of my first two weeks, I'd written three songs. One was finished, one was being edited, and the last one was just a draft; I hadn't even figured out the chorus.

Still, I felt the need to show Drew. I'd never wanted to show something like that to anyone before. My parents didn't give a single fuck when I aced tests or brought home crafts I'd done in art class. Over time, I didn't even attempt to show them or win drops of affection from them. I knew the words of validation and love that I sought would never come.

Somehow, I'd blown Drew away with my voice, and singing for him felt almost as natural as breathing once I got used to it. Sometimes I wondered if that's what had made him kiss me in the first place. I shook my head as I trotted down the steps that lead to the basement and told myself not to think about that night *again*.

Drew had that Friday off, and he was napping on the couch with a movie muted in the background. I was ready to slap my pages of lyrics on the coffee table in front of him, but instead, his peaceful presence caught me off guard.

I stared at him from the entryway and felt the blood burn my cheeks as my eyes swept down his body greedily. His lips were parted, and his breaths were long and even. He had one hand atop his broad chest, and the other behind his head, cradling his messy waves. He wore no shirt and a pair of simple black sweatpants, and as I took in each curve and hard edge of his muscular torso, I forgot how to breathe properly. I forced a breath and squeezed my eyes shut before loosening the borrowed tie from its chokehold around my neck.

When I opened my eyes, he hadn't moved. I almost wished he would have woken up when he sensed my presence, but he was too encompassed by sleep. Slowly, I took a few steps closer to him. I couldn't help it. He had a small dusting of chest hair and an impressive happy trail. The heat in my cheeks intensified, but I couldn't tear my starved eyes away from his body. Even from where I stood, I could smell the fresh scent of his deodorant mixed with the summer sun. Something caught my eye, and I noticed he had a ring in his left nipple.

I felt like I was fucking hyperventilating. My dick strained in my slacks, and I was about to stroke myself—just once—when his eyes opened groggily. I sat down immediately near his legs and plopped a flimsy pillow over my lap to hide my arousal.

"Hey." Drew grinned. He stretched his toned arms above his head in a feline-like stretch, and all his other muscles tensed with him. I looked away and begged my erection to go away, but no matter what awful things I tried to conjure up in my mind to distract myself from him, the blood down south wouldn't ease up.

"You okay?" he asked with a gravelly voice. I looked back at him as he sat up and bent over in my direction to look me in the eye.

I nodded. Why had I come down here in a rush, again?

"Oh!" The lyrics.

Drew arched a brow. "Oh?"

I fumbled around in the pockets of my slacks underneath the pillow until I felt the folded-up pieces of paper I'd neatly stored in there before I left the office. A last-minute rush of nerves entered my bloodstream, but it was too late. I'd handed him the pages.

Drew unfolded them slowly with a curious expression written on his face. He bent his head to read, and his waves hung almost down to his eyes. He pushed back his locks and smiled at me a little before turning back to the words.

"You did these?" he asked at almost a whisper when he was done.

"Uh, yeah." I nodded apprehensively. "Thoughts?"

He set the pages on the coffee table and turned so that he was facing me again. "I love them." I paled a bit and he patted me on the shoulder. "I'm not just saying that, man. I really do. All drafts need work, but those are some damn good drafts. Do you have a beat?"

And just like that, my heart started soaring.

After showing Drew my songs, he helped me conjure a beat. We played with different melodies and octaves; experimented with a combination of my singing and screaming the lyrics, and after a couple of weeks, we had two songs that were our pride and joy. The only problem was that we needed more than a singer and a drummer.

I hadn't seen Sean since we'd graduated because I'd been a bit preoccupied with, well, Drew. And work. But mostly Drew. One night after we'd practiced the songs as well as a couple of covers, we drank a few beers on the couch, drenched in sweat from all our work, and I took my phone out and texted Sean whether or not he was still interested in starting a band.

It took less than a minute for him to reply that duh, of course, he was.

I had never told Sean about my love for singing and explaining that to him via a text message didn't feel right. So, I just told him we had a couple of people—a singer and a drummer—who were looking for a guitar player and a bassist.

After texting back and forth for about five minutes, Sean was set to come over with one of his buddies who he played with the next night. When I mentioned it to Drew, he was nothing but smiles. That night, we each had several beers, watched dumb movies, and for the first time in a long time, allowed ourselves to sit close to the other on the couch.

AUGUST WAS ALMOST over when Sean came over with Brian one night. In less than a week, Drew would be going back to school, and I could tell by his fluctuating moods that he didn't want to go back.

I didn't bring it up, though. He was happy when playing the drums or talking music, so I let him be. I knew he'd come to me if he needed it.

Sean and his new roommate, Brian, came over for dinner because Drew's mom insisted on cooking *arroz con gandules*. I'd never met Brian but liked him instantly. When Drew opened the door to let them in, he smiled and immediately came over to hug me. The dude was a little shorter than me, but not by much.

When he released me, he beamed and smiled at me. "I feel like I know so much about you from Sean. Sorry, I get a little carried away sometimes," he said.

I couldn't help but smile at him. Brian wore his hair in twists, had large, purple gauges in his ears, and had a contagious smile. He was on the stockier side but had thick muscles, which made his hamstrings practically pop out of his black skinny jeans.

After we made our way to the dinner table, we all sat down and helped ourselves to Drew's mother's *Pernil Asado.* Amy's senior year had already begun, and she was over at a friend's house studying and Mr. Dawson was working late, so it was just us and Mama Dawson.

"So, what're you boys up to tonight?" Drew's mom asked with a cocked and perfectly lined brow.

Drew didn't talk to his parents much about his drumming, even though I'm sure they'd heard us practicing. I didn't understand why. His parents were as good as they could come in my book. Drew opened his mouth to speak, but Sean beat him to it.

"I guess we're playing some music after this, yeah?" he asked with a clueless grin.

Drew's mother nodded and took a bite of her dinner. "Sounds fun. Not going out?"

Drew shook his head. "No, I think we're going to see about maybe..." he trailed off and pretended to clear his throat. His eyes dropped to the plate in front of him. His mother looked confused.

"We're just going to play some music and see how we all play together," I answered for him. "And maybe after that, we'll play video games or something." I shrugged as nonchalantly as possible.

The next thirty minutes were spent answering Drew's mother's questions, though she'd stopped asking about the music not long after we started eating. I wanted to ask Drew why he was so hesitant about it with his parents, and why they weren't eager to talk about his drumming but thought better of it. I'd ask him later when Sean and Brian were gone.

With full stomachs, the four of us made our way down to the

basement after we helped clear the table. I had offered to help with the dishes, but Drew's mom simply gave me a peck on the cheek and waved me away. After only being in their home for a month, Mama Dawson (a nickname I'd started calling her after I became more settled) had become more of a parent to me than anyone else. I dreaded the day I'd have to move out. She squeezed my cheeks and said, *"¡Que se diviertan!"* and smacked my ass with a cleaning towel as I jogged away.

Once in the basement, Sean and Brian took out their instruments and began tuning. Drew was grinning like a wildebeest, and I retrieved a few beers from the fridge and passed them out, too eager to stand still while they prepped.

After I handed them their beers, Sean looked at me pointedly. "Alright. Who's this singer?"

Drew stared at me, probably because he'd assumed I'd told Sean about my voice already. "Seriously?" Drew questioned. He slapped my back a little harder than was necessary and then shook my shoulders playfully. He rolled his light brown eyes dramatically and turned to Sean. "*Ash* is the singer."

"No shit?" Sean exclaimed.

"No shit," I mumbled.

"And he's really fucking good," Drew said. He caught my eye and winked, and my stomach exploded in somersaults. "Seriously."

Sean tied up his mane and shook his head in fake contempt. "You been holding out on me, Asher Lance?"

It was my turn to roll my eyes. "No—I-I just—" I stuttered.

"So, you *have* been holding out on me." He placed a hand on his heart and dropped his head back before dramatically sticking out his tongue and playing dead. "And here I thought I was your oldest, dearest friend," he cried.

"Oh my God, Sean," I huffed.

Brian took in the whole scene with a broad grin as he put on the strap of his gorgeous acoustic guitar. "So." Brian looked between us. "What's the game plan?"

The basement suddenly felt claustrophobic around me. The walls pressed in and the air became too hot. I locked eyes with Drew while a fresh dose of nerves coursed through me from head to foot. I was reliving that same terror as the night I sang for Drew the first time, but it was more severe.

"How about you guys sit on the couch, and we play you what we've been working on?" Drew suggested.

Sean and Brian nodded, then made their way over to the couch with their instruments strapped on and their beers in hand.

They looked back at me as Drew sat on his stool and brought out his drumsticks. I stood in my usual place near him but felt awkward without an instrument or microphone to hold. I took several large gulps of the beer, and Drew must have been able to sense the panic rolling off of me.

"Can you guys turn your backs? Just for the first song," Drew clarified.

Sean was about to protest, but I gave him a silent, pleading look. He sighed and turned around to face the television, and Brian followed suit.

Drew motioned for me to breathe before hitting the drums for the first time. I took a deep breath and he smiled at me with twinkling eyes. As he drummed louder and louder, and we approached the first set of lyrics, my heartbeat thundered in my throat. I forced in the breaths and looked at Drew instead of my oldest and newest friends on the couch.

Without thinking, I belted out the first set of lyrics without missing a beat. I started soft and began my crescendo in the middle before screaming near the end. Sweat beaded at my hairline, and I felt the urge to pull off my shirt from how hot I felt, but I continued. At the very end, I sang fast and soft, almost like a rap, and then Drew finished us up.

By the end, I was panting. Drew bit his lip as he smiled up at me from where he sat. Though unspoken, I knew he was proud of me.

Sean and Brian turned around in their seats the second the music stopped. They both had grins on their faces, and Sean's eyes were so round they looked ready to pop. He took off his guitar, hopped over the couch, and consumed me in what could only be described as a bear hug. "Are you *fucking kidding me, Asher?*" he belted as he jumped up and down. "Son of a bitch!"

CHAPTER FOURTEEN

AUGUST 2012

The night that Sean and Brian came over was the night we unofficially became a band. It was also the night that Ash's confidence grew. After we performed that first song—which was the first one Ash had written— he saw the genuine surprise and love radiating off Sean, and absorbed Brian's compliments, he understood that I was sincere about the talent he had. I'd be lying if I said it didn't do me good to hear them compliment my skills, too. It was one thing for Ash to cheer me on but having two semi-strangers praise me as well–made me feel like I could accomplish the dreams that seemed so far from reach.

It was one of the best nights of my entire life.

We stayed up well past midnight jamming and drinking. We'd moved on from beer to rum and Coke, and by the end, we were all so elated from the session, and tired, that we had to call it a night around one in the morning.

Brian was the designated driver, and even though I insisted they crash in the basement, Brian was adamant that he had to be up early for work, and Sean wanted to be in his own bed, which was under-standable.

We high-fived, hugged, and laughed before they made their way back to Sean's van in a clear, late summer night sky. There was hope that our dreams would come to fruition heavily coating the humid air around us.

The house was silent, but my heart rang loud. Amy had come home hours ago and was more than likely asleep upstairs. Mom went to bed early and Dad was never up past eleven. The dogs were asleep with them in bed as per usual. It was eerily quiet in the living room without the sound of dog claws ticking on the tile in the kitchen and without Dad *hmm*-ing as he and Mom watched the news.

Ash closed the door and locked it behind him after he waved one more time to Sean and Brian. He turned around to face me with a contented smile and leaned against the door. Pure joy radiated off him and straight into me.

We had hardly touched since that night after he sang for me. It took all my control not to push it with him, but I'd kept myself in check despite my hormones taking over every time he was near me. That kiss crossed my mind before I fell asleep, and it was what I felt on my lips each morning when I was still stuck inside my dreams.

As Ash stood there against the door, I wanted to push my luck. I was dying to feel him again.

"You were amazing," I said softly.

I took a tentative step toward him, which put us only a couple of feet apart.

Ash threw his head back and chuckled lightly. "I couldn't have been amazing without you and all of your help." He took a small step forward, bridging the gap between us even more. "Thank you." It came out as a whisper and my skin vibrated in response.

To test the waters, I stepped in more so that we were only an inch or two away. When he didn't move, I pressed my right hand on his chest and felt his heart beating hard and fast underneath my touch. Still, he didn't move.

"Are you ashamed? Of what we did?" I asked quietly.

His eyes had drifted to look at his feet, but they snapped back up to meet my own at the question. He licked his bottom lip and shook his head.

"I feel..." he trailed off but slid his hands over my own on top of his chest. "Embarrassed. And confused, I think?"

I nodded. I'd felt those things over the last couple of weeks, too. My own pulse quickened with the contact of his hands, and I wanted to be bold, but I also wanted him to feel comfortable. I didn't know what this meant for our friendship or the possible band we were forming. I didn't really want to know. Because the smell of the sweet sweat on his clothes mixed with the washed-out aroma of the cologne he'd put on this morning—the quick breaths emerging from his pink lips, and the fire in his eyes—was about to send me over the edge.

I leaned in slowly, giving him the time to stop me if that's what he wanted. His breaths grew ragged and sharp as I slid my hand up his chest to his neck and gripped the back of it. At the same time, I pressed my lips to that perfect spot right underneath his incredibly defined jawline. I gripped him tenderly on his neck, but my grip hardened when I felt Ash's fingertips press into my hips. I pressed my body into him and sucked at his neck.

A soft moan came from his lips, and whatever small sense of control I'd had left vanished. One of my arms wrapped his torso, and the other cupped his jaw as I slammed us roughly into the back of the door. I couldn't get to his lips fast enough, but he met me halfway. When we collided, I felt like I was drifting inside of a lightning bolt.

Ash's hands moved from my hips to my hair, and he gripped my locks to deepen our kiss, to pull me in as much as possible. I desperately needed to get closer even though every inch of me was on every inch of him. He bit my bottom lip, right where my lip ring was, and it took every ounce of willpower not to scream out. I had to remind myself more than once that we weren't alone, but I couldn't break the euphoric moment, either. There was something even more exciting about knowing we could be caught at any moment, and even though I'd never willingly do that to my family, it had my blood boiling.

I'd been imagining this for days. Nothing I did took away the itch to have him. No amount of porn or rubbing helped. And I'd never been big into that, anyway. I needed *him*.

Ash became more adventurous amidst our heated make-out, and soon enough I felt his hands sliding up my torso, underneath my shirt. The skin-to-skin contact jolted me. He breathed hard against me, and I broke the kiss, panting, even though it was the last thing I wanted to do.

I swallowed hard and caressed his jaw. "My room?" I whispered. My voice was deep and coated in what could only be described as pure lust.

A large part of me expected Ash to freak out at my invitation, or for him to run away like he'd done last time. Instead, he grabbed my hand and led the way up the stairs.

In the hallway, Ash pushed me silently against the wall by my bedroom door and kissed me, but this time the kiss was so light it was barely a brush of his lips on mine. I brought him into me and trailed kisses down his jaw and throat, and then led him into my bedroom. We had only been in the room for seconds before the door was locked, and we were on each other again.

I had no idea what we were doing aside from kissing and touching. In my fantasies, I'd always pictured Ash doing all sorts of things to me, but now, I felt anxious and inexperienced. Sure, I knew how certain things were done, but I wasn't sure about the prep work... and I didn't want to hurt him, either. I wondered if he'd ever been with a guy before.

As though sensing my worries, Ash pushed me onto my queen-sized mattress and straddled me. His confidence and demeanor were so much different from the last time we'd touched. The change in him since our last encounter was startling–and incredibly hot.

He stripped off his shirt, and I lost my breath. He was a thin guy, but he was perfect. Not very hairy, natural muscles, and skin so smooth I could lick him all day and night. I trailed my fingertips from his sternum down, down to his abs, and further, until my fingers toyed with the button on his jeans.

"Fuck," he gasped.

In the dark, I couldn't see the length of him through his pants, but I ventured further south and gasped at the feel of him which filled up most of my hand. He hissed between his teeth as I stroked him through the material, and he rocked his body into mine as he threw his head back in an exuberant way that I knew had everything to do with my hand on his cock.

Ash clutched my wrist to stop my movements, then swung off me. I thought it was over that time, for sure. Thankfully, I was wrong again. He kneeled on the bed and lifted me up just enough to yank my shirt off. Then he was back on top of me, kissing everywhere he could on my chest. His sweet lips found the ring in my nipple, and he licked and sucked at it, which almost made me finish then and there.

"You—can—-can't keep—" I groaned.

His lips met mine again and I thanked fucking God. But it was abrupt. He pulled back and whispered to me, "I'll do what I want, and you'll like it."

I squeezed his ass, hard, and he moaned my name. My eyes rolled back in pure bliss. I wanted him to say my name like that for the rest of my life.

Ash's nails scraped lightly against my sides as he worked his way down. He found the button on my pants and undid them. The sound of my tight zipper followed. He stood in front of me, where I was positioned on the bed, and he forced my pants down and off.

"Is this okay?" Ash's eyes met mine, questioning and heated from what little I could see.

"Yes."

Fuck, yes.

"I've never done this before," Ash said.

I shook my head. "Me neither."

"No," he paused. "I mean..." he sighed. "I've never done any of this before. With...anyone."

It took a moment for me to understand.

"Oh, well we don't have to do anything you don't wa—" I was cut off by him kneeling in between my legs, right in front of my cock which had burst from my boxers. I was harder than I'd ever been before; painfully so. And as much as I wanted him to touch me, stroke me, suck me, the urge to do the same to him was almost as great.

"Fucking gorgeous," Ash murmured.

I propped my upper half up on my elbows, wanting to look at him. I had no idea what he would do, but if he kept fucking me with his eyes like that, I'd have to start begging him to touch me.

Ash held my gaze for a long moment, and then he dipped his head down and licked the tip of me while his dominant hand gripped my shaft. He licked slowly, then fast, exploring me and watching my reactions. It was a little sloppy at first as he experimented, but it didn't take him long to figure out how to work me just right. I moaned his name and ran my fingers through his hair to show him how fucking much I liked it. Soon enough, he became more adventurous and placed half of my length in his mouth. I groaned way too loud with my sister's room being close by, but I was taken over by ecstasy. Manners be damned. He continued to take me deeper and deeper, stroking me with his hand as he sucked and swirled his tongue on the tip, and I couldn't fucking last any longer.

Without much of a warning, I came hard. So hard that I saw the cosmos. I panted his name as he swallowed me whole.

He stared at me in disbelief, but he was grinning. Ash stood up from where he'd been kneeling and unbuttoned his own pants. He slid them down with his boxers and palmed his cock, and it was then I knew exactly what he meant by it being *fucking gorgeous*.

Ash started stroking himself as he looked down at me, and that was unacceptable, because that was my job, and I was itching to touch him.

I grabbed his free hand and pulled him down onto the bed beside me. We were both naked and panting, and for the first time ever, I didn't feel awkward while being intimate with another person. With Emma, the lights had always been off on purpose. With the girl before Emma, I could barely make myself come. With Ash, I was almost instantly hard again just looking at him.

Desire pooled in his eyes as I lifted him up and put a pillow under his head. I hovered my body over his and kissed him tenderly on his swollen lips. His hand was still stroking himself, and I roughly pulled it away and pinned both his hands above his head. He squirmed a bit in protest, which was the cutest thing. I chuckled in his ear and kissed his earlobe just as I touched the tip of my cock against his own. Ash's body lurched and I felt his pre-cum on my fingertips as I moved my hand down to grip him.

"Drew," he breathed desperately.

"Yes?" I asked, delighted to have him right where he was pinned underneath me.

"*Please.*"

He tried so hard to get me to move my hand on him. I grinned and looked down at his flushed face. "Please, what?" I whispered against his lips. His arms jerked from where I had them trapped. "So impatient," I mused.

I decided to torture him just a little bit longer because his need was the biggest turn on I'd ever seen. His breaths were shallow, and he couldn't stop moving his hips in a feeble attempt to find friction. Ash bit his lower lip and cried for me. That's when I unpinned him and stroked his long length.

A shudder coursed through me as I watched myself touch him.

Fucking gorgeous.

I licked the tip of his cock and stared up at him while I savored the taste. Both of his hands fisted my hair. I placed both of my hands on his hips and squeezed, taunting him once more with my mouth, slowly and lightly.

"Do you want me to make you come?"

"Drew—I swear to God—please—" He gripped my hair so hard

that my scalp burned, and my dick twitched in response, already craving round two.

I only worked the head for a few minutes, shamelessly delighted by the sounds that came from him as I did so. One of my thumbs came down from his hip and stroked the vein on the underside of his cock. His eyes closed tightly, and he sucked in a sharp breath in response.

"I'm going to lose my shit if you don't—"

I took his full length into my mouth and his words were forgotten and replaced with the most beautiful moan. It was hard to fit all of him in my mouth, and I was worried my teeth would hurt him. I moved slowly at first as I got used to the feeling, but I knew he needed me fast and deep. I gagged a bit as I took him as far as he could go and bobbed my head until he was practically ripping my hair out. Ash cursed under his breath as I picked up the pace.

"You feel so fucking *good*—"

He came undone when I forced him farther than I thought I could go, and he spilled into my mouth. I swallowed eagerly and continued to suck as he rode out the waves of his climax. When he was finished, I came back up to the head of the bed and laid beside him.

We both panted and looked at each other with wild eyes. I pulled a throw blanket that had been pushed to the foot of the bed up and over our bodies. We didn't get dressed. We didn't speak. Ash took my hand in his own and kissed my knuckles. In the dark, I did my best to memorize how he tasted and smelled.

It wasn't long before we drifted to sleep together. I had an urge at one point to go and make sure my bedroom door was locked, but I didn't dare move.

In the early hours of the morning, I woke up sweating and rock hard. My erection was pressed into his lower back as we spooned, and I did my best to breathe and go back to sleep. Instead, Ash turned to face me and enveloped me in a deep kiss. Before I could wake up fully, he was stroking me and slipping his tongue into my mouth.

We didn't get a lot of sleep that night.

CHAPTER FIFTEEN

I never want to see him look at me like this, ever again–the devastated look of grief and rage and everything in between that he gave me when I admitted the proposal. It's the same look he gave me when Lizette announced our news to the world, and he's throwing me the same look now as we board the tour bus.

Luckily, the rest of the band and even Mike is oblivious to the feud brewing between me and Drew. They take their usual spots on the bus, make their coffee, and keep to themselves as we head toward the airport to board our flight to California for a few shows. After that, we'll hit a couple cities on the East Coast, and then we're done.

Lizette stayed with me last night. She kept me awake for most of the night, kissing me and touching me and wanting to make love more than once. I was only able to get it up twice while thinking of Drew, and I never came. I had to rush to the bathroom both times and hide the evidence that there was nothing in the condoms.

Tears streamed down my face as I looked at the traitor staring back at me in the mirror. Each time I closed my eyes, I saw the hurt in Drew's brown eyes. The eyes I'd gazed into on too many occasions to count. The eyelids I'd kissed in the dark, and the bridge of his nose which I'd pressed against my own.

Even before I'd met his scornful glance in my direction on the bus, I'd wanted to take it all back.

Hell, even before I'd proposed to Lizzy, I'd spent many nights wishing I'd never asked her out. Every night before bed, I beg the universe to allow me to find the strength to break it off so that I can be with Drew. And each morning, I wake up the same coward as the day before.

Drew makes it obvious that he won't be joining me in the back room of the bus today. He lounges on one of the couches near the breakfast nook and immediately puts in his headphones. I want to take him with me to the back so we can talk. I want to assure him that it'll be okay, that I'll change, that I'll find a way to get us out of this fucked up hole I dug.

But I can't. So, I don't.

IT WAS one of those days at the airport where fans demanded our attention at seemingly every turn. No one prepares you for becoming famous. It's tiring not being able to do the things I once did in private without any peace. In the beginning, I thought I would surely get used to it, but I never did. Sometimes, my patience is too thin to remember that our fans look up to us, love us, and want to support us. Sometimes, I want to blend in.

I'd signed three autographs, taken pictures, and had people ask me about the engagement a total of six times before we even made it through security. Once we made it to the gate, the plane was ready for first class to board, and I thanked fuck for that.

We took up all of first class with the band members, Mike, and our security and sound team.

My seat was at the back, and I knew that Drew's seat would be next to my own. My brain goes into overdrive as I try to find the words to make things okay between us, even though I know that there's nothing I can say at this point to help.

Drew eventually strolls down the aisle and sits beside me without a word. His headphones are still in, and he makes his intentions known when he stares straight ahead, as though I'm not even here.

"Drew?" I ask after a while. The main cabin is boarding now, and it's no longer as quiet on the plane. The bodyguards that sit next to us on the other side of the aisle are already snoring, as is the majority of our crew. Sean watches a movie and sips an energy drink in front of us, and Mike plays a game on his phone near the front.

Drew says nothing.

I force a deep inhale and exhale as I look out the window. My eyes sting and my throat constricts as I hear the flight attendant's speech on safety, and I don't bother taking in the words I've heard hundreds of times before.

Once we're up in the air and the plane levels out, I venture a look at Drew. His eyes are closed, but he's not asleep. When he sleeps, his lips part and his fingers twitch. Drew's as still as stone.

I want to take his hand in mine, but I clench my fists in my lap instead.

After a few moments, Drew gets up and heads to the bathroom situated right behind our seats. Without thinking, I follow him and quickly enter the room before he can object or cause a scene. He throws daggers at me with cold, brown eyes as I lock the door.

Wordlessly, he turns toward the toilet and relieves himself. I lean against the door on the verge of tears, with a scream lodged in the back of my throat.

"Drew."

He doesn't look back. He finishes and flushes, then goes to the sink and washes his hands. The first class bathroom is still incredibly small, and the two of us are just able to have a couple of feet between us. Slowly, Drew turns and looks at me with *that look* as he dries his hands.

"What, Ash? What could you possibly want?" Drew asks with venom coating each word.

I look down at my feet. "To talk."

Drew laughs. "About what? You made your decision, man. Now I know my worth."

His words are like a stab in the center of my heart. He can't possibly think that I don't care for him—that I don't love him.

I step close to him and invade his space, even though his body language grows rigid as I close in on him.

"I'm sorry." I grab one of his hands, but it's limp in mine, like he's not here. "Drew, please."

"Please, what? How long have I been begging you, Ash?" He gets in my face and his nostrils flare. "How many times have I asked you to take a chance on me or at least just come *out* already? But no." He shakes his head, and a lock of his wavy hair falls in his eyes. "All you've done in ten fucking years is feed me empty promises while keeping me as your plaything on the side so you can be the world's influential and *straight* leading man." He spits the words at me, and I feel every syllable.

"I just—you're right, Drew. I just need to figure out—"

"Figure out 'how to come out properly?' Or what about, 'I just need to figure out a good time to come out to the world. I don't want to let our fans down or hurt the band.'" He quotes my past excuses word for word and my skin stings. "What do you need to figure out *now*, Asher?" I flinch at the sound of my full name.

When I don't answer, he nods. "That's what I thought."

He moves to the door, and I grip his wrist. I can feel the hatred rolling off him as he turns and glares down at where I hold him.

I don't know why I do it. I crush myself into him and force a kiss on his lips. I can't stand the hostility and I can't bear the blatant disgust and disappointment he's feeling toward me, even though I deserve it. He painfully grips my head and ravages my lips with his own before thrusting me back against the small countertop. He touches his lips in surprise before pointing a finger at me.

"Fuck you," he spits. "Don't fucking touch me."

He leaves the bathroom and everything around me blurs. I feel needles in my chest and face, and nausea rolls through my core. I barely make it in time to puke into the toilet with a silent sob.

I never wanted any of this, but I know I'm the one to blame for our demise.

CHAPTER SIXTEEN

OCTOBER 2012

A lot can happen in a month and a half.

A lot *did* happen in those weeks.

After the night that we unofficially became a band, Sean and Brian started coming over almost every night during the work week, save for when Brian had to get up early the next morning.

We jammed, we laughed, we came up with beats and melodies. We brainstormed band names and when and where to play our first show. It was tiring and liberating.

Every Friday at the office, I spent my downtime editing the songs I'd written, or composing new ones. The more I practiced singing with the guys, the more I started to understand different rhythms. Drew had been teaching me how to play the piano on the side so that I could learn to read music, and test different notes for future songs when I needed to.

Whenever Sean and Brian weren't at the house, and we weren't busy playing piano or hanging out with Drew's family, his lips were almost always on mine. Or somewhere on my body.

I tried my hardest not to think about what we were doing, because I would only end up guilty, confused, outrageously hard, and then confused all over again. I didn't know why I felt like that–but it was a vicious cycle I was trying to break.

Some nights I went to bed swearing I wouldn't touch him again. Not like that, anyway. Other nights, I crawled into his bed and begged him to touch me.

He was always willing to oblige.

We didn't talk about it.

There were a lot of things about sex that I was curious about. My parents had never given me a sex talk other than reminding me to use a condom, so I wasn't "left with a little mistake" of my own.

Sex Ed in high school was a fucking joke, and they hardly touched on what can happen sexually between two people with dicks. In my spare time away from Drew, which was hard to come by, I researched how it was done. Specifically, I taught myself how we could work our way up to penetration. If it would hurt...how to make it hurt less. It usually ended with me slamming my laptop shut and trying to convince myself we weren't going to do that, and then I'd have thoughts for the rest of the day about *only* that.

We'd already done everything else, and a part of me—a large part of me—wanted to know what it would be like. And by the way Drew's hands had started to roam toward my ass more and more, I would say he was feeling the same. I wondered if he'd been doing his research, too?

The thought of Drew looking up ways to please me sent my pulse skyrocketing. Christ, I was a mess.

One day in early October, Sean jumped around like a cat on crack as soon as he entered the house. Drew's mother eyed him coolly. She was a great mom, but I didn't think she loved having the other guys around so often. Still, she didn't say anything about it. She made us food, gave us privacy, and left us alone.

Drew and I led the way down to the basement as usual. I was aware that Sean had something to share, but Drew had shot him a look that said *Wait until we're downstairs.* We'd all gotten to be close friends throughout our exhausting rehearsals, and I was thankful for it, because sometimes Sean had no filter, but he could read Drew well enough by then to keep his mouth closed.

Once we were downstairs, Drew slumped down on his stool. I leaned against the wall near his drums and tried not to admire his toned, tan arms that his loose, black tank-top showed off deliciously. I could practically taste his cock on my tongue as I stood near him, and I couldn't help but think he should have come with an XXX warning label. The arm holes of his shirt were cut farther down than necessary, allowing me to move my gaze down his chest, almost to his navel. My cock twitched in response. As Brian and Sean laid their instrument cases down, he looked up at me and licked his lips, pure seduction swirling in his eyes.

Drew flipped his baseball cap backwards and winked at me with a knowing look. I had to force myself to walk further away from him to concentrate.

"Alright, Sean, what is it?" I asked.

Sean's face broke out in the biggest grin I'd ever seen him wear. "We got a gig."

"What?" Drew and I asked in unison. I looked over at the drum set and saw that Drew had jumped up from his stool in his excitement.

"Are you fucking with us?" I asked. Sean was a prankster, and I loved and trusted him, but I also knew he loved to fuck around. Still, I didn't think he'd joke about something like that.

He shook his head wildly and I knew his words must have been genuine. "You'll never believe where the venue is. We go on first, which is scary as hell, but you gotta start somewhere, right?"

I stared at Sean in disbelief. I looked back at Drew and noticed his mouth hanging open. He looked just as shocked as I did. Brian grinned smugly. I'm sure he'd already gotten the details on their ride over.

"Well?" Drew asked impatiently. "Where? And when?"

Sean and Brian shared a shit-eating grin. "It's November ninth. At the one and only..." he trailed off and pretended to drum with his index fingers on the couch. Brian joined in. They looked ridiculous, and I loved them for it. "The Madder Hatter!"

My chest lurched in excited anticipation. *The Madder Hatter?* Drew came up to stand closer to us and gave high fives to Sean and Brian. Sean went out back for his before-jam-session smoke break, and Brian went to use the facilities. Drew and I looked at each other in amazement. The Madder Hatter...where we'd met that one night in April not so long ago. It felt like fate. While we waited on the others, we stared at each other, smiling and unmoving.

Before the others came back, Drew nipped at my bottom lip and I moaned into his mouth. When he pulled back, I anxiously looked around the room. He chuckled and stole one more kiss before heading back to the drum set, leaving me needy and breathless.

Sean strolled back inside with the same grin he'd had on as before and patted me on the back. "You good, man? You look like a cat's got your tongue." He snickered at his own joke, the marijuana already working on him. Drew looked at me and gave me a knowing smile.

A cat didn't have my tongue, but Drew most certainly did.

Later that evening, after Sean and Brian left, Drew and I lounged on the sofa in the basement. We had just gotten done chugging some well-deserved water. We were both sweaty from practice. We didn't say anything or touch each other for a long time. I think we both needed the silence to wrap our heads around everything.

"I'm going to drop out of college, Ash," Drew said softly.

His face was turned toward mine, and I looked at him to let him know I was listening. "My parents won't be happy. But I can't work, go to school, and do the band. I don't even want to go to school."

I placed a hand on top of his thigh, right above his knee, and gave him a light squeeze. "I know."

"I'm scared," Drew admitted after a drawn-out silence.

I took his hand in mine. "Do you want me to be there? When you talk to them about it?"

He looked at me and ran his fingers along my jawline. "I think I need to do it myself. Rip the Band-Aid off or whatever."

I scooted into him closer, and he moved his head so that it rested on my shoulder. I leaned my head on top of his and kissed his hair. "I think it'll be okay, Drew," I murmured. "Really. Your parents love you so much. Hell, I think they even love *me* now. They have big hearts. Kind hearts. They might not love the idea at first, but even if that's the case, I think they'll come around to it."

Drew let out a shaky sigh and shrugged. "I hope so."

"When are you going to do it?"

"Tomorrow."

Right as I was about to do something—kiss him or hug him, or hell, I didn't know—my phone buzzed with a text from Sean.

Sean: Wait. Do we even have a band name?!

CHAPTER SEVENTEEN

OCTOBER 2012

Of course, the one time I really needed Dad to be around for family dinner, he was running late.

Amy was at a friend's house, as per usual, and Ash had gone over to Sean and Brian's house to give me the space I needed to talk with my parents.

Each minute that ticked by that Dad didn't walk through the front door made my courage dwindle down to almost nothing. My forehead was coated in sweat, and I couldn't stop twitching my hands as I moved around the kitchen and helped Mom prepare dinner.

When Dad was thirty minutes late, I finally asked, "Where's Dad?"

Mom wiped her hands on her pastel pink apron and shrugged. "I think he was running by the office and then getting a beer with a coworker."

I wanted to lash out at my own mother just because she didn't know where he was or when he'd be home. I clutched the kitchen counter with both hands and forced air into my lungs. I could feel Mom's piercing stare on me from where she stood. When I looked over at her, she had one of her eyebrows raised in that questioning look that mothers have when they know something's wrong.

"Dinner is ready. Your father can take it or leave it. Fix us a couple of plates and I'll pour us some lemonade. Then, we are going to sit down and you're going to spill whatever it is you're holding back." Her accent was thick, which only happened when she was mad or serious about something. All I could do was nod in agreement.

After sitting down at the table and sending up a half-assed prayer, she didn't bother touching her food. Mom took a long sip of her lemonade and crossed her arms.

"Well?" Mom asked, expectantly.

My hands trembled underneath the table. "I wanted to talk to you and Dad."

Mom shrugged. "You know how your dad is. He may not even be home for another hour or so. Talk to me, *amorcito.*"

Mom always knew when something was up. She could sense these things from miles away, almost like she could smell it on my skin. With gritted teeth, I forced the words out of my mouth, because if I didn't do it now, I wouldn't. And that would just upset her even more.

"I want to drop out. Of school," I clarified. I immediately cursed myself in my head for saying it *like that.* I refused to look her way. "Because I want to focus on music." I looked down at the food on my plate which only made me nauseous. I could feel her eyes on me, but I couldn't look up. Instead, I swallowed down the uncomfortable knot in my throat.

"Okay," Mom said slowly. "Can you elaborate a little more?"

"I know you and Dad want me to be in school. And you might not let me live here if I drop out...I–I just don't like it, Mom. The classes bore me, and no area of concentration sounds right. Nothing *fits.* The only time I'm happy and can see a future for myself is when I'm drumming."

My breaths were shallow, and my fingertips felt numb, but I decided to meet her gaze. To my surprise, they weren't squinty or cold like they sometimes got when she was upset. She nodded and took a bite of dinner.

"Did you want this before or after Asher came to live here?" Mom asked after several awkward minutes of silence.

Out of all the questions I'd feared, I hadn't thought she would ask something like that.

I shook my head. "Before."

Mom clucked her tongue and took another bite. "Are you— forming a band? With those two young men who are always over these days?"

Her question made me smirk a little, despite my nerves. "Brian and Sean, Mom. And yes. We just got our first show lined up."

Mom nodded thoughtfully, then reached out across the table for me. I placed a large, clammy hand in her small one.

"*Mijo*, if this is something you want to pursue, then you must. *No puedes ignorar tu corazón*. It's not healthy to ignore your passions. I do worry about this path, and I'm sure your father will, too, but that's not because we do not support you, okay?" She squeezed my hand. "Anything with the arts is hard, but that doesn't mean it's not worth it. Just promise me two things?"

"Yeah?" I breathed.

She moved her thumb over my hand, and I felt my shoulders relax an inch. "First, if it doesn't work out or you make no progress after several years, promise to reevaluate." I nodded. "Second, don't threaten me with moving out yet. You are still working, and you work *hard*. We want you here until you want to be on your own. Just don't leave quite yet." Mom winked at me as a couple of tears ran down my cheeks and onto my dinner plate.

"*¿Nene?*"

I looked at her.

"Why were you so scared to tell me this? Hmm?"

I shrugged and wiped my eyes. "I know you want me to get a degree. Get a successful job, and all that."

Mom laughed. "Well, not everyone can do what your father does.

119

I know I couldn't." We both shared a chuckle. "You know I support you. Dad supports you. No matter."

After that, we finally ate, though I could barely stomach the food after our talk. The lemonade was great, though. We talked about Mom's newest design project and then we figured out the details of my withdrawal from community college. The air was lighter, and I could breathe again. I felt a text go off in my pocket, but I ignored it as we talked. I knew it was more than likely Ash. I couldn't wait to tell him how well things had gone—with Mom, at least.

Right as I gathered the plates in preparation to take them to the kitchen, Mom lightly grabbed my wrist.

"Is there anything else you want to talk about, *mijo?*" Mom asked softly. Something in her neutral expression told me she knew. About me. And Ash. What our relationship had evolved into. My heart picked up so fast, that I could feel the lemonade tickle the back of my throat as another wave of nausea rolled through me.

"W-what?"

"You can tell me. I don't expect you to tell me everything." She smiled gently. "I know you're grown. But...I feel like you need to tell me something else?"

Oh, God. I really wasn't expecting that.

"Ash?" I questioned weakly. Why was Mom so good at knowing these things? Were all mothers like this, or was she especially gifted?

She gave me a curt nod.

"How do you know?" I whispered. "*What* do you know?"

I rubbed my fingertips over the phone in my pocket, desperate to run away from the conversation and call Ash.

Mom shrugged. "You know I try to give you boys privacy. Truly." She paused and took a breath. "But, uh, there was one night I went down to the basement to check in on you. It was late, and I wondered why you weren't in bed. "You were both asleep on the couch, but Ash was laying on you. Your hands were—"

"Okay, okay. I get it." I held up a hand to her and prayed she'd stop talking. I gulped and resisted the urge to run. Mom pursed her lips together and allowed me time to answer. "I—I don't know, Mom. Something just...happened between us. Not that long ago. Not before he moved in or anything." My voice cracked and my cheeks flooded with a violent blush. "Did you tell Dad?"

She shook her head. "No. That's not my place."

"Are you...shocked?"

Mom shook her head again. "No. Not shocked. With Emma, you never seemed like yourself. Something was missing."

"I don't know if I'm gay, or bisexual, or..." I trailed off and brushed away a couple of tears.

Mom got up and wrapped her arms around me as I sat there in my chair. She kissed my temple and moved the hair from my eyes. "Drew, it doesn't matter. You don't have to label your relationship with Ash." A sob I didn't know I was forcing down broke out. Mom ran her hands over my shoulders as she continued. "You don't have to label your sexuality, either. Everyone is different." She moved her head so I could turn to face her, then tipped my chin up so I was looking at her. "You are perfect. Just as Drew. Okay? Just be safe about it all."

Another sob burst from my chest as she held me once more.

"Estoy orgullosa de tenerte como mi hijo." I am proud to have you as my son.

Her words made me cry harder, but she stayed there with her arms around me, brushing her fingers through my hair and telling me how good I was. Finally, when all the tears were gone, after my breathing steadied, I stood up and gave her a proper hug.

"I'll tell your father about school. You tell him about the band. The rest—you tell him when you're ready."

I latched on to my mother again and let her absorb all my worries and fears in the special way only a parent can before we finally moved into the kitchen to clean.

As we cleaned the dishes, she asked, "So, what is the band name?"

There was a heavy blanket of exhaustion draped over my body

after our emotional dinner, but I smiled at the plate I was scrubbing, happy that she asked. "April Renegade."

Mom smirked. "Why April?"

I shook my head and hid a grin. There were some things that were only for myself and Ash to share.

CHAPTER EIGHTEEN

By the time we get off the plane in California, my rage is so heavy, I'm clenching my fists as we walk through the airport, because I don't trust myself not to throw a punch at Ash.

The way he tried to corner me in the bathroom was laughable. As if he can just get me alone for a little while and that'll fix all his fuck ups from the past few years? He should know better.

The fucking audacity he had to corner me and put his lips on mine after proposing to his fucking girlfriend the night before makes my skin itch and buzz. I want to take a shower so I can scrub my skin raw and force my skin cells to forget every time he's touched me.

I was up until the early hours of the morning, torturing myself by scrolling through the comments about their engagement on social media. When I was done with that, I moved on to the numerous articles that had already been written about Ash and Lizette.

My anger radiates from my core. It's so severe that I'm shaking as we make our way to the limo after exiting the airport.

I sit as far away from him as I can manage, in between Trish and Sean. Still, Ash stares at me from his seat. His eyes are rimmed red, and I know he's upset, but that doesn't change things. For years, he's promised to change. That he'd come out when the time was right. Promised me he and Lizette weren't serious, even though it was blatantly obvious that Lizette was serious about *him*.

For a long time, I convinced myself that he had trouble showing his true colors because of how he was raised. I know that's part of it. But after a while, the same excuses didn't work anymore, and the more lies he told, the less I believed him. It's been a decade, and he still expects me to be his plaything on the side while he passes as straight to the rest of the world?

Fuck that.

Sean brings me back to reality when he bumps my knee with his and offers me a soda.

"You good, my dude?" Sean asks.

I nod and stare at the soda can in my hand. I'm sick of lying. I don't want to hide anymore. I crack the top of the soda open and chug half of it, just to have something to do other than avoid his eyes. This time, I won't go back to him like I've done in the past. I don't want to be the person who hides. I don't want to be the *other lover* of April Renegade's leading man. It leaves a bad taste in my mouth just thinking about it, because I've already been his side piece for too long.

"We rented out a whole set of boutique lofts right in the center of L.A." Mike grins from beside Ash. "They're brand new, and no one's moved in yet. I figured more privacy would be nice for the last leg of the tour."

"Heck, yeah, Mike. Thanks," Brian says. "Are they gonna be, like, super bougie? We are in L.A., after all." He and Sean snicker at that.

Mike shrugs and rolls his eyes halfheartedly. "Honestly? Yeah. They're kind of 'bougie.'"

Sean and Brian share a look of humor, then howl in laughter. Mike never talks like that. Hell, Mike hardly ever jokes. Even I crack a smile.

"Okay, okay." Mike grimaces as the laughter intensifies. Sean and Brian sit back and look like two scolded school children with their arms crossed and smug smiles on their lips. "You all ready for the last few shows?"

I nod and finish off my soda as the others hoot and holler some more. All except for Ash. Mike gives Ash the side-eye but doesn't say anything.

"We've got L.A. tonight, then a few days off before we head to San Diego so you all can rest up a bit. After that, we'll fly up to San Francisco before going back to the East Coast," Mike says.

As burned out as I am from the tour, this is the first time I've ever wanted the tour to end prematurely. And it has nothing to do with the shows or the fans or the traveling.

"And then it's D.C., right?" Trish asks.

Mike nods. "D.C. and then we end the tour at Madison Square Garden in March after another break." He sighs in content at the thought of getting to go home soon. Looking at Mike going home to his wife reminds me I still haven't called Mom and Dad. I set a reminder in my phone to do so on one of our days in between shows.

When we arrive at the lofts and walk into the lobby, my jaw drops. Floor to ceiling windows let in an abundance of natural light. The place is surrounded by freshly cut flowers in glass vases with natural-colored rocks at the bottom, there's exposed brick on the main wall that houses the stairs and elevator, and massive, exquisite paintings decorate the walls. The hardwood underneath my feet looks real and recently stained, and the rugs on top of them are boho and cushy under my feet. Even the woman who greets us in the foyer is dressed up and pristine. She wears a tight, blood-red pencil skirt, a frilly white blouse, and red bottom pumps. Her lipstick matches the shade of red from her skirt perfectly.

"You weren't kidding, Mike," Brian sighs as he looks all around, running a calloused hand over the top of his head of thickly braided twists. Even Trish, who is usually too cool to be impressed, looks downright mesmerized.

"Welcome, April Renegade and crew," the finely dressed woman greets. "We are so happy to be able to house you for the next few nights while you are in the city." She smiles and shows off a set of perfect, white teeth. "Shall we?"

We all enter the spacious elevator after Ellie—that's the woman's name—and listen as she talks about the building's history. It was apparently an old warehouse before it was converted into lofts last year. "The bottom level houses the lobby, a couple of offices, and a communal game room."

I can't help but notice that Ellie's eyes drag down my body as she talks. She doesn't bother trying to hide her attraction, either. She barely looks at anyone else. "On the second and third floors are the loft apartments. There are ten total; six smaller on the second floor and four larger lofts on the top."

She stops on the second floor, and we follow her out.

"Trish, you'll be on this floor with me," Mike says, "along with Jim, Evan, Connor, and Alex." Trish doesn't look thrilled to be separated from the main band, but she keeps quiet. Connor and Alex accompanied us to most places for travel—Connor is the main sound tech who's been with us since our very first tour, and Alex is Mike's assistant. Sometimes, they stay with the other roadies, but I think Mike wanted to treat them to a few nights at the loft as a thank you.

Ellie turns to those of us going up to the third floor and hands us all our keys. Looking down at my key card, I notice an old-fashioned 3 printed on it in bold letters. "You gentlemen let me know if you need anything," Ellie says. She places a hand on my bicep and sends me a sultry smile before walking back to Mike and the others.

We enter the elevator again, and Brian immediately begins snickering. "I think Ellie has the hots for you, Drew."

Ash stares at his feet from where he's slumped against the elevator wall.

Because I'm in the mood to be a total prick, I smile at Sean and Brian. "Yeah? She *is* pretty hot."

"You gonna go for that, bro?" Sean nudges my ribs with his elbow.

126

Sean and Brian think I've been single for so long because I'm a bachelor who enjoys his privacy. So be it. I shrug nonchalantly and wink at them to give them the answer they expect as the elevator comes to a stop.

MAYBE IT'S because he's so down, but Ash puts on an incredible show. More incredible than the previous ones.

I feel like my performance is better than usual, too. Not to say that I slack off or don't try my best each night, but tonight I channel all my fury into hitting the drums. I don't focus on Ash or his tight ass in his jeans. Don't think about Lizette planning their fucking wedding. I just drum. It's not hot by any means, but from how much I've strained myself on the drums, I end up sweating and taking my shirt off, which always makes the crowd go crazy.

Ash looks back at me once my shirt's off, and I feel a sense of satisfaction as his eyes dip to my six-pack and the V that juts out from my pants. I make sure not to look at him or pay him any mind. He won't be getting any of this during the encore, and he better well know it.

He ends the song on a high note, scream-singing at the top of his lungs, and then my drums fade out until I'm barely tapping, the guitar and bass go silent for less than a second, and we seamlessly move along into the next song—the song our album is named after. As soon as it begins, a knot forms in my throat. I tell myself to keep my shit together, but "Home by June" always gets to me. I guess it doesn't matter how mad I am at Ash; the song digs its way underneath my skin, into the deep crevices and cracks of my being, and brings back a flood of memories.

When Ash first showed me the lyrics, tears fell down my cheeks and they didn't stop for a long time. "Home by June" is primarily about my mother; how she noticed Ash and took him in when he was struggling to get out of his parents' house. The first time Ash showed the song to Mom, she sobbed and clutched both of us. I wonder what she thinks about him getting engaged. Has she called him? In a way, Ash is her second son.

Not only is the song touching and haunting, but it brings up memories that I'd rather block out. I shut my eyes and wipe the sweat from my brows as I'm tortured with the memory of our first kiss, the family dinners we shared, the movies we watched while snuggled up in the basement—I see it all like it happened days ago.

I open my eyes and stare up at the blinding stage lights up above me so I can feel something other than the sinking weight that pulls at my chest.

"I'll be home by June, I just don't know it yet. I never knew home could feel like you..." Ash sings low and slow as he stands unmoving at center stage. His hands wrap around the mic as he continues, his voice growing a little louder. He sings about falling in love and being home with family for the first time. As the song comes to its end, I try to wipe my eyes as discreetly as possible.

We exit the stage in between the last song and the encore, and I make a point not to go to my dressing room. Ash walks past me and into his, and his body being close in proximity to my own makes the hair all over my body stand up. I'm angry and devastated and longing for him all at once. My head spins with the rush of emotions and from the exhaustion I've felt over the past twenty-four hours.

I make my way to a small fridge in the lounge area backstage and grab an energy drink. I chug half of it before I realize the local opening band, whose name I regrettably already forgot, watches me from the futons. I'm sweaty and a little embarrassed as they look at me with big, star-stricken smiles.

"Uh, sorry. Didn't see you guys there," I murmur.

One of the members, a guy a little shorter than me with short platinum hair on one side and teal hair on the other, rises to his feet and comes up to me. The rest of the band continues on in whatever conversation they were having before I came in.

"Hi," the guy says. He's got very blue eyes, like the clearest of beaches. His face is more feminine than my own—fewer sharp edges and more soft curves along his jawline and cheekbones. But, he's admittedly handsome. A light dusting of facial hair decorates his jaw and neck. "I'm Theo."

Theo stretches out his hand and I take it in my own. "Hi. Drew."

He grins which reveals a smiley piercing dangling by his front teeth. "You guys are even more phenomenal in person. I've been a fan for a long time." Theo shifts his feet where he stands, clearly a little nervous. "Sorry, I'm not trying to be weird." He laughs. "I was just really excited when I learned we got to open for you."

I take a long swig of my drink. I can hear the crowd going nuts, and know it'll be time to go back on stage in a minute or so. "Thanks. And no need to apologize. It's always fun to meet new bands while on the road."

Theo's eyes twinkle a little. "Listen—I know you're busy as fuck, but if you want to hang with us later, I think we may be going to a couple of bars. We're from around here, so we could show you the lesser-known places." Theo winks. Is he flirting with me? God, I've been wrapped up in the same man for so long that I don't even know if he's simply being nice or flirting. I feel pitiful.

"Uh, sure. Maybe," I say. I don't want to commit to anything, but I don't really want to say no, either, which surprises me.

He pulls out a cracked iPhone and opens his contacts. I quickly type in my number and rush off to the stage.

CHAPTER NINETEEN

NOVEMBER 9, 2012

The Madder Hatter didn't have much of a backstage area, but they made it comfortable by pushing a few couches and loveseats against the back wall, which was made up of old, exposed brick.

I refused to drink or smoke before going on stage because I wanted to be completely present for our first show, and I didn't want to risk messing anything up. The buzzing inside of my head was becoming obnoxious, though, and I begged my nerves to calm down as we sat backstage. More than once, I thought I might puke.

Drew was nervous, too, but he was handling it better than me. Meanwhile, Sean and Brian were all smiles. I wished I could be like that. I sat on one of the couches with my head in my hands, tapping my right foot. I'd already sweat so much, it felt like I'd stepped into a sauna. My shirt was plastered to my back like someone had glued it on.

"How long?" I asked Drew.

He paused, presumably to check the time. "About fifteen minutes."

I puffed out a giant breath and rubbed at my temples. Less than a year prior, I hadn't even sung for anyone besides myself. Now, I was going to step on stage and sing in front of hundreds. The bitter taste of vomit rose in the back of my throat. I forced it down and groaned uncomfortably.

"Here," Drew said as he placed a cold plastic bottle full of water in my hands.

"Thanks."

I managed a small sip, then ran over our very small setlist of six songs in my head for the hundredth time. My very scuffed Converse stared back at me from where I looked down at the floor while silently rehearsing lyrics. Three of the songs were of our own creation. The other three were covers of well-known songs—a slower, acoustic version of My Chemical Romance's "I'm Not Okay" was one of them, and I found myself identifying with the lyrics more than ever.

The other bands hung around on some of the other couches, or stood outside on the back patio to smoke before they went on. I'd never heard of the other two bands, and I looked forward to the part of the show where we would be done performing, and we could stick around and listen to them play.

"You gonna be okay?" Drew whispered close to my ear. He smelled like something spicy, which usually turned me on. Instead, it worsened my nausea.

I did my best to give him a convincing nod. Carefully, I lifted my head from where I'd hanged it between my knees and leaned back against the couch.

Drew discreetly bumped his knee against mine. The small gesture made my heart squeeze, and one look at him made my throat dry up. He wore a simple, black V-neck t-shirt, ash gray skinny jeans with rips and tears from the bottoms of his pockets all the way down to his ankles, black Docs, and a maroon beanie. To put it simply, he looked fine as hell. He'd even let his mom trim his hair up before we left; his waves were curlier than what I had grown used to, and they framed his sharp, masculine features in a way that very well could have brought me to my knees.

"Okay. Let's come up with a game plan."

"What?" I hissed, suddenly worried. Had I forgotten something?

His knee touched mine again, and the small bump sent heat curling down from my sternum, past my stomach, and down to my toes. "Yeah. A game plan," Drew said. "Let's come up with something *now* that will help you chill out whenever we go on stage."

I almost asked how he knew I'd freak out but thought better of it. Drew had known me long enough by now—*really* knew me. We both knew there was no way to predict how I'd be once I took the stage. I might be cool as a fucking cucumber, or I could pass out, piss myself, and refuse to perform ever again.

Drew leaned back against the couch so that we were shoulder to shoulder. He took the water bottle from me and took a swig. "You need something neutral to look at. Not the crowd, or the lights. Something...calming."

I doubted there would be anything neutral or calming enough on that stage to make his recommendation possible.

"You could look a few feet in front of where the mic will be," he offered. "It'll just be the floor, but that's good, right? You stare at the floor all the time. Shit, you were looking down at your shoes a second ago. Easy," Drew joked. "Neutral. Not exciting."

The nagging feeling in my gut remained. "I can try that. But— what if that doesn't work?"

He shrugged and his shoulder rubbed against mine. "You can always close your eyes for a bit. Not for too long, cuz that might be weird. But, if it gets bad, shut your eyes for a bit. Pretend you're somewhere you feel safe."

I scoffed. "Did you just turn into my therapist?" I laughed for the first time since we'd arrived. The tension in my shoulders eased away from my ears just a little. Then, Drew winked at me, and my stage fright was suddenly replaced with butterflies of a completely different nature.

He leaned over a bit, his lips mere centimeters from my ear, and whispered, "You're going to be great, Ash. And afterward, we'll go home and celebrate. Just us."

Drew pulled away, and goosebumps emerged along the skin on my neck where his warm breath had been. No one else could see his features in the low light backstage, but the look he gave me was dripping with sin, and his wicked smile held a promise that he had plans for us later in the night that had nothing to do with music and everything to do with us being naked in his bed.

EVERY NERVE inside of me sent my body into a fit of uncontrollable vibrations as I walked onto the stage. I told myself that I wouldn't look at the faces in the crowd, but despite the blinding lights situated toward us, I was able to make out the outlines of those closest to the stage.

Everything moved fast and dreadfully slow all at once as we took our places. People clapped around us, but the noise was faint through the blood whooshing in my ears. I wrapped my hands tightly around the microphone and felt a little faint. My knuckles bleached with the strain of my grip. After repeating Drew's advice in my mind, I closed my eyes, counted to three, and took a breath.

"How's everyone doing tonight?" I asked into the mic. A few shouts and claps sounded in the audience. My heart thudded restlessly, but as I talked, it became less distracting. "We're so happy to be here tonight. A few of us met here for the first time a while ago." My voice cracked in the mic, but I trudged on. "So, we wouldn't really be here without the Madder Hatter." I smiled and looked down at the spot on the floor a few feet in front of the mic stand. "We're April Renegade." Drew excitedly clicked his drumsticks together behind me as Brian strummed at the guitar. "And we hope you're ready to rock."

Cheers came from all around me—right in front of the stage, from the sides, and up from those seated on the upper level. The smile that crept up to my lips was genuine. I turned my back to the audience as the music began. Drew locked his warm eyes on mine, and it turned out that was all I needed to find some confidence. I jumped a few times and turned around in time for the first set of lyrics.

I started off a little rough around the edges but trained my eyes to find that one part of the floor whenever my voice shook or if I became overwhelmed. I stood in the center, unmoving as I adjusted to my new surroundings, but by the time I was screaming into the mic at the tail end of our first song, I'd moved around the stage a bit and even headbanged with Sean. A quarter of the way through our set, my voice leveled out and I'd found my footing on the stage.

Out of all the possible scenarios I'd obsessed over leading up to our first show—like whether I'd forget the lyrics or face-plant on stage—fell to the wayside as soon as the crowd exploded into a roar of excitement after our first song ended. And it was *our* song—not a cover. It was the first song I'd written and shown Drew, which I'd named "Dark." I stared at the crowd in awe as the instruments faded out. Groups of people came closer to the stage from where they'd been standing back near the bar. Several people whistled while others held their hands up in the rock 'n roll salute.

It felt like a dream. One I'd be content to stay in forever.

"Thank you so much," I breathed into the mic. "We appreciate you. We really do." I paused and grinned while staring at the floor. "This is our first show. We wouldn't want to have it anywhere else."

More screams sounded as the guys began playing our cover of "I'm Not Okay." To my surprise, as the song began, I was okay.

I was *more* than okay.

IT WAS one of the greatest nights of my entire life. It was one of those defining moments that would be etched permanently into my memory. I replayed the night over and over in my head as soon as we were finished so I could cherish each song, each round of applause, every time I turned around and Drew looked at me in awe, and all of the other minor details, like the thick feel of the air from the people dancing by the stage, the smell of mixed perfumes and colognes along with sweat and beer, and the cool, light blue color of the lights that surrounded us.

After we exited the stage, I felt high; like I was floating somewhere above my body, looking down on myself. I didn't feel like Asher Lance from the trailer park who had to hide from his parents or Asher Lance who was terrified to sing in front of others. I felt like Ash. Ash, who had an energetic stage presence despite his anxiety; Ash, who was praised for his unique voice after the show by the other bands and several people in the audience.

As I shook hands with the other bands and then got hauled into a massive group hug from the guys, I decided I wasn't Asher Lance anymore. I never really was. So many artists had stage names or pen names, so maybe I'd be Ash Lancing. I'd always dreamed of Lancing instead of Lance. It rolled off the tongue better and sounded stronger. Ash Lancing was the lead singer of an up-and-coming band, and though Asher Lance had been a stepping stone to Ash, maybe it was time to move on and evolve.

Drew grabbed my face in his hands as the other guys jumped around in post-show ecstasy, pulling me out of my thoughts. For a second, I thought he might kiss me. Instead, he grinned at me and shouted over the music overhead, "You did it! We did it! We fucking *did* it!"

The four of us walked outside to the smoking patio right as the next band hit the stage. A few people lingered, but as they finished their smokes, they went back inside the venue. We got a few compliments as people made their way back in, and one woman ogled Drew so obviously on her way back inside that I was filled with the insurmountable urge to trip her. Instead, I let her look. She'd never have him, but I would—because I *had* had him.

Once the four of us were alone, Sean brought out a fat blunt and lit it. "This one's for all of us. What a fucking show!"

"You were great, dude," Brian told me pointedly. "Seriously. After you got used to it all, it was like you belonged on that stage." Brian took the blunt from Sean, inhaled deeply, and choked on the smoke. He was sent into a coughing fit that lasted a concerning amount of time.

He turned to Sean once he recovered. "Christ, dude, what *is* this?"

Sean grinned maniacally. "The good shit."

Brian handed the blunt to me, and I took a small hit. I didn't want to be high off my ass or cough up a lung, but I did want to celebrate.

"You do belong on the stage." Drew grinned as I took a puff. I offered the blunt to him, but he shook his head and pulled out a half-empty pack of cigarettes that he'd bought over a month ago. I handed the blunt back to Sean. Drew placed one of the cigs in between my fingers, then lit it for me, pausing a little when he cradled my fingers in his cupped hand. Brian and Sean kept smoking and got higher off their asses with each puff. They all but giggled as they announced that they were going to the bar for a drink.

"You belong up there, too, you know," I told Drew after the door shut behind our friends. He lit his own cigarette and inhaled before stepping closer to me. He exhaled to the side, careful not to blow smoke in my face.

We stood in the corner farthest from the door, drenched in the dim October moonlight. Drew walked into me until my back pressed against a tall privacy fence that was covered in thick foliage. He took the cigarette from his lips, and I knew he was about to ravage me, just for a minute or so. I brought my own cigarette down from my lips.

Drew devoured me, and the feel of his lush lips along with my small high, the nicotine, and the thrill of ending our first show had me groaning into his open mouth. He caressed my jaw with his free hand, but eventually got greedy and dropped his cigarette to the ground so he could grab me with both hands.

I did the same.

Drew slid his tongue over my own while we ground into each other there in the shadows, holding onto one another for dear life.

"How long until we go home?" I asked after I nipped at his bottom lip.

He grinned against my lips. "Just say the word, Ash. I'm ready when you are." Drew slid his hands over my chest and kissed me deeply one last time before he let me go and retrieved his half-smoked cigarette from the ground.

CHAPTER TWENTY

NOVEMBER 9, 2012

We stayed through the second band and halfway through the last band before practically running through the city streets back to my car. Sean and Brian chose to stay. Brian insisted he'd only taken a few hits from Sean's jumbo joint and he was drinking water, so he was fine to drive after the show. I was relieved, and it was a damn good thing we'd all driven separately, because there was no way in hell I was going to wait to take Ash home any longer.

It wasn't a short trip home. From D.C., getting back to my place would take around an hour. For most of the ride, we left each other alone and stayed in our own headspaces. It was one of those nights that's one of a kind. One you know you'll never experience again, even though I knew things were only getting started for April Renegade. The way the crowd consumed our music was extraordinary, as was the feedback we got after. Whatever doubts we all had before we walked onto that stage had lessened significantly by the end of our set.

There was no doubt in my mind that Ash belonged on the stage. Front and center. I could tell when his energy heightened and his anxieties fell away during our set, and watching his transformation while singing his heart out was brilliant. At first, he'd stayed near the mic, almost unmoving. His fingers had twitched restlessly, and his head was bent down a bit, more than likely looking at the floor.

Then, something shifted. As Ash sang on, the crowd lifted him up. He loosened up and walked around the stage, danced with the microphone stand, at one point he head-banged with Sean, and he even came over to where I was near the end and pretended to bang on the drums.

Ash's newly found self-confidence was well-deserved. It also made me incredibly hot for him. My thoughts lingered on the way he'd looked on the stage as we hit the home stretch back home, and I found that I was having trouble paying attention to the road.

A couple of miles out, after I'd exited the interstate, I slid my hand over to rest on his thigh. I had expected him to hold my hand until we got home. Instead, he brought our joined hands up to his mouth and kissed each of my knuckles slowly.

I leaned my head back and tried to focus on the road. Having his lips on any part of me while I was driving was incredibly dangerous. He leaned over across the center console and kissed my neck lightly.

"Ash..." I warned with a rough, pained rasp. "I don't want to swerve off this road and kill us."

He chuckled against my neck and slid his tongue along my jawline, tracing the hard line and setting my whole body on fire. Our hands untangled as he stroked me all over–over my neck, down my chest, and that sweet spot in between my thighs. My skinny jeans became painfully tight. Ash couldn't be tamed, and it took every brain cell of mine to not veer off the road and throw his ass in the back seat. Ash cupped my growing bulge as soon as we turned into my neighborhood, leaving me with blurred vision and shallow breaths.

Finally, I turned into the driveway and parked abruptly in my designated spot. Ash was on top of me in an instant as soon as he unbuckled himself. He straddled me, and I fumbled around in the dark for the lever to push my seat back so we wouldn't lean back against the horn and alert my family of our arrival.

After sliding us back, Ash wasted no time grinding into me, delirious and lost in his need. His delectable lips hovered above mine as I gripped his ass and felt him through his jeans. I reached for him, and the distance between us disappeared. His lips were soft, and he tasted faintly like the one drink we'd had accompanied by old smoke and the fresh mint of the gum he'd chewed on the ride home. He trailed a hand underneath my shirt and down to the waistband of my jeans, teasing me until I couldn't stand it.

"Inside," I ordered. Ash could be such a tease, and if we didn't stop, I was going to finish in my car with my pants still on, which is *not* what I had planned.

Ash looked at me and smirked. He knew exactly what he'd been doing. He loved to rile me up. He clumsily hopped off my lap and we made our way to the house. I wondered for only a second if Sean and Brian had handled my drum set carefully enough when they packed everything up—and then Ash was on me again, shoving me back into the wall of the house by the front door. I yelped a little as my back hit the siding, and he laughed huskily into my neck.

The front light was off, so I assumed everyone was in bed. I let him have his way with me for a moment because I knew I was going to drag his ass inside at some point. Ash drew back from a lengthy kiss and pressed his forehead against mine.

"You're so beautiful," he murmured. My cheeks heated instantaneously. I cupped the back of his head and left a trail of kisses down his neck. Ash pushed himself into me, and the friction he gave me was pure torture through our jeans.

I raked my hands down his back right as the light by the door turned on, casting a yellow glow over us. Ash jumped off me and took a step into the yard to avoid the light...and to tuck himself up into his waistband. I did the same with shaky hands. How the abrupt interruption didn't make my dick soft immediately, I had no clue.

As soon as Ash came back to the front door, it opened.

"¿*Mis amores?*"

I jumped away from where I stood pressed against the house, walked into the foyer, and smiled at my mother. Ash walked in after me. Inside, the house smelled like chocolate chip cookies, which I knew meant Mom stayed up and waited for us. She closed the door and locked it behind us.

"I thought I'd turned that light on." Mom tapped herself lightly on the forehead. "I got so caught up in my tele-novella and making cookies, I must have forgotten." She rolled her eyes and motioned for us to follow her into the kitchen.

"Mom, you didn't have to wait on us," I said. The clock in the kitchen read that it was almost half-past midnight.

She scoffed and made us sit down at the small breakfast table on one side of the room. "I wasn't going to go to sleep and *not* hear about your first show."

"Well," I chuckled. "Dad did."

Mom placed a fresh plate of cookies between me and Ash on the table, then poured us a couple of glasses of milk. Ash's cheeks were flushed, and his lips were swollen. He looked embarrassed, and it was cute as hell.

Mom came back with the milk. "I am *not* your father, Andrew." She rolled her eyes again and sat in a chair by me. "Tell me about it, and then I'll go to sleep."

When I first told Mom about dropping my classes and focusing on the band, I'd been so freaked out about how she would take it, but as she sat at the table and demanded we tell her every detail of the show, I felt like an idiot for worrying about it in the first place. Even Dad didn't take it too hard—like her, he wanted me to be happy.

I took a large bite of the warm cookie and moaned a little. Mom smacked me lightly on the shoulder. "*¡No lo excites!*" *Don't excite him!* My eyes bulged and I choked on a laugh. Mom was smarter than to forget to turn the light on. She wanted to give us a moment alone before interfering.

Ash's face was twisted up in confusion as he looked between me and Mom. Then, he let it go and took a bite of his own cookie.

"Oh my God," he whispered. "This is the best."

We sat there and ate our cookies while we told Mom all the details about the show. When Ash finished his last cookie, I shamelessly stared at him while he licked the melted chocolate off his thumb and index finger. I loved my mother to death, but if I didn't get Ash alone–

Mom faked a yawn and stood up, obviously understanding where my thoughts had gone. She bent down and kissed my cheek. "I'm glad it was a great night. Tell me more in the morning? *Buenas noches.*" Mom winked at me from the doorway before she retreated to her and Dad's room.

I stood up and washed our glasses out as fast as I could while Ash threw away the paper plate we'd shared. As I rinsed the second glass, he came up behind me and wrapped his arms around me.

"We're that obvious to your mom?" His voice was deeper than normal, and I felt my heart pick right back up like we were back in the car.

I turned my face to meet his. "What do you think?"

"I think it's time for bed."

IT TOOK us longer than necessary to make it to my room.

Ash grabbed my ass on our way up the stairs which resulted in my pressing him into the wall and feeling him up right there in between the photos of past family portraits. After we got to the second floor, he stopped us before we entered my room, reminding me of the first time we'd ventured into my room together in the late hours of the night. Ash nipped at my lip ring, stealing ragged and excited breaths as he did so.

"I swear to God, *Asher*—if you don't take me into that room right fucking now—"

He breathed a chuckle. "You'll do what?"

"Just you fucking wait," I growled.

"I love when you're demanding." He licked his lips.

For a moment we stared at one another. Undeniable heat pooled in his eyes as he raked his eyes up and down my body. Finally, he released me, yanked at my hand, and thrust us into my bedroom. I hurriedly locked the door behind us.

I'd made plans a few weeks prior on how we'd celebrate our first show, and I was more than ready to share my plans with him. *Fucking finally.* I greedily shoved him onto my bed. Earlier that morning, I'd cleaned the sheets and bedspread. When they were dry, I spent my time making the bed nice and pretty for the sole purpose of defiling it when we got home. Ash rumpled the bedspread as he stretched out, then placed his hands behind his head and grinned up at me from where he lay.

I'd recently purchased a small light for my room. It looked like a little orb, and sat on my bedside table. It had different color settings to choose from, and I bought it just so I could look at him while he sucked me, ravaged me, and marked me as his. Doing everything in the dark was overrated. I turned the little light on and chose a deep blue, which cast the room in a shadowy twilight.

Ash started stroking himself through his jeans, and he'd somehow unbuttoned his jeans already. He caught me eyeing his hand and threw me a knowing smile. He continued to stroke, completely comfortable letting me watch.

"So, what *are* you going to do to me?" He purred.

Such a cocky asshole.

Throughout the past few weeks, we became more comfortable in our exploration of one another. Our relationship was the most intimate thing I'd ever experienced. We'd gone from a little reserved and confused in the beginning to needing more, more, *more* each time. What once felt a little odd or embarrassing was now second nature. I knew exactly where to touch and suck and stroke, and I'd figured out the perfect times to do so.

The first time I'd ventured into unfamiliar territory, I was hesitant. I didn't want to make him uncomfortable with anything we did. One day in the basement, while I had my lips secured around his throbbing cock, I found the confidence to run my fingers up and back so I could lightly squeeze his balls. He liked that so much, his knuckles turned white from clenching the arm of the couch, and his grip in my hair burned.

After that, I continued farther, stroking the rim of his tight hole and teasing. At first, his eyes shot open, but then he eased into my touch and took me so good. I'd successfully hit that sweet spot after I'd gotten my whole finger in, using my spit to get him nice and slick, and Ash had never come so fucking hard. It was the sexiest thing I'd ever seen, giving him an intense kind of pleasure he'd never experienced before. After that, he started begging for my fingers when I didn't immediately touch him there. Sometimes, he even guided my hand back and shifted his hips up, begging me with his body instead of his words.

For days, I'd been priming him to take something bigger.

He hadn't ventured into that area of my body yet. I wanted him to, but I didn't want to rush him or bring him out of his comfort zone. I was more than happy to give him whatever he wanted, whenever; but I did wonder what one of his long, smooth fingers would feel like inside of me.

I realized I'd been lost in my thoughts when Ash repeated the question.

I crawled on top of him and hovered on my forearms so that my face was close to his. "What do you want me to do to you, Ash?" I asked, licking my lips. I sat up and straddled him, slowly undoing his zipper, driving him a little crazy with the anticipation of what was to come. As soon as it was down, his cock burst out and I palmed it. Ash lurched and his head fell back with the contact.

"*Fuck*, Drew."

I loved when he said my name like that—like he could barely speak through the thick lust that coated the back of his throat. He panted as I gripped him harder.

"I have many things I want to do to you, Ash." I maneuvered him so I could strip him of his godforsaken pants and shoes. "And I plan to do them. Right now."

Ash looked up at me with wide eyes and a slack jaw.

"But before I begin…" I threw his pants to the ground and slid his boxers from his hips. "Is there anything you *don't* want from me?"

Ash bit his bottom lip only for a split second. "No. I want it. All of it. I want all of you."

I exhaled roughly at his words and from the feel of pre-cum which coated my palm. I squeezed and teased his cockhead after throwing his boxers off to the side. I sucked him, and slowly cleaned up his seed. He'd only been in my mouth for less than a minute when I got off the bed and opened the drawer of my bedside table.

He propped himself up on the bed, and I could tell he was miffed about my abrupt decision to take his dick out of my mouth.

"Patience." I winked. "And take that stupid shirt off."

Ash shot me an incredulous look before sitting up and ripping his shirt off.

"Good."

"You take off *yours*," he whisper-shouted.

I shook my head, and he licked his bottom lip in impatience. He was itching to touch himself; I could tell by the way his fingers twitched at his sides and the way his cock from where it stood at attention.

"I'm not taking orders from you," I said huskily. "You'll have your turn when you earn it."

Ash scoffed but obeyed, which made my own cock throb from where it was still trapped in my pants. I hurriedly rummaged around in the drawer until I found the CVS bag stored at the very back. After opening the bag, I felt for the cool tube of lube I'd bought the day before. I sat the tube on the table and I turned to Ash to gauge his reaction. He eyed the lube and moaned. He couldn't take it anymore. His dominant hand gripped his shaft and he worked himself as I slowly, tauntingly pulled my shirt over my head.

"I've been...prepping," Ash said quietly, his hand mid-stroke, eyes unwavering from mine.

God damn. I didn't think I could get any harder. "You've been wanting me, haven't you? *All* of me." I unbuttoned my jeans.

Ash nodded and parted his lips, panting hard for me already. He continued to stroke and eye-fuck me while I undressed.

"I'm going to be very upset with you if I'm not the one to make you come," I said.

Ash's hand immediately stopped. He ground his teeth and inhaled deeply while I pulled my zipper down and peeled my pants off.

Ash sat up and pulled down the covers. He slipped under the sheets just as I was finally free of clothes. I joined him restlessly and turned my body toward his so that we could face each other. Hot anticipation coursed through me–the kind that had my nerves shooting through my body at lightning speed, leaving me giddy and breathless.

Ash's kiss was soft, his lips barely brushed against my own. He'd been prepping for this. For me. Picturing him playing with himself and fantasizing about all the things I'd do to him had my breath stalling.

"What?" he asked.

I shook my head. "Just you."

"Me?"

"I love how bad you want me inside of you," I growled against his neck and moved lower, leaving kisses and sucking on each stretch of untouched flesh, inhaling as I did so. He gasped and slid a hand to the back of my neck. "Love how badly you want me to take your v-card."

Ash groaned. "I love that you're going to take it from me." My head shot up and I stared up at him in the violet darkness. His eyes were hooded. "I'm serious, Drew. I wouldn't want to do this with anyone other than you." The sincerity in his gleaming eyes showed me how serious he was.

"I wouldn't want to do this with anyone else, either," I said hoarsely.

It was the truth. The attraction was one thing, but Ash had also easily become my favorite person. Being around him made me feel alive for the first time in a long time. I ignored the heavy feeling in my gut which questioned how long this would—or could—last. How we would come out to the band. It wasn't something we had discussed, and I wasn't about to discuss it while we were naked in my bed.

Underneath the covers, I couldn't see his roaming hands, and when he grabbed my shaft and began stroking me, I let out a surprised moan. Ash looked down at my face with a devilish smile before he moved his head and kissed my neck. He slid his tongue over my collarbones and all the way down my chest. His free hand played with my chest hair as he worked himself lower.

I wanted to take him, but I also wanted him to take me into that sweet mouth of his. Ash loved to suck me and lick up everything I expelled. Hell, he'd done it that morning when we had the house to ourselves.

I wasn't complaining.

Ash's fingers dug into my hip bones, and his head disappeared under the covers. Using no hands for aid, he licked my entire length then sucked my head into his hot, wet mouth.

"Fucking *hell,*" I grunted. My dominant hand found his head under the covers. He didn't have a lot of hair to grip, but I managed to grasp at whatever I could manage in my frenzy.

Ash moaned with me in his mouth, and I felt my cock twitch against his tongue. He worked me deeper and deeper until he was taking my entire length, swallowing me down as far as possible. Heat curled low in my stomach and was accompanied by a faint, familiar pressure. I knew I was a goner—there was no way in hell I'd be able to hold off.

"Ash—" I breathed.

He lifted the covers up so I could watch him consume me. The sucking sounds paired with his talented tongue made my eyes roll back. To my surprise, the next thing he did was cradle my balls, just like how he liked. A different kind of pleasure pulsed through me as he tugged.

"That okay?" Ash whispered after taking me out of his mouth.

"God. Yes. *Please.* Harder," I begged, moving my hips against him.

"Not so big and bad when I'm the one getting you off," he quipped. *Such a cocky little*—his finger teased in between my cheeks, caressing my hole as he licked the tip of me slowly. My skin was on fire, and I was dizzy with pleasure. Ash reached over to where the lube sat on the table, opened it, and put some on his fingertips. Without a word, he resumed his position, sucked all of me into his exquisite mouth, then swirled the lube from his fingers all around my entrance. He pushed a finger in, ever so slightly and my hips bucked a little off the bed, craving more.

I hadn't mentioned to Ash that I'd been experimenting on my own. I wanted to be primed for him, too. When he wasn't around and I had to get the job done myself, I took some long showers. Still, I'd never gone deeper than the first knuckle because I wanted him to take the rest of me.

"You're so ready for me, aren't you?" Ash asked as he stared up at me through thick lashes.

All I could manage was a nod and a weak whimper. Oh, how the roles had reversed.

Without breaking eye contact, Ash sucked all of me into the back of his throat, then pressed his digit inside of me much deeper than I'd ever gone. A bolt of ecstasy hit me out of nowhere. My grip, which had fallen to his shoulders, tightened as I spilled into his mouth. He didn't stop suckling me until I reopened my eyes and let out a pleasurable sigh.

Ash joined me back under the covers, and I gripped him eagerly. I met his lips and pried his sweet mouth open with my tongue as he wrapped his body around mine hungrily.

I had a feeling it wouldn't take long for me to get hard for him again.

CHAPTER TWENTY-ONE

The morning after our Los Angeles show, I wake up with a rare ailment—a hangover.

Well, it's a rare thing for me to have, anyway.

My head feels like a rubber band several sizes too small is wrapped around it, and it takes me several minutes in my cloudy, in-between sleeping and waking state to realize that the room doesn't smell bad. *I* smell bad.

"Fucking *hell*," I groan. I lift my head up a couple of inches and notice I'm on top of the expensive duvet in my loft. I apparently didn't even take my shoes off last night before collapsing onto the plush mattress. The bright California sun shines down on me and the sparkling hardwoods through the large windows, and I realize the sun is high enough that it must be well into the morning. No wonder I feel like I was stomped on by a whole ass stampede.

I manage to prop myself up a bit on my elbows and wince at the screaming throb in my temples and across my forehead. I muster up the majority of my strength and shove the pillow beside me underneath my head, fluffing it so I can stay propped up.

Thank goodness we have the next few nights off until we head to San Diego.

I feel for my cell phone on the bedside table, and exhale in relief when I grab onto the pop socket secured to my phone case. In the past, I've left my phone, wallets, and keys in various places when I got drunk. There was a party several years back at Tre Cool's place up in Oakland, and my phone somehow ended up in his fish tank by the end of the night, which was something I knew the partygoers still hadn't forgotten.

After unlocking my phone, I grimace at all the notifications that pop up.

My social media accounts have gotten more attention than usual due to the wedding announcement, and even though I silenced most of the notifications long ago, some still manage to come in. I open my home screen and ignore the red bubbles littering various applications. I have eight text messages—five from Lizzy, which is normal for how often she's on her phone, a couple from Mike, and... one from *Drew*.

Nausea hits me in the gut when I see the unread message. I force a shaky breath and tap on his contact. I don't remember a lot about my night once we got settled in Trish's room after the show, but I do remember that Drew wasn't there, and I was concerned about where he was, even though I knew it wasn't my place to worry.

Drew: I knew I was done for as we lay on that rooftop, cig dangling from your fingertips. Nothing I could do would make it stop, because you were you, and I kept dreaming of your lips.

My heart somersaults. I stumble into the bathroom and retch over the toilet before I can fully process what he sent me. I squeeze my eyes shut against tears and vomit, riding out the sickness as best I can. By the time I'm no longer gagging, I clutch a hand to my heart and rake at the skin and bone and tissue that keeps me from the beating organ with my fingertips, like maybe I can rip it from my chest with nothing more than my nails and my overwhelming desperation.

I knew I was done for as we lay on that rooftop, cig dangling from your lips. Emma's rooftop—when they were still dating.

Nothing I could do would make it stop because you were you —Drew. My Drew. *And I kept dreaming of your hips.* More tears drip down as I remember how badly I'd obsessed over Drew and every single thing about him that made him, *him* in those months leading up to the day we crossed the line from friendship to lust; lust that quickly evolved into something much deeper.

It was one of the last songs I wrote for our self-titled album back in 2013. My secret love song to Drew.

Once I regained my strength enough to stand, I went back to where I'd been on the bed and carefully laid back down. Breathless and hot, I check the text again and look at the time stamp: 3:07 am. He was up late. I sit there, staring at the words I wrote years ago, mocking me. 2013 Ash wouldn't even recognize 2022 Ash. What have I done? I want to reply, but I'm at a loss.

I open the texts from Lizette. The photo I have of her in my phone's contact is from when we'd been dating a little less than a year. We made goofy faces for the camera as we sat together in a movie theater with piss poor lighting, waiting for the previews to start. She didn't wear any makeup that day, and she looked gorgeous, especially with her crossed eyes and crazy smile.

The worst part of the last couple of years is that I've continuously hurt Drew over and over, but I've also dragged Lizzy down into it, too. My fist meets my forehead and I lightly pound onto my stupid head a little while more tears spill over onto my rank t-shirt.

The phone buzzes in my hand. A split second of hope that it's from Drew fades away immediately.

Lizzy: Don't freak, but California Rocker wants to do an interview with us today at 3...is that ok?? I'm sorry. I went ahead and said yes before I checked in with you.

"Motherfucker—" Another buzz.

Lizzy: I can always cancel. You're prob too tired?

Through clenched teeth, I agree to do it even though I'm well aware that I'm digging the hole of my grave deeper and deeper each day that I live this lie.

THE ENTIRE MORNING, I lay in bed wearing my filthy, vomit-crusted clothes. I watch every single music video we've ever released in chronological order. The first one I watched made me sob so hard I thought I would surely throw up again, but the nausea was replaced with a gnawing sense of anguish.

Watching twenty-year-old Drew on the drums was like falling for him all over again. At one point, I knew I was torturing myself, but I couldn't stop. His hair was a little longer back then, and his complexion was darker from the days he spent working out in the yard. He didn't have any tattoos yet. He was slimmer, but still cut. Drew. *My* Drew. The man who saw a light inside of me and would never do anything to hurt me. Younger Drew wasn't so different from Drew now. My throat burns and my eyes sting with more tears.

Around one in the afternoon, I haul my worthless ass into the spacious shower and sit on the shower bench as the scalding water beats down on my back and neck. I stay in there until my skin hurts, then I manage to bathe and get out.

I wipe the foggy, oval mirror that rests above the sink, and scold my reflection.

"You're an idiot," I tell myself. "Truly useless."

The shadows underneath my eyes are alarming. Even the color of my eyes seems duller than usual. I look like I'm ten years older than I am. I can only imagine what the tabloids or the *California Rocker* will say about that.

I dress up a little more than I usually would for our interview—black, form-fitting jeans, black Doc Martens, and a light gray button-down. As I put on deodorant and shave, I decide I'll try and track Trish down and see if she can put some concealer or something under my eyes to make me look less ghastly.

The urge to stop by Drew's loft on my way to the elevator is strong. I stand and look at the door that's across from my own in the open hallway. I almost step up to the door and knock but think better of it. I want to check on him. Instead, I go to the elevator and press the down button.

With a light *ding,* the elevator doors slide open. I walk in, and right as I'm about to hit the button to take me downstairs, Drew's door opens. I hit the button to keep the elevator open as my heart shoots up to the back of my throat, but when the door closes to Drew's loft, it's not Drew who exits, but one of the band members from the opening band who played before we went on last night.

It's past two in the afternoon, but the guy looks like he just woke up. He gives me a lazy half-smile as I begrudgingly hold the door for him, and as the doors slide close, he says hello. He reaches across to me in the small space and presses the button for the ground floor. Right underneath the hood of his black sweatshirt, I notice a light trail of bite marks. I know exactly what they are because I've worn and cherished the same ones on and off for years. My sense of worry for Drew is replaced with rage and jealousy so thick that I want to bash the blue-haired fuck's face in.

"It's nice to meet you." The weaselly fuck grins. I repeat the fact that this guy did nothing wrong over and over again in my head as I clench my fists at my sides. "I've been a fan of yours forever." He laughs and shyly runs his hands through his stupid hair.

"You, too," I bite out.

I want to ask him what he was doing with Drew. *My* Drew. I want to ask him how whatever happened between them even started.

154

I want to grip him by his stupid, bright hair and slam his face into the steel doors of the elevator.

When the elevator dings again, and the doors open to the second floor, it takes every ounce of willpower not to do something rash. I give the guy a halfhearted wave and rush out like my life depends on it.

In the hallway, I slide down against the wall and sit with my head in my hands as I try to make sense of what happened. It takes me a long time to get my shit together, stand up, and knock on Trish's door.

LIZZY and I meet the reporter for the *California Rocker* at a quaint cafe near the loft. Mike managed to rent out the small cafe for an hour so we could do the interview in peace, without distractions from fans or onlookers.

The reporter is a young man only a few years younger than me. I can tell he's nervous because he takes sporadic sips of his ice water when we haven't started with the questions yet. His name is Barry, and he graduated from New York University not long ago. He wears thick-framed, maroon-colored glasses and a tie to match. He sips from a cappuccino in between water with hands that shake a little, and I wonder whether the guy should be drinking caffeine at all.

Lizette looks like a dreamy sun goddess. Even though we won't take photos for the issue until tomorrow, she's dressed in a sand-colored, floor-length dress with spaghetti straps and golden sandals. The dress makes all of her features pop. She proudly shows off the engagement ring on her left hand as she places her slender hand on top of mine.

"So." Barry takes yet another sip of his water. He glances at me as he presses the record button on his iPhone. "Let's go ahead and get to it! Ash—how are you feeling now that you've proposed?"

Barry smiles at me, and Lizzy beams. She pats my hand lovingly, and I want to scream. Despite being at the cafe with them, my mind is hyper fixated on the person who waltzed out of Drew's loft. The bite marks. The smug, lazy grin spread across his face in the elevator.

I shoot Barry my best fake smile. "I'm feeling good, Barry. I'm feeling good."

CHAPTER TWENTY-TWO

NOVEMBER 10, 2012

I'd never felt so high in my whole life. Nervous and giddy and impatient and—*God*, every inch of my skin was alive for him.

Drew's cheeks were flushed as he pressed his cheek against my own in the dim light of his bedroom. His wavy hair was damp with sweat, and his breaths were shallow and hot. He stared at me as I skidded my fingertips down his bare, sweaty back. He gasped when I squeezed his ass from under the covers, then lunged at me. My tongue flicked at his, and when I pulled back for air, I nipped at his lip ring on my way back down. He let out a throaty moan of pleasure, and I knew he was ready to go again. Which was good—because I didn't know how much longer I could wait for him to take me.

The night was perfect in all the best ways, albeit unexpected— whenever I'd daydreamed about singing at a live show before Drew entered my life, I would have never thought that my fantasy would end with me in Drew's bed, begging him for his touch and pleading with him to fill me up.

Drew nuzzled into my neck. "You're sure you want this?" He laughed huskily. "I swear I'm not trying to talk you out of it." His voice became serious. "I want you to want it...I don't want to make you uncomfortable or anyth—"

I put an end to his rambling by tenderly pressing a kiss to his forehead. Drew always smelled like something warm and spicy, and I wanted to roll around in it, even with him coated in a fine, salty layer of sweat. I tilted his face to meet mine and kissed him deeply on his swollen, delectable mouth. Ran my tongue along his bottom lip with a small, purposeful groan which told him how badly I needed him. The last thing I wanted was for him to worry about whether I was uncomfortable or unwilling. Still, my heart warmed at his gentlemanly intentions. I was well aware that many people—couples or fuck buddies, or whatever—didn't have that kind of communication. My parents certainly didn't. I shoved the thoughts of them down and away. There was no room for their interference in my safe space.

Drew placed his rough hands on either side of my face and kissed me softly. He looked up at me and said, "I never thought I'd get so lucky. You're—*shit*. I feel weird saying this to you, but you've become so important to me, Ash." The last part was barely a whisper, and then his gaze flicked away from me. I cupped his chin to bring him back.

"I've never known anyone like I know you, Drew."

He huffed a laugh. "Not even Sean?"

I rolled my eyes. "Sean and I are close. But not *this* close."

Drew snickered into my neck. "Asshole."

In a flash, Drew's body was on top of mine. One of his hands pinned my arms above my head, binding my wrists together with his strong fingers, and a low grumble sounded from his throat. My pulse picked up speed and I hissed through a wave of ecstasy. Drew teased me underneath the covers; finally allowing his need to take over and his doubts to fall to the wayside.

"I *do* love your ass," he purred.

Drew pinned me down a little harder as I shifted my hips up to rub against him. My bones ached, craving the friction. He grazed his teeth down my body slowly, inch by inch, biting me on my chest, my rib cage, below my belly button, and on the tender dips of my waist until I whimpered from the torture he was obviously basking in. My hands clenched against his hold, itching to dig my fingers down his back and pull him in closer.

My dick twitched as his hand fondled my sack, and I couldn't control my back as it arched from the contact. Drew panted heavily and let my wrists go. He sat up and fumbled around in the semi-darkness until he found where I'd discarded the lube.

With my arms free, I sat up so I could run my hands down his bare thighs. Drew let out a rough exhale as I heard the top of the lube open. Before squeezing any into his hand, he leaned into me.

"I'm going to let you lead me," he said roughly, trying to keep his composure. "Stop me if it's too much?"

"Okay." I ran both of my hands over his hips and down his thighs once more, then laid back down on the pillow.

Drew ripped the covers away from us, then pried my thighs apart and bent my knees up so that I was completely exposed to him. He settled in between my legs with a contented sigh. We moaned in unison as our cockheads brushed up against each other. Somehow, he was harder than he was when I'd sucked him off. I was practically drooling for him. I rubbed both of us at the same time in urgent, languid strokes that had Drew dropping his head back for a moment before he came to and resumed positioning us.

He gripped me behind my knees and hauled my legs up around his midsection. Drew reached for his pillow and tucked it underneath my ass while I continued stroking us. I could have easily come for him like that, but I didn't want to. I needed all of him; I had been fantasizing about this moment for weeks.

Every wicked sound he made had me working us harder and faster in my hands. A rumble came from his chest and if I thought I'd been impatient before this, well, I'd been mistaken.

"You're incredibly needy for me, aren't you?" he asked.

"If you think otherwise, you haven't been paying attention."

He leaned forward once more to meet my lips, and I met him in the middle with fervor. Drew desecrated my mouth in a way he'd never done before; he pressed into me so hard, I knew I'd surely be bruised come morning. His hot tongue darted into my mouth and moved with my own in a perfectly choreographed dance.

The second we parted for air, I was begging. "Drew, *please.* I can't fucking stand this anymore. Take me, or I'm going to flip you over and take you."

I expected him to punish me for my words—in the most thrilling way, of course. His eyes were wild, and I knew he was contemplating his next move.

Drew eased back a little and put some of the lube on his fingertips.

"You like touching me so much, then put some of this on me while I finger fuck you." His voice deepened to an octave I wasn't aware he could reach, the order and his words steady and firm, and holy hell, I'd do whatever he wanted me to. An exhilarating shudder ran through me as he thrust the tube into my hand.

As soon as I'd gotten some lube in my hand, he adjusted us in a swift movement that I envied. If I'd been on top, I wasn't sure I'd have been so graceful. Right as I slid my slick hand around his length, he pressed half a finger into my hole. I lurched forward at the pleasure one of his knuckles brought.

"That's right, baby," Drew panted. "You're going to take all of me so well. I know it."

Something about the way Drew spoke dirty to me made my breath hitch. My cheeks burned, and I made a mental note to put some of his beautifully foul words into future lyrics, but that thought vanished as soon as his whole finger went in as deep as it could.

"*More,*" I demanded through the ripples of pleasure coursing through me.

His face lit up as he watched his finger thrust into me and slid in a second. He scissored inside of me, and I jerked beneath him and halted in my strokes. The sensation was so intense I could hardly stand it, but I knew his fingers wouldn't be enough to satiate my craving this time.

Drew lifted my legs around him more, then took his cock from my hand. I didn't dare touch my own, not when he was about to fuck me. I savagely watched him add more lube to himself and basked in the face he made when his tip pressed into my hole.

"Ash—" Drew had barely gone in, but his head fell back. "Oh, *fuck*. You're the best thing I've ever felt." He breathed hard and slid in a little bit more. "You're so tight," he panted. "Fuck. *Fuck!* You're taking me so good, baby." He was mesmerized by the sight, and I was mesmerized by his words, his movements, and his gluttonous eyes as he watched himself press into me more and more—all of it. "Can you take more?"

"*Please.*"

Drew moaned and slid in deeper. The stretching sensation was a little painful, but the ecstasy of having his beautiful cock inside me overwhelmed any discomfort I felt.

"How far are you?" I whispered.

"A little past the head."

Oh God. Neither one of us had been paying my cock any attention, but it didn't seem to matter. I was so sensitive that when I gripped my shaft right underneath the head, I had to distract myself from coming.

Drew's eyes flicked down. He licked his lips and watched me jerk myself, then he thrust his hips farther in. I bit my lower lip to keep from screaming.

"Almost all the way in," Drew panted.

Despite feeling past full, I wanted it all. I reached my free arm around his waist and dug my nails into the soft flesh of skin right above his ass. "Go all the way," I breathed. "I'm not going to last— I'm—" Apparently, Drew couldn't go any longer, either. Before I could finish my thought, he pounded his way all the way in, hitting my sweet spot over and over with quick movements until I cursed through gritted teeth, coming harder than ever from my G-spot. My cock was about to blow, too, and I couldn't hold on any longer. The feel of him inside of me and the grip of my own fingers on my bulging cock sent me over the edge. My vision blurred, and a tidal wave of intense pleasure flooded through me.

As I came down, I stared at him through hooded eyes. I gripped his ass in both hands and pressed, making him go as deep as possible. "Come for me, Drew. I want to feel you come inside of me," I moaned.

"Oh God," Drew gasped. "Ash—*Ash!*" With one last thrust, his body tensed, and his muscles flexed around me until he finally let out a violent shudder and collapsed. Drew's breaths were heavy and labored as he leaned into me. He nuzzled his nose and lips into the crook between my neck and collarbone, riding out the waves, unable to move.

Feeling him pant while snuggled into my chest was the cherry on top of the best night of my life. I ran my fingers through his hair and swept his locks back from his face. He let out a giant, contented sigh right as I reached down and kissed his cheek, right below his eye.

It took us several minutes to come down. Drew was still inside of me, and every time he shifted on top of me, my cock threatened to come back for another round.

Drew kissed along my jawline and met my lips softly, then he slid out of me. I instantly felt the loss of his body tangled with mine as he stumbled from the bed and grabbed a couple of hand towels from his closet. He'd started keeping towels in there not long after we started doing more than kissing.

Once he cleaned himself up, he came over to me and wiped up the beautiful mess from my stomach and in between my legs with a relaxed, lopsided smile plastered on his face. Wordlessly, we shared some water from the bottle on his bedside table.

I got out from under the covers with a ton of effort and swung my legs over the edge of the bed. I bent down to reach for my boxers, but Drew's hand wrapped around my wrist. He pulled me into him.

"We're dirty. Don't you think we should take a shower?" he asked in my ear.

Well. We *did* need to clean up. Not only were we both covered in each other, but we'd spent a lot of time sweating up on the stage.

The clock read that the sun would be rising in a few hours, and despite the overwhelming exhaustion deep in my bones, I wasn't ready to part from Drew yet.

CHAPTER TWENTY-THREE

NOVEMBER 10, 2012

It was hard to keep my head up. Performing at the Madder Hatter had been such an exhilarating experience that I'd been tired since the time we'd gotten into my car to head back to my house. Somehow, Ash's presence and all the promises of what I'd had planned for us gave me enough energy to properly fuck him and then some.

Despite my heavy eyes, I was glad we didn't go to bed.

Glorious hot water rained down from above the showerhead, drenching both of us from where we stood underneath the stream. You'd think after everything we'd done that we'd be done kissing each other.

We weren't.

After we got in, I grabbed my loofah and soaped it up with a nice, earthy smelling body wash my mom always bought. I got down on my knees before Ash and cleaned him thoroughly from head to toe. As I scrubbed his ass, I couldn't help but grin as his beautiful member got semi-hard for me again.

Once I was standing again, I thoroughly washed his hair, then lathered his shoulders and kneaded my fingertips into the tension that had built there. He moaned in a similar way to how he moaned my name when I'd been inside him, and that sound had my skin heating all over again. You'd think my body would have collapsed by now, but Ash had a way of riling me up by simply breathing, and there he was, getting me all hot and bothered all over again.

After I finished with him, he rinsed the loofah, added fresh soap, and took his turn with me.

"You don't have to do that," I said groggily, looking down to where he knelt before me. Ash ran the loofah down the back of my thighs and kissed the soft spot over my right knee. He batted his wet lashes up to me and winked in response.

When he was closer to where I stood and took his time washing my chest, I finally got the guts to ask the burning question that had been on my mind since we left my bedroom. "Was it—okay?" He seemed perfectly fine during and after our sexcapades, but I'd never forgive myself if I'd hurt him.

Ash traced my lips with his wet thumb and looked me in the eye. "Stop worrying. I know that's a hypocritical comment, seeing as I almost puked before we went on the stage tonight." He rolled his hazel eyes and grinned at me sheepishly. "But seriously. Stop. It was..." He chewed on the inside of his cheek. "It was otherworldly, and I can't wait for you to experience what I got to experience."

A blush worked its way into my cheeks as I murmured, "Ditto."

Even when I was deep inside of him, seeing stars and rolling my head back with each thrust, I wondered how it would be if our roles were reversed. I was glad he was more than willing to switch it up in the future.

We stayed under the water, holding each other, tracing one another's skin, and kissing long after we were squeaky clean.

When we were out of the shower, finally dry and about to collapse from our eventful day, night, and morning, I led him back to my room.

"Sleep with me tonight?" I asked once I shut the door. I didn't bother locking it, but Ash reached around me and flipped it.

"Yes," he said. He looked at the lock and worried his bottom lip. "I just don't want to freak your mom out if she comes in here."

We sluggishly moved over to the bed and curled up in the sheets that had grown cold in our absence.

"Something tells me my mom won't be checking in on us tomorrow. At least, not until well into afternoon," I said.

Ash ran his fingers through my damp hair from where he laid on my chest. He loved to play with my hair, and his soft caresses had my eyes fluttering closed. Emotion rushed my chest and clogged my throat. What had I done to deserve someone like him?

"Hey, Ash?" I whispered just in case he'd already fallen asleep.

"Mmm?" His fingers continued.

My heart skipped a beat. "Are you going to freak out if I tell you that I love you?"

To my surprise, he laughed and pulled me in closer. "As long as you didn't tell me in the middle of screwing me, because if you'd done that, I'd hold it over your head for the rest of our lives." His nose ran along my neck in a deep inhale. "I love you, Drew."

My eyes warmed and stung. I wiped away a couple of stray tears, and felt like an idiot for getting so gushy. Then again, I guess it was an appropriate time to feel that way.

"I love you, too, Ash," I whispered.

Within a minute or so, Ash's breathing grew heavy, and his hand fell from my hair. His body twitched a little as he fell farther into dreamland. As I held him, I replayed the last twenty-four hours in my head. I cradled his body as close to mine as I could and tried my best to memorize the duet that was his steady heartbeat and even breaths as I slowly entered the realm of dreams.

CHAPTER TWENTY-FOUR

"I've seen Ash in the news quite a bit lately." Mom's words hang heavy in the air. She takes a breath before continuing. "With the engagement, and all."

I scoff over the phone. I'd much rather FaceTime her, but Mom always insists she doesn't like the way that she looks on camera, which is stupid because even as she grows older each year, she's always been beautiful, inside and out.

For once, I'm grateful she can't see me. Over the past couple of days, I haven't done much aside from entertaining the cruel seductress that is self-destruction. The others have been busy tooling around L.A. while I've holed up in my room in the dark. The bright light from the large windows pissed me off so much on the first day that I called down to the desk and asked if there was any way for me to live in complete darkness for a while. Luckily, there was—and of course, the blinds were controlled through a fucking app. When did buttons and switches go out of style? Why did everything need to be on my phone? Either way, once I downloaded the app and closed the blinds, I hadn't bothered to open them back up.

Over the forty-eight hours of solitude after Theo left, I watched movies and bad reality television, ordered and ate takeout, and drank a concerning amount of alcohol. It wasn't enough to be belligerent, but enough to keep the sharp, intense edges of my pain at bay.

Theo had been an intriguing idea for me after the show the other night, but once we hung out with his band and ended up back at the loft, I wanted nothing to do with him.

Even though I know I have to get over Ash, I'm not ready, and no amount of lying to myself while trying to screw my problems away would help. Theo and I had made out a bit and then fell asleep. In the morning, he proposed that we go out to brunch. Instead of lying to him, I told him I was in love with someone else and I needed time before doing things like that. Thankfully, Theo understood.

"I was wondering if you'd heard the big announcement," I say dully.

Mom replies with a *mmhmm* and a cluck of her tongue. "He texted me not long after he proposed."

Well, at least he'd done that. After all, my mother considers Ash as her second son, and he still spends some holidays with us. A heavy, unwelcome weight twists in my belly as I wonder what the holidays will be like without him.

"And what did you say?" I ask, not able to hide my curiosity.

Mom had us figured out from the very beginning. I wasn't sure if Ash was aware, but she definitely *still* knew about us, even after Lizette entered the picture. I never talk about my romantic or sexual relationships with Dad or my sisters, because I figure, what's the point if we aren't out in the open? But Mom is a different story.

I stare at the hardwood and feel grateful that I didn't tell my other family members about Ash and me after all this time.

A few years back, I sat everyone down during one of the holidays when Ash wasn't in attendance and told them I was gay. My sisters couldn't have cared less. Mom gave me a wink, probably laughing internally after being in on my secret for so long. Dad simply clapped a hand on my shoulder and squeezed. Occasionally, they ask if I've met anyone special. I always tell them no, and when I do, whatever secret humor Mom keeps to herself about me and Ash turns into something icy—despite her love for Ash, she's disappointed in his actions. I know that as a mother, her heart aches for me, and I hate that.

Mom makes a disapproving sound over the phone. "Well, he didn't even *call* me to let me know. I was not happy about that *or* the news."

I chuckle. "That doesn't answer my question, Mom." I can practically feel her responsive eye roll through the phone.

"You will not like it."

I wait, knowing damn well that she'll cave and tell me eventually.

"Aye, dios mio." Mom sighs harshly into the phone. "I said, and I quote, 'You already know Drew is *el alma gemela.*"

My eyes swell at her words–she told Ash that he was my soul twin. My throat closes up like someone is pressing on my larynx. I roughly slide my free hand down my face. The facade I have been living in for the past ten years is crumbling all around me, and there's nothing I can do about it.

After a moment, I say, "Well, knowing you, that's a pretty tame response."

She snorts, then grows quiet. "Are you okay, *mi amorcito?*" Her voice cracks with worry, and I can picture the line in between her eyebrows, etched deep with worry.

I'm not okay; not even close. I want to tell her that I am, but she will know it's bullshit, anyway. So, I force out a "no" in a voice that is deep and throaty and ready to burst.

"May I say one thing before you force a subject change?" She knows me so well. My heart now aches in a different way, because I'm far away from home, and all I want is to sit at the dining room table of my childhood and have Mom sweep the hair from my face and wrap me in a tight hug. As a young man, those hugs used to embarrass me. Now, I realize how idiotic that was.

"Yeah?"

She sniffs a bit and clears her throat. "As someone who loves you both, I do have hope that *he* will come to his senses and break this engagement off." I smile sadly at her avoidance of his name. "He is a good person, and I know you know that. But—" Mom takes a breath. "As *your* mother, I think it's time to walk away from him in... that way." I stay silent. "I will be so happy if he comes to his senses, Drew, but if he doesn't, you do not deserve to be in the dark anymore, *mi hijo querido*. You have too much love in your heart to give. Either way, you know I am here and I support you." Her voice cracks again and I can tell she's crying by the way her voice quivers and grows soft. "I only want you to be happy."

As soon as we hang up, I break. My soul and my heart shatter into millions of jagged pieces as I let out a wail and fall from the bed onto the floor.

I relive it all as I cry and scream into my fists. Our first kiss. Our first show, and all that came after. Writing lyrics and coming up with beats in my parents' basement. When he told me he loved me for the first time. The world tour as a band after our first signed album was released—all of the extravagant places across the globe where we performed and then retreated to one of our rooms to kiss and touch and laugh underneath heavy duvets, content with keeping our eyes on one another instead of exploring each city that passed us by.

Ash is the only person I've ever been in love with. I don't know how to go about life without his love or his friendship. Mom is right, though. I have to close the door on him–I've given him more time and patience than most people would have.

I try my hardest to convince myself to pull away from Ash, but the small voice in the back of my head tells me I don't have the strength to go through with it.

IN THE MORNING, I rip myself off the floor where I had slept and cried throughout the night, and painfully force myself to get my sorry ass up, pack up all my shit, and turn into a human being again. Over the past seventy-two hours, I felt like nothing more than a carcass. Each pang of aching heartbreak and bitter betrayal ate me up like a buzzard ravaging my entrails. Each breath that left my lungs felt like a dull stab. I ran out of tears hours ago, and now my eyes feel dry and agitated. Moving my body to pack up the few belongings I'd used while in the loft was a harrowing task at best, especially with my body sore and stiff from being on the floor.

We are headed to San Diego in less than an hour and have a show tomorrow night. At the rate I'm feeling now, I wonder if I'll even remember how to bang on my drums or if I'll be able to hold a beat.

I'm sure the amount of alcohol I consumed while in L.A. doesn't help my current state. The refrigerator in my loft still has some booze in it, but I'm done with the binge I was on. I have to be. Despite the hole I crawled in, I refuse to stay in it. I owe myself more than that, and I owe my fans and family more than that, too.

There's a light rap on the door as I finish washing my face. Deep purple shadows are cast underneath my eyes, the whites are a milky pink, almost like when I smoke pot, and my appearance is sickly to say the least. That shit will not fly. I'll hit the gym and eat something decent in San Diego if I get the chance. I nod at myself in the mirror as if making my reflection a promise, then drag my ass to the door.

As I grip the door handle with a clammy palm, I know it's him. It's the kind of thing I have come to sense after being with him for so long and spending countless hours by his side. I could always tell if my phone lit up with a text whether it was him or someone else. Sometimes I'd get out of the shower, and I'd know he'd texted me or tried to call on the rare occasions that he did so. Other times, I could feel his presence outside of my brownstone before he walked up the steps. I knew when he was asleep or faking it. I knew if there was something on his mind that he was withholding from me–because I knew Ash Lancing better than the back of my own hand. I wonder if *she* can feel him the way that I do. I highly fucking doubt it.

With a shake of my head, I open the door and stalk over to the bed where my suitcase is laid out, not bothering to look his way. The door shuts behind him softly, and adrenaline runs through me while deep-rooted anger latches onto my rib cage. Blood whooshes in my ears and I grind my teeth together.

After a long, awkward couple of minutes where he watches me throw my charging cable into my backpack and put on deodorant and a fresh t-shirt—because, yeah, I want him to see what he's missing out on—I finally look at him.

In all honesty, he looks shittier than I do. That shouldn't make me happy, but it does. I defensively cross my arms over my chest and sit on the bed.

"What's up?" I ask. I'm horrified at the sound of my raspy voice, so I clear my throat. I refuse to look him in the eye, so I focus on the door behind him.

Ash leans against the wall by the door. I want nothing more than to go to him like I should be able to, wrap my arms around this man, this person whom I've loved for almost a third of my life, but I can't. So, I remain seated.

He shifts a little against the wall. He's wearing a ratty old band shirt—one of our first, before we were signed—torn up jeans and Chucks. I can smell his aftershave from where I sit, so I opt to breathe through my mouth because his smell mixed with his after-shave and deodorant is so perfectly *him* that I might lose whatever ounce of self-control I have left.

Ash lets out a sigh and crosses his arms. "So. I saw that guy from the opening band come out of your room the day after the show."

"Okay?" I ask, defensively. There is no reason for me to feel guilty, and that's what I tell myself.

Anger rolls off of Ash in heavy waves. His hands clench and bleach his knuckles. "Do you, like, have a thing for him?"

Before I can stop myself, I snap my eyes up and purposely meet his venomous gaze. "Are you fucking kidding me right now with this shit?" I spit.

Ash looks away, and the next thing I know, I'm on my feet,

closing the small distance between us. Ash's jaw twitches, and he exhales roughly through his nose. He refuses to look at me now, and that's not acceptable.

In a couple of strides, I make it so I'm right in front of him, and I roughly grab his chin in my hand and force the asshole to look at me. I'll be damned if he doesn't look me in the eye while I speak. His eyes grow wide with fury, but I don't release my grip on him. In fact, I squeeze. His eyes flutter shut and he gasps, then tries to pull away from me.

"No," I breathe. "No, Asher. You don't get to come in here and look at me like that. And you don't get to ask me about who I'm interested in or who I fuck." I don't miss the grimace that decorates his face as he takes in my heated words. "And you *definitely* don't get to talk to me or scold me like I'm your boyfriend or your partner or your god damn husband. We've been over this shit for years. Over and over." I take a desperate breath and release his chin, but stay where I am.

A deep laugh rumbles out of me that has nothing to do with humor and everything to do with days and months and *years* of disappointment. "You could have avoided this." I open my arms wide and gesture to the loft as though it holds the key to all our memories; everything we've been through, and all the ways he screwed it all up. "Remember how I wanted to come out to the label before we signed with them? When we were meeting with lawyers and signing papers and nondisclosure agreements and all that?" Ash recoils, then nods slowly. "Yeah. But what did you do? *Nothing.* Because you needed time, and I understood that, but that was eight years ago!"

Ash doesn't say a word, so I continue, unable to stop. "As our fan base grew, it got harder and harder to come to terms with it all; with coming out. And you know what? You never asked *me* if *I* was scared, too. Do you realize that? I was petrified! But it's always been about you. Then, as time went on and you started dating that fucking model—" I refuse to use her name because the thought of her wrapping her body around his makes me want to throw punches.

"—I realized when you started dating *her* that it was never about your desire to come clean with the world or waiting for the 'right time.' You didn't want to, and you still don't. You've never asked me how tired I am of being your fucking side-dish, when it's *my name* you scream when I get you off, and *my bed* you seek when you need comfort. It's always been *me*. You could have broken it off thousands of times, but you keep me leashed to you like I'm a fucking pet. You live in a fake world, and I swear to God, you're content with it all."

Anger boils my blood, and my breathing picks up its pace as the words spill from my mouth, raw and unfiltered. Remembering the day when Ash started dating Lizette never ceases to raise my hackles. I'd tried so hard back then to leave him alone in his made-up, fantasy world. To allow him to live his lie. I'd held strong for eleven days–up until the point he showed up at my place, said all the right things, and hypnotized me with his touch. You'd think I would have learned my lesson after that–when he didn't break up with her–but I didn't.

Nauseating flashes of what could happen in the future speed through my mind, and fury rises inside of me, to the back of my throat, until I'm spewing venom. "Will you be fine in a few years when you have a baby with your wife and you're still closeted? How about when you cry yourself to sleep at night, wishing I was beside you? Will you be fine when I'm so miserable I have to leave the band? Is that what you want?" I'm trembling now. Tears stream down Ash's cheeks and neck, dampening the collar of his tee.

"No," Ash whispers after several moments pass. "I won't be fine."

"Good," I grunt as I step back from him.

I turn my back in time to hide the tears that fall. Nothing has ever hurt this bad. I've never been so full of anger and grief in my entire life, but that doesn't mean I want him to see it.

"You've made me wait way too long, Ash," I say quietly, my back still turned. "You've filled me with empty promises, keeping me shackled to you in secret, when I could have been out there finding someone who accepts me, someone who would flaunt me around and be proud to have me as their partner." The last part is uttered barely above a whisper.

The door opens, and I force a breath into my aching lungs, but the door doesn't close.

I'm about to turn around to make sure he's still in the room with me, when I hear him say, "You're right, Drew. About it all." His voice cracks, and if I didn't want to bash his skull in, I'd hug him. "The truth is, Drew, I've never been worthy of you."

When I turn around, Ash is gone.

CHAPTER TWENTY-FIVE

JUNE 2013

It had been thirteen months since Asher Lance walked into my life on that chilly night in Washington, D.C., and eleven months since he came to hang out with me at my house and never left. It only took us a little over a month to kiss, and from there, I was completely lost in him.

The only time my thoughts didn't revolve around Ash was when we were playing live shows at local venues—in D.C., Fredericksburg, Alexandria, Boston, Richmond, even Baltimore and Philadelphia— still, during the rush and pandemonium of being on stage, my eyes still drifted to our lead singer, even when I tried to focus. Watching the transformation of Asher Lance to Ash Lancing, the stage name he chose as representation of his breaking away from parents as well as a reminder of his self-confidence and growth, was something I'd forever cherish. The young man who sang to me for the first time in my parents' basement now belted his lungs out on stage almost every weekend, slick with sweat and soul ablaze from jumping around, no matter how big or small the venue was. And, once we exited the stage after our last song, his eyes glittered with something I'd never seen during those first few months after I'd met him.

Ash had come alive.

He had the same sparkle in his eyes whenever we were alone, which hadn't been as often due to our busy schedules, which left us exhausted. I'd been promoted to manager at the gas station, and my hours had changed from during the day to a rotating schedule of early morning until noon, or midnight until the early crack of dawn. Ash continued to work at Dad's office, and in his spare time, Ash practiced the piano and composed more songs.

Our first show of the summer was in Richmond. It would be our second show there, as the city had a lively music scene, and the drive wasn't too far away. Somehow, Sean had worked his magic on the owners of a well-known, underground venue called The Antidote. I'd never heard of it before, and it was hard to find anything about it online. Sean said that the club was secretive on purpose—a lot of well-known artists performed at The Antidote, and only those who know about the club from word of mouth were able to buy tickets.

"How the hell did you score us a spot, then?" Ash balked after Sean came over and told us the news. Brian had to go over to his folks' house, and it felt weird for it to be the three of us instead of our usual four.

Ash and I sat next to one another on the couch while Sean perched in front of us on the coffee table with a half-chugged beer in between his thighs. Ash's face was littered with skepticism, and I feared mine probably looked similar. It seemed way too good to be true.

Sean huffed an impatient breath and took a swig of his Corona. He set the beer down next to him and leaned forward, placing his elbows on his knees. "I need you both to look at me and absorb what I'm about to tell you."

I shot Ash an inquisitive look which he returned. If Sean wasn't there, I'd pull his sweet ass on top of me on the couch and kiss him. It had been a long work week, and I'd barely gotten any one-on-one time with him.

We studied Sean, ready to hear him out, despite our better judgment.

"Yes, a lot of famous artists and bands play there, *but* so do a lot of local bands. The venue is big on representing new talent. So, I was like, fuck it, I'll reach out and see what happens, because the worst thing that can happen is they say no."

I nodded in agreement. Perhaps we'd teased Sean a little too much. Though he was the joker of our group, whenever he put his mind to something, he tended to go all out.

Sean took another swig from his beer and then continued. "Instead of sending an email or calling them up, I decided to drive down and request to meet with the owner."

"Wait," Ash said. "Sorry to interrupt, but how do *you* know about this place?"

Sean flashed his friend a smile and a wink. "I have my ways."

I ignored the urge to roll my eyes, but Ash couldn't help letting out an impatient groan and a snarky shake of the head.

"Anyway—the two people who own the place were hesitant to meet with me, but I insisted that they just watch a couple of our live show videos, and if they didn't like our sound, I'd peace out. They took me into their shared office connected to the club—they're a cute, fashionable couple, did I mention that?" We shook our heads impatiently. "Yeah. They're cool. Well, we all scooched around one of their desktops and I played one of the videos from our Baltimore show last month."

The Baltimore show was easily our greatest performance to date. After having performed more than a handful of times on stage, we had become more comfortable and increasingly confident with each show that passed us by. Our music was crisper, we communicated better, and though we still stumbled with a few things, we'd improved immensely. In Baltimore, we played all of our own songs, with the exception of one cover. The venue was a large one, and the crowd was lively. Ash ended up crowd surfing after one of the last songs, and the memory of him diving fearlessly into a sea of rambunctious bodies would forever live rent-free in my head.

"Which song?" I asked.

Sean smirked. "The best one, obviously." When I stared at him, expectant with a solid answer, he chuckled and said, "It's One A.M. on Sunday Morning."

The song had easily been a favorite of our growing fan base. It was also my favorite for reasons Sean was oblivious to. Ash presented me with the lyrics to the song only a few days after our first live show —after he'd spent the night with me in my room. There were secretive lyrics strewn throughout that only Ash and I knew the truth behind, even though it was obviously a song about love and sex. When Sean asked who Ash had written it about, he shrugged nonchalantly, winked at his friend, and snarkily told him to mind his business.

I wished people knew Ash had written the song for me, but Ash wasn't in the headspace to come to terms with taking our relationship to the next level and coming out. Not yet, anyway. With each day that passed, I hoped he would tell me he was ready, but I knew better than to rush him with something like that.

"Good choice." Ash nodded, bringing me back to the conversation.

Sean grinned. "Well, they thought so, too. Leah and Jeff—they're the owners—were really impressed. So impressed that they've given us a gift even greater than being the second opener at their venue Saturday."

The second? "We aren't going on first?" I asked. At every show to date, we had gone on first in the lineup, which was custom for a newer band just getting started.

"Nope. There's one band before us, then we will play, and then the headliner. Care to know who the headliner is?"

Ash and I leaned in so close to Sean in anticipation that our knees bumped into him.

"Sean," Ash warned. Sean's smile turned absolutely feline.

"Green Day."

Ash and I yelled out, and the three of us stood up so we could hop around and hug. We must have been loud enough to alert Mom because she bounded down the stairs in no time, wine in her glass sloshing around, wearing a bewildered expression.

"*¿Qué diablos está pasando?*" Mom shrieked with a worried hand trembling at her throat.

I ran to Mom in excitement and lifted her off her feet, then I launched her in the air and spun her around, making the wine in her glass splash on my shirt, but I didn't give a damn. When I set her down, all three of us bombarded her in a group hug, which had her yelling profanities in Spanish.

"Mom!" I kissed her right cheek, then her left. "We're playing a show in Richmond and we get to open for *Green Day!*"

Her attitude perked up immediately. She joined us in jumping up and down, forgetting about the glass in her hands. Green Day was one of her favorites of all time, which was a large reason I'd been exposed to their music from a young age. Mom had gone to one of their big concerts in 1994, and she'd wanted to see them again ever since.

"Can I come?" she squealed.

Mom hadn't been able to attend one of our shows yet, even though she'd seen the videos and heard all our songs. Just the other day, she'd commented on how badly she wanted to come see us perform and that she'd force Dad to come, too, even though he wasn't a fan of crowds.

I looked at Sean with Mom's question in my eyes.

"Of course, Mrs. Dawson. The owners were super chill and told us we could bring a few people with us, so long as it didn't exceed ten."

Mom squealed again and hugged me tightly. We had caught Dad's attention, too, because I heard his heavy footsteps on the stairs not long after.

Before I opened my mouth to tell Dad the news, Mom rushed up to him. "Drew and the band are going to open for *Green Day!* Green Day!" She repeated the name like she couldn't believe it. I couldn't believe it myself.

Dad looked at her with adoration in his eyes as he caressed her cheek with his fingertips. He kissed the top of her head, looked at me, and said, "I guess that means we're going to a concert." Dad winked at me. They were so supportive, but I still felt the need to show them what I was capable of, and knowing they'd be at the show had my stomach somersaulting.

Mom and Dad disappeared upstairs and came back moments later with a cold bottle of unopened champagne and plastic flutes.

"To April Renegade!" Dad said as he popped the bottle open.

We lifted our plastic flutes and cheered. Tears welled in Mom's eyes as she patted all of us, even Sean, on the back.

THE CHAMPAGNE from our little impromptu celebration gave me a warm, tingly buzz. I'd never had champagne before, and I liked how the bubbles fizzed on my tongue with each sip I'd taken.

All I wanted as soon as the celebration began was to lean over to Ash and smother him in a kiss. He was so handsome, especially when the alcohol heated his face and left the apples of his fair cheeks a rosy pink. Without him, I don't know if I would've joined a band or formed my own. There was a good chance I may have stayed in college without a plan or any inspiration to find one.

The excitement from the evening had me riled up. Instead of trying to sleep, I swiped through photos on our band's Facebook page. We'd recently hired Emma to do some professional photos for us as well as some live shots from a few shows.

I was fortunate to have an ex-girlfriend who was willing to be in my life. It had taken a few months, but eventually, we started to see movies together again. We occasionally grabbed coffee or lunch and were back to texting each other most days. After my shower, I texted her the news about The Antidote and invited her to the show—not to be our photographer, but to attend for fun. Despite the late hour, she texted me back almost immediately and let me know that she would be there.

I had just finished looking at the photos, mainly to look at the gorgeous snapshots Emma had taken of Ash on stage, when a light knock sounded at my door.

I sat up and said, "Come in."

My heart thundered in anticipation before Ash had opened the door. When we realized there was no use in keeping our hands to ourselves, and that we didn't *want* to keep to ourselves, Ash got into the habit of sneaking away from his room to visit me most nights, but they'd come less and less in the past few months.

We took turns with who was top and who was bottom, who gave the orders and who obeyed. It turned out we both loved to dominate as much as we enjoyed being on the receiving end. Ash fucked me for the first time a few weeks after I took his v-card. After that, all sense of self-control flew out the window.

Ash sat down on the bed next to me. He smelled fresh, and I knew he must have recently gotten out of the shower because of the strong aroma of his deodorant and body wash in the air around us.

"Hey," I said softly. I pulled him into my lap so that we were chest to chest.

"Hi." Ash leaned in and kissed me tenderly.

Though the gesture was mostly innocent and sweet, I was already growing hard underneath him. He felt it, too, because he parted from my lips with a low chuckle.

Ash ran his hands down my bare chest, and I wondered if he could feel how intense my heart thundered in my chest. I tugged playfully at his tank top, and he pulled it up and over his head wordlessly. Both of us wore only our boxers, and that riled me up even more, especially when he got off me, lifted the covers, and slid into bed.

We laid down and I rubbed my nose over his cheek. Sure, I'd missed the amount of sexy time we'd had before our schedules picked up, but I missed having him next to me in my bed more.

"Are you nervous?" I asked after several moments of heavy breathing and greedy kisses. My fingers trailed his side, from the top of his shoulder, down his ribs and hip, where I caressed his flesh with my thumb.

"Yes," Ash said. His voice was breathless and uneven from my touch. "Are you?"

I chuckled and gripped him a little harder, unable to resist the feel of his plump ass against my fingertips when my hands slid lower. "Of course, I am."

He sighed, but it was one of contentment. He played with my hair and moaned while I worshiped his body. It wasn't long before I took his length from his boxers and began stroking him. Ash kissed me deeply, savoring my mouth before biting down on my lip ring and lapping at it to soften the sting. I needed to ravage him, but I wanted Ash to stay in my bed more than that; I didn't want to rush our alone time together.

"Drew?" Ash whispered as we broke apart to take a breather. I stopped working his shaft and gave him my full attention.

"Yeah, babe?" I whispered.

"I've really fucking missed you these last few weeks," he whispered. We hadn't addressed our busy schedules much. At his words, I exhaled a sigh of relief that I hadn't realized I'd been holding onto. I didn't want to come across as needy, so I'd let him come to me for the most part over the past few weeks. Maybe that had been a mistake.

I rubbed his back and pulled him even closer to me. "I've missed you so fucking much."

Though it was late, we stayed up for another hour, kissing and touching like we were starving, and when I woke up in the morning, I grinned when the fog cleared from my eyes, and I noticed him sleeping peacefully on the pillow next to me.

THE ANTIDOTE WAS the coolest venue I'd ever seen.

We arrived a couple of hours early to go over things with the owners, meet the other bands (I was afraid I might piss myself whenever we got to meet Green Day, but I tried not to focus on that) and prepare for the show.

The four of us practiced nonstop on the days leading up to the event. We wanted to make a good impression on the owners, the crowd, and the small group of friends and family that were set to arrive closer to showtime. Brian's parents, Sean's mom, my parents, and Emma and a girlfriend of hers were coming, and that fact made my stomach churn a bit. I was upset because Ash hadn't invited anyone, even though I knew it was because he didn't want to. When I'd brought it up to him the night before, he simply shrugged and told me he was happy my parents would come.

Sean pressed the buzzer by the door on the side of an old building. There wasn't a sign, but I figured that was done on purpose. The way the venue operated reminded me of a speakeasy. I pondered if there was a password you had to know to get into the venue as we waited.

After a few minutes with no response, Sean pressed the buzzer again.

"That's weird," Sean said with knit brows. He pulled out his phone and checked the time. "They said to be here by seven."

The door clicked and unlocked on the other side of us, and when it opened there was a middle-aged man wearing a sheepish look on his face. It didn't take us long to figure out why he hadn't answered the door the first time. His glasses were askew on his face, and it was hard to overlook his disheveled hair, and the slight smear of coral-red lipstick near his Adam's apple.

"Sorry, guys!" Jeff reached out a hand to me, then Ash. "I

promise I'm a professional. I'm Jeff, one of the owners." He laughed a little before shaking Sean and Brian's hands.

Sean wiggled his eyebrows as we walked into the warehouse-like building. We entered what looked like a giant storage room. Chairs were stacked on one side of the room, as were a few tables. Empty boxes that held liquor at one time or another sat by the door.

"Having a little pre-concert fun with your lovely lady?" Sean smirked.

I almost yelled at Sean for joking like that with Jeff, but I quickly understood that Jeff enjoyed that kind of humor and took absolutely no offense to it. Jeff shook his head and laughed once more. Sean raised a closed hand in front of Jeff, and after adjusting his glasses, Jeff met Sean's knuckles in a fist bump.

"We try to keep things exciting around here," Jeff said and motioned for us to follow him. We followed him to one side of the room which had two doors. He pointed to the one on the right. "That's our office. We like to keep it separate from the actual venue, which is downstairs." His eyes looked at the door and he shot us a wolfish grin. "We'll let Leah clean up a bit and meet us downstairs."

Jeff opened the door on the left-hand side, which revealed a wide staircase with steep steps constructed of brick. There wasn't a lot of light, and the air smelled like lemon Pledge had been sprayed all over to try and cover up the underlying aroma of cigarette smoke and booze.

When we reached the bottom of the stairs, Jeff pulled out a remote from his pocket, pressed a few buttons, and the venue came to life before our eyes.

"You're the first to arrive, though I imagine the others won't be long behind you."

The Antidote was larger than I thought it would be. In front of us, all the way across the room from where we stood, was the stage. I think I stopped breathing from the beauty of it all. The backdrop was old, maroon velvet. Matching curtains were pulled back to the sides of the stage. A banner with "The Antidote" written in old-fashioned lettering hung across the top of the backdrop.

Small round tables and chairs with red velvet cushions that matched the curtains were positioned along the walls, leaving plenty of standing room in front of the stage. Unlit candles sat on every table, and antique gas lamps hung on the walls.

A huge bar sat to the side of the stage. Bulbous stage mirror lights illuminated each shelf of liquor behind the bar. Empty (at least I think they were empty) antique liquor bottles lined the top shelves, and modern bottles crowded the shelves closer to the bottom.

The walls of the club were gold and decorated with a swirly, royal blue pattern. The colors went well with the coffee-stained wooden floors beneath our feet.

"Um, holy shit?" Brian asked. His eyes were wide, and his mouth was agape. The place wasn't just classy and gorgeous. It had soul. I could sense it with each step we took.

"Like it?" Jeff asked.

"Of course, they do," a woman's voice came from behind us. "How could they not?"

Leah was a tall woman with dark, bluish-black, shoulder-length hair that framed her angular face. Mischief sparkled in her brown eyes as she sauntered over and greeted us. She was a gorgeous woman, and Brian looked at her like he was in the middle of a dream. Not only was she naturally gorgeous, but she dressed in a powerful, confident, all-black jumpsuit paired with red pumps. If I'd been straight, I'd probably be drooling a bit like Brian and Sean were, too.

"Okay, be honest," I said. "How often do you have to escape drunken attendees during these shows?" I raised a brow.

I was relieved when they both laughed. Jeff kissed Leah on the cheek and winked at me.

Leah served me a coy smile. "Often, if I'm being honest."

The duo showed us around their pride and joy, and afterward, Leah waltzed behind the bar, leaned over on her elbows to prop herself up, and asked for our drink orders—if we wanted them. Leah and Jeff had something special. At the other shows we'd played, the managers and owners were down to business or barely present, but as Leah slid me a rum and Coke and proceeded to take the drink orders of the others while Jeff joked around and got to know us, I noticed they'd made their place of business homey.

After Leah made our drinks, Jeff motioned for us to follow him. The doorbell rang from upstairs, and Leah winked at Jeff before bounding up to the top level to retrieve whoever had arrived. My pulse quickened as I wondered if it was Green Day at the door.

Jeff explained that he had expanded and converted old storage closets behind the stage into quaint dressing rooms a few years back. The four of us were a little cramped in our room, which was basically a couple of vanities and a loveseat. Luckily, there was an area outside of the room with a couch and another loveseat where we could stretch out a bit more.

"I'd give you guys the biggest room, but I'm trying to impress Green Day." Jeff grinned. "It's their second time here, but they haven't been back since we renovated."

Sean smirked. "It's all good, Jeff. Maybe next time we play, we'll be successful enough to have the big room." He winked to let Jeff know he was playing around, and then they clinked their beer glasses together.

"Alright, guys, I wanted to talk with you before the other bands get here." Jeff perched on an arm of the loveseat next to Sean and Brian. Sean and Brian's mutual looks of humor turned into something serious in an instant. "It's not a bad thing, I promise," Jeff went on. "Actually, it's a great thing." He paused. "There will be a couple of A&R scouts in the audience tonight. They should be arriving soon."

Jeff paused and took in our mutual shocked faces with a bright grin. "So, I told them both about you. Sean is very convincing, and I'm glad that Leah and I took the time to hear him out because we really think you have something special." My heart thrummed erratically as his words set in. Representatives from record labels were coming to listen to *us?* I desperately wanted to grab Ash's hand and use it as an anchor. It felt like everything was happening at lightning speed. "They're going to talk to you before the show—probably while the first band is on. Not that they aren't great, too, but I asked them to come specifically for April Renegade tonight."

I didn't know whether it was appropriate to hug Jeff, and I didn't have to ponder the thought for long, because Sean beat me to it, and Brian joined in right after.

When they let go, Ash rolled his eyes and said, "Sorry about them. They're like lovable teddy bears with bad jokes."

Jeff laughed and held up his hands. "I like it. Trust me. And we like *you* all. I can't wait to hear you live."

CHAPTER TWENTY-SIX

E ver since our interview was released, Lizette and I are plastered all over the news and social media. A few sites have started the rumor that Lizzy's pregnant. I guess they don't care about being original with the lies they spew.

I'm grateful for the plane ride to San Diego because I can turn my phone off for a while. I'm at the point in my stress and anxiety where I'm constantly nauseous, and each notification I get makes my churning stomach worse. It would be easy to connect to the WiFi, but I refuse the modern technology. I can't see more news stories on our upcoming wedding or read about the rumors. Especially when I'm sitting so close to Drew.

Guilt tugs me in two different directions. It gnaws on my insides as I think of my last confrontation with Drew. What had I been thinking, going to his room and asking him shit like I deserve the right to know his business? On the other hand, I haven't bothered responding to Lizzy's texts or the missed FaceTime call from last night. Ever since we sat down and did our interview together, I've been MIA.

Neither one of them deserves someone like me.

Drew sits in the row ahead of mine, off to the left, so I can see his side profile from where he lounges next to Brian. On the way to the airport, I asked Sean if I could sit next to him for this flight, and though that was a peculiar request as I was usually inseparable from Drew, he nodded and didn't make it weird. Still, I can tell by the way he glances over at me every so often that he knows something's amiss. I'm grateful when he puts his headphones in and closes his eyes.

For once, I'm not in the mood to listen to music. Instead, I torture myself by looking at Drew as often as I can manage without him feeling my gaze. He's watching some action movie on the screen in front of him and sipping on a Ginger Ale, which is strange because I've never once seen him drink that except for when he had the stomach flu.

I look him over to make sure he's okay.

I look at him because I can't stop.

When we land in San Diego, my mind and body are on autopilot. I can't tell what the others are joking about as we make our way through the airport terminal, and I barely register the setlist or our plan for the night as we ride to the hotel. I cry silently in the shower before we leave for the amphitheater; it's like my body can't even manage the usual groans of sadness that accompany tears anymore. Like I'm shutting down completely.

As we ride to the venue, I look at Drew, unable to help myself. He avoids me and pretends to look at his phone. That, or perhaps he's texting *Theo* from the other night. My jaw clenches with the possibility.

Drew is right, and I know it. I've known it and ignored the fact for years. I don't have a say in what he does, who he's with, whether he leaves the band, or any of his other decisions. I'm not his boyfriend, his partner, his husband. Hell, I might not even be his best friend anymore.

I look down at my feet as my vision fogs up. If Drew isn't in my life anymore, I don't know if I will survive. A large part of becoming who I am was because of Drew and his family. If he left...I shake my head and resist the urge to slap my cheeks to keep the thoughts away. But I don't know what to do. I've never known what to do.

As we pull up to the theater, I dread going onto the stage because I'm a shell of Ash Lancing. I'm a shell, a void, and our fans deserve so much more than that.

Just like Drew.

THE MUSIC IS DEAFENING ONCE we hit the stage, even through my in-ears—but I'm thankful for the heavy bass that booms through the venue like deep thunderclaps. It allows me to get lost in my element and leave all my worries and guilt behind for a couple of hours.

Once the last song ends and we walk behind the stage in preparation for the encore, everything hits me all at once, all over again. I spiral down deep, barely able to make it to my dressing room before hurling in the trash can. I splash some water on my face from my water bottle and sit down with my head in between my knees, forcing deep, even breaths.

More than once, I look at the closed door and pray I hear Drew's voice on the other side of it.

Unsurprisingly, he never comes.

I tense up as I stare at my cell phone that rests on the coffee table in front of where I hang my head. I haven't turned it back on. There's no way in hell I can stand to look at the notifications or the texts and missed calls from Lizzy.

The crowd roars in the distance. I lean my forehead against my knee and take a shaky breath in through my nose and out through my mouth. I force myself into a sense of fake calm by counting backward from one hundred, and as I start to feel less faint, a loud knock on my door signals that it's time to come out for the encore. My bones rattle inside of me as I force myself up and out of the room.

I'm the last one to go onto the stage, as usual, which is beneficial because I have a few seconds longer to get my shit together, but it also makes matters worse because Drew goes out right before I do. He strides past me and takes his place in the lineup, and I inhale the scent of him. A visceral reaction to his presence consumes me, leaving me weaker in the knees than I was to begin with. I pinch the inside of my arm and concentrate on the fact that we're about to run back onto the stage even though all I want is to wrap my arms around my best friend and apologize for all of the shitty things I've put him through.

Normally, Drew would look back at me from his place in line, flash me a wicked, shit-eating grin, and say something cheesy like, "Go get 'em, tiger."

When he doesn't turn around, I feel like I'm being gutted—like someone is slowly ripping me open and discarding my entrails.

Before I have a chance to compose myself, I'm running onto the stage and screaming into the mic with a fake bravado that might have made me a decent actor in another life.

As much as I've dreaded the entire evening, the next song has my rib cage breaking and my undeserving heart pouring from my chest cavity. One of our popular, fast-paced songs ends and transitions seamlessly into my very favorite song. One that we don't typically play. Of course, Mike insisted we perform it tonight.

The lights dim all around and transition into a cool violet as the drum and bass stop playing temporarily and the guitar sends out soft, treacherously solemn notes through the amphitheater.

It's hard to breathe, yet I find the air and make my lungs expand in my breaking chest. *"It's April now, and it's come so soon, come so soon, and I didn't even realize that I'd needed you."* The tears well up, and I turn my back to the audience and wipe my eyes discreetly while making it seem like I'm telling Sean something. *"And the thing about April is it's gone too soon, but then I blinked, and it's turned to June."* I can feel his eyes on me when I turn back to face the audience. His gaze burns my backside like the sun is beating down on me on a cloudless day. *"I'll be home by June, I'll* come home to you, and I didn't know it then, how you'd make my dreams come true."

My love song to Drew. Most people don't mention or ask for it at concerts, but the audience sings along with me, and they don't miss a single word. Cell phone lights fly up into the air as the crowd sways.

The lyrics are simple, but the meaning behind them has never been that. *"My lips touched yours on that day in June, and there in your arms, I wondered if we'd be doomed."* My heart lurches as I remember writing the song at the law firm nine years ago. More tears emerge as I sit in my own misery. Nothing has changed since I wrote the song, except for our fame. *"But you see, I love you, and this day in June, and all the days after that I have with you."*

It's the hardest performance I've ever had to live through. Several times, I feel my voice crack as my emotions well up and rise within me, trying to escape. I push them down as far as I can, and though the word of the last verse comes out a little rusty, it's over, and the audience screams for us at a deafening volume.

The final song in our encore is lighthearted and runs at a fast tempo, which I thought would be relieving, but instead, it leaves me numb. I'm a robot in my own body, going through the motions of living, but completely cold inside.

I wonder if, when I dive off the stage into the hands of our fans, they might not catch me this time, and instead, I'll get what I deserve and land face-first on the concrete below.

IT's a relief to not have to keep myself together in front of thousands of people anymore. Or in front of Drew and the rest of the band. But it hurts. *God,* it hurts.

Drinking after the concert made everything worse. I couldn't get drunk or even tipsy, and the alcohol in my system made my anxiety escalate into pure panic.

I lay in the fetal position on the cold floor of my hotel room's bathroom, close to the toilet in case my body decides to rid itself of toxins. The bathmat underneath my head is soaked from my tears. My moans of anguish echo off the bathroom tiles and haunt me. My body shakes. I feel both hot and cold all at once.

My doctor prescribed me Xanax for emergencies a couple of years ago, but I know I'm too far gone at this point for it to help me, and even if it could, I can't move from the floor. A tingling numbness dances through my fingertips, my toes, my face, and the sensation mocks me and reminds me how shitty it can be to be alive.

Especially without Drew.

Sweat tickles my skin and drenches the back of my shirt. I wail into the crook of my elbow and tremble. For the first time in a long time, I let myself fall apart instead of trying to tape the broken pieces of myself back together.

I hear the door of my hotel room beep and then open, and the sound rattles me. What the fuck? I don't want anyone to see me like this. How the hell did someone get a key–? My heart accelerates its violent pumping, and I wonder if it'll make me pass out. I hope it does.

"Ash?"

My eyes flood at the sound of Drew's voice.

"Dude, if you're here, just let me know, okay? Your fucking *fiancée* is freaking out because she can't get ahold of you, and neither can Mike or anyone else." He pauses, and I hear him rustle around the room until he's right by the bathroom.

"Are you—?" Drew opens the door and immediately looks down at me.

I refuse to look at him. I don't want him here. Not when I'm like this–and we're not *us*.

"Oh God," Drew sighs. Without hesitation, Drew turns on the sink. I know he's wetting a washcloth to put on my face and neck, and I despise the act of service he's providing after all the heartache I've caused him.

To make matters worse, I can't stop sobbing and shaking now that he's here. I want him to leave me alone. I don't ever want him to let me go. When he crouches down and rubs the cool cloth over my forehead, I wail like I'm dying, but I can't control any of it anymore, and Drew, *my Drew,* is here and he's taking care of me despite everything. I scream into my arms and feel hot tears and snot coat my skin.

I'd like to evaporate into nothing.

"Ash...Ash!" Drew shakes me by the shoulders. "You have to *breathe,* Ash."

Breathe.

I'm not sure I can do that.

Instead, I start hyperventilating, because I don't know what to do anymore. About anything. Drew curses under his breath and then stands up, but I don't know where he goes. My lips tremble and treacherous waves of heat roll through me, followed by a cold, sickly sweat that makes my teeth clatter.

There's the faint sound of the shower running in the distance, and then freezing water drenches the back of my head and neck, drenching the majority of my upper body.

I yell out through my ragged breaths. The cold water stings. I shake violently, but my breathing evens out and the tingling in my extremities starts to fade.

"There," Drew huffs. He sits down on the toilet seat in front of where I'm curled up. "You need to get out of your head. Were you just going to let it get worse?" Drew scolds.

I don't respond to him, which makes him grumble under his breath.

"Where are the pills your doctor gave you for this?" he demands.

I turn my head a little to meet his gaze for the first time. "Front pocket. Backpack," I whisper.

Drew's out of the bathroom instantly and comes back in no time with the pill bottle in hand. "Can you sit up?"

That sounds like the last thing I want to do, but I nod. Drew places the pill bottle on the counter and stretches a hand out to me. It's a small gesture, but it makes my throat tight, nonetheless. I grab his warm, rough hand and he pulls me up and into him.

For a second, I think we both purposely forget everything. Drew holds me to his chest and brushes the water droplets off my face with a hand towel.

Slowly, Drew guides me into the bedroom and helps me sit on the bed. He disappears and comes back with the pills and a bottle of water from the outrageously priced mini bar by the kitchenette. He uncaps the water and hands it to me. My hands tremble, but I take it. Drew unscrews the pill bottle, takes out a tiny white pill, and motions for me to open my mouth. I obey and swallow the pill down carefully. The bitter aftertaste of chemicals plagues my mouth, so I manage another small sip.

Drew props a couple of pillows up by the headboard and eases me back on them before covering me with the blanket at the foot of the bed.

"I'll be right back."

I close my eyes and count the seconds until Drew returns. Almost five minutes have passed by the time he returns. He comes over and sits next to me.

"I had to call Mike. He's calling Lizette. I—" He turns his face away from me. "I don't feel comfortable calling her." He sighs and forces a deep breath. "I told Mike to tell her that you lost your phone. So...just go along with that, I guess."

Pain is etched into the fine details of the face I've loved for years. I wonder if anyone else would be able to see it, besides myself and his mother. His mouth, which is seemingly neutral, is tugged down a bit on the right-hand side, and though he doesn't wear the crinkled brow like when he's upset or thinking hard about something, his eyes and brows look frozen. His nostrils flare out, but only ever so often–like he's trying to breathe through the knife I placed in his chest.

Against my better judgment, I reach for his hand. He flinches at first but doesn't pull back. My hand slips inside of his in the most perfect fit, like a key inside of a lock.

"Thank you," I rasp.

Drew scoffs. "You can't do that shit, Ash."

I nod and lick my chapped lips, which taste like saltwater. "I know. I'm sorry. I'm so sorry. For...all of it."

Drew tries to take his hand back, but I tug at it and keep him with me. I don't know what to say or how to say it, but I want to try and figure it out. His head falls toward his collarbones and he studies the carpet. It takes me a moment in the dark to notice the tears that cascade down his face.

Using all my strength, I force myself up into a sitting position and wrap my arms around him. A treacherous sob escapes from his throat. He covers his face with a hand like he's embarrassed to have me see him like this when I'm the one who's caused it all.

I feel him break within my hold and somehow, I'm eighteen again, and the ugly reality that I did this to him replaces all of my guilt with irrefutable anger and hatred for who I've become. Drew's shoulders quiver and the sounds that come from him as he cries will surely haunt my nightmares until my dying day. This—*this*—is so much worse than his anger over the last few days. I never wanted him to feel like this. It was the last thing I'd ever wanted. Yet, somehow, it came to fruition due to my own decisions. I made Drew a promise forever ago that we would come out, and I've broken that promise every single day since.

There's so much to say and figure out, but exhaustion envelops me like a heavy quilt wrapping around my shoulders, and as the Xanax hits me, I have to lay back down.

My thoughts fog and my head becomes heavy. I tug on Drew. Hesitantly, he lays down next to me. We face each other, keeping a foot of distance between us, and I use the last bit of strength I can muster to wipe the tears away from his cheeks.

"Rest," Drew sniffs.

I don't want to rest. I want to go back to Emma's rooftop after the Blink-182 show and do everything differently. I want to move in with Drew and his family, fall in love with him, and never hide it. Not for a second.

Despite my attempts to stay awake, I drift off into a deep sleep that has nothing to do with the Xanax and everything to do with Drew beside me.

A SOFT MELODY stirs me from my slumber. My sore eyes crack open in the dark and strain to adjust to the lack of light. There's something heavy on my chest. I take in the scent of spice. Locks of hair tickle my chin from where he lays on my chest.

Drew.

His hand soothes my arm in continuous, lazy strokes from my shoulder to forearm. I stay still because I don't want him to stop singing, and he hasn't figured out that I'm awake yet.

Drew has a deep singing voice, much different than my own. It's rich and coated in a baritone of secrets. I can't remember the last time *he* sang for *me*. It's been years. He's never thought his voice was any good, but I'd beg to differ.

"I'm glad we met when we were so young, it means I get to hold you longer..." Drew sings barely above a whisper. *"If only I'd had you from the start, maybe then I'd be stronger..."*

My eyes sting while he sings an untitled song we wrote together for our latest album. It didn't make the cut to be on the final version of the album because it was "too slow" and different from our usual sound. I blink back tears as he moves onto the chorus. *"No one knows about us, oh, oh, oh, no one can see, can see how your fire has taken over me..."*

I lay there while he finishes the song. Near the end, I feel something drop on my chest. It leaves a warm sensation in its wake, and I finally become lucid enough and understand that he's crying. The warm tears continue to fall, and his shoulders shake slightly with each breath he takes.

It's past time for me to be the person Drew has needed me to be—and I hate that it took him crying in my arms, exposing his pain instead of running from it, for me to wrap my head around it all.

The consequences of my actions hit me like a semi-truck.

I've wasted *so much time.*

All along, we could have had this. I could have slept with him by my side every night, woken up to him each morning, made love to him whenever, wherever—I should have been there for him entirely. Instead, I've left him in the shadows, only coming around when it's been convenient for me.

Despite the hardships that are surely on the horizon, I know they will be nothing in comparison to what I've put Drew through. Lizette will hurt. Some fans will be outraged. I don't even want to think about the heyday the media will have. It's going to be overwhelming and a lot to handle, but so be it, because I *never* want him to feel like this again. My pulse quickens in my throat as I contemplate whether or not he will be able to forgive me after so many years of empty promises. If he can't forgive me, well—I deserve it. I do. But at least I can give him what he needs to move on.

Drew's tears slowly stop not long after he finishes the last verse of our song. I let him know that I'm awake by wrapping my arms around him tightly and pressing a kiss to the top of his head.

He sluggishly moves off of my chest and props himself up on the pillow next to me. He wipes away the wetness on his face and looks down at the bed to avoid my stare, even in the dark. I move onto my side and gently grasp his chin so that he knows I'm looking at him, that I'm present, that I mean everything I'm about to say.

"Drew, I have never deserved you. At least, not since I first promised you that we'd come out and..." I trail off. I want to run away. Instead, I inch in closer to him. I know that to be there wholeheartedly for the person I love more than anyone and anything, I have to be strong and confess to all of the thoughts running wild in my mind. I need to reveal my deepest layer of soul to him, just as he's always done for me.

"You've loved me unconditionally since we were teenagers, Drew. Your family...is my family." I swallow down the knot that's formed in my throat. "What I'm trying to say is—*you* are my family. Whenever we're apart, I'm miserable. Whenever I'm faking it with Lizette, I lose whatever grasp I have on who I am. You're right about everything. You've always been right. My promises haven't meant anything in the past. Honestly, I think I held onto hope that I would act one day and keep those promises, but I never actively *tried* to change things. All I've done is sit back and force us to do the same thing we've always done, despite your pleas." A hot tear falls from my eye and hits my upper lip on its way down.

Drew, forever patient, stays silent and lets me talk.

I take another breath to ground myself as much as I can. "I'm not going to give you any more excuses, Drew. You know my past, and you know why it's been hard for me to accept this side of myself. You know me better than anyone. I'm scared of coming out and the uproar it's going to cause. But if I have to choose between every one of our fans dropping us or having you in my life, I choose you. Every fucking time. And the fact that I didn't get that until tonight makes me the biggest asshole in the world."

Drew hums a chuckle, which makes my heart leap against my rib cage.

"I'm a total idiot. I don't know how you've put up with me and all the hiding and all my bullshit for so long, baby," I choke. "You're the love of my life. Sometimes I think I knew that from the first time I heard your laugh. Before I even saw your face, knew your name, or knew all the things that make you, *you.*" I press my forehead against his. "I don't expect you to want to be with me after a decade of broken promises, watching me go around with Lizette —*Christ,* I'm such a dick." I heave a sigh and force the rest out because there's no way in hell I'm stopping now. "Either way, I'm done with it."

Drew sits up, and from what little light is in the room, I scarcely make out his eyes growing wider.

"I'm done, Drew. I don't have a plan yet. I need to make one—and soon. I can't put Lizette through any more of this shit, either. Like you, she deserves the truth, and she deserves someone who will love her, and *only* her." Drew places a hand on my chest, which beats so fast I can feel it pounding. "The first thing I want to do is tell Sean." I nod in confirmation to myself. "And then I'll consult with Mike and tell Brian, too. You don't have to be there for any of this. In fact—I don't want you to be unless you want to. You've been through enough."

"Ash—"

"And then I'll tell Lizzy."

Drew sits unmoving, almost blending in with the shadows around us. He's so still; I wonder if he's breathing. "And what about...coming out to the world?" Drew asks in a raspy voice, thick with stale sorrow. "How can I be sure you're going to follow through, Ash? It's been so long... I've heard these words before–I–" Drew trails off, his voice cracking on more sorrow.

I sit up and wrap my arms around him. His shoulders stiffen at my touch. "Drew, I will never, *ever*, put you through this pain again. I know my promises don't mean shit after years of the same worthless excuses, but please. Please, Drew. Please believe me this time? Let me prove to you how serious I am."

His shoulders soften a little as he exhales a sigh.

I release him and give him some breathing room. "This is why I need to talk to Mike about everything. I doubt Mike will care about this aside from the initial shock factor. Either way, I think he can help me come up with a plan. I hope he can–I need his words of wisdom in order to do this right." After a moment, Drew exhales roughly, then he crawls into my lap and hugs me tightly, squeezing the air from my lungs. I don't complain a bit.

"That's why we pay him the big bucks, after all," Drew murmurs. His small joke gives me hope.

I move back a bit so I can cradle Drew's face in my hands. I'm flooded with relief because he's no longer crying, but I know my promise is only the beginning of making everything up to him.

I touch my nose to his. He doesn't scowl at me. He doesn't sob or scream. Instead, he sits on my lap and we hold each other. We sit there for a long time, listening to each other breathe while I run my fingers through his hair.

"You've left one major thing out of your plan," Drew says, breaking our prolonged silence.

"Mmm?"

Drew smiles against me; I can feel the corners of his lips turn up from where his face is planted against my neck. "You owe my mother one hell of a visit."

We share a hearty laugh, and afterward, I lean in slowly to kiss him, allowing him more than enough time to protest if it's not what he wants. I'm shocked when he meets me halfway and brushes his lips against mine without another word.

It's a long time before we stop kissing.

Eventually, we get underneath the covers, despite our dirty clothes. After what seems like hours of silence, Drew's eyes flutter closed. Right as I shut my eyes, he pulls me in closer and whispers, "I always knew you'd come around. I'm not going anywhere. But don't fuck it up this time. I'll leave for good if you don't stick to your word."

Drew yawns and nestles snugly into my chest. It's a long time before I fall asleep despite my grogginess from the panic attack and the Xanax I took. *Don't fuck it up this time. I'll leave for good if you don't stick to your word.* I repeat those two sentences until I turn his warning words into a game plan. Only then do I allow myself to sleep.

CHAPTER TWENTY-SEVEN

JUNE 2013

We barely had any time to talk with the other opening band when the A&R scouts arrived. Green Day was bound to arrive at any moment, but talking with those who represented actual recording labels was more exciting than meeting the famous band that had inspired me so long.

Two scouts came down the stairs after Leah retrieved them from upstairs, and they hugged both Leah and Jeff like they were the best of friends.

The first scout was a very tall, pale man with striking black hair braided down his back. He wore all black, almost as if to match his hair, and he clutched a tablet in one hand. The other scout was a Black woman who was on the shorter side, but she stood tall next to the man with her chin lifted and shoulders squared. Thick box braids sat on top of her head and had been pinned up and secured in a way which made me think of a crown.

Leah casually led the other band to their dressing room so that the scouts could talk to us. Once she was gone, the two approached us with Jeff at their side.

It was the woman who spoke first. "April Renegade in the flesh," she beamed. She held out her hand and we took turns shaking it. I could feel Sean's excitement vibrating off him from where he stood next to me. "I'm Laura Rose. I represent Tidal Wave Records."

My breath caught in my throat. Tidal Wave Records had become quite well-known in the last couple of years. They took an interest in everything to do with rock and all the many sub-genres within it. I wasn't aware of who they'd signed recently, but I'd read an article about them and their CEO in *Rolling Stone* only a couple of months back.

"I am super stoked about the show. I've been watching some of the videos you posted on your channels." Laura grinned and dipped her chin, then took a step back and allowed the other A&R rep to introduce himself.

Though the contrast between his hair and skin was a little off-putting, he smiled a boyish smile as he shook our hands, and I felt nothing but warmth radiate from him. Tattoos peeked out from underneath his t-shirt, and he smelled faintly of smoke.

"I'm very happy to be meeting you all. I have a feeling we might owe Jeff a favor after tonight." He winked at Jeff and my stomach jolted. Did that mean he was already thinking of signing us?

After he shook our hands, he crossed his arms casually, making sure he had a good grip on his tablet as he did so. "I'm Pete, and I'm here on behalf of Peter P.B.G. Records."

Drew's jaw dropped, as did Brian's, and then Sean's, as we all figured out that the "P" in Pete must also stand for Peter Browning Gould Records. He seemed too young, but if it was him, he held a lot of power in the music industry and had signed many, *many* extremely talented artists.

Pete's eyes shone with amusement at our faces. "Yes, I'm Peter, but my father is the one who started the label, not me. I'm Peter Browning Gould Junior. Pete." He shrugged like it wasn't a big deal.

"He's still with the company, but taking less on now that he's nearing his retirement, and I decided it would be cool to keep the business in the family as much as possible." He grinned and looked us over. "We've had our eyes on you since the beginning. Your first show was in D.C., at The Madder Hatter, right?" He asked it like it was a question, but I had a feeling he already knew.

"Uh, yeah. That's right," Drew said.

Pete nodded. "My girlfriend just so happened to be at that show and showed me some of the footage she took."

Well, that was insanely lucky. We all gaped at Pete, then back at Laura. We were all at a loss for words.

The doorbell rang, and it made me jump. Jeff held up a finger and bounded up the stairs. We made small talk with Laura and Pete as best we could while we waited for Jeff to come back. Laughter and shuffling footsteps sounded from the top level of the building, and a moment later, Jeff came back downstairs with a shit-eating grin plastered on his face. Trailing behind him was Green Day.

THE NIGHT BECAME a blur after Green Day arrived. We were introduced to Green Day alongside the opening band and chatted for a bit before they left to get settled in their dressing room. Meanwhile, the first band got situated on the stage. During the surrounding chaos, we sat at the bar with Pete and Laura and answered some of their questions. After a little while, we got over the initial shock of who they worked for, and we transformed from nervous young men to self-confident, passionate musicians.

I sipped on warm lemon water thanks to Leah and watched everything as though it happened in slow-mo: the first band performed their stage tests, Billie Joe Armstrong came out front with the rest of Green Day and helped them set up—I took in the sound crew dancing around the venue in a wild flutter of pre-show excitement, and noticed the way Leah and Jeff treated their staff with the utmost kindness as each bartender, server, and security guard arrived for the night.

We made our way backstage once the first people trickled in. The candles lit up the space in a dreamy way that made me want to sit amongst the audience, but it was getting crowded, and I had vocal warm-ups to do. I wondered if once we were backstage, I'd be able to sneak in a good luck kiss from Drew.

There was something about Drew at The Antidote. I knew he was as nervous as the rest of us with the prospective labels here, but despite that, he glowed. His hair was a bit shorter than he usually wore it; his curls were tamer than I liked, but the way they poked out around his face from beneath his deep green beanie brought out all the perfect, angular features of his face. He'd bulked up a little in the past few months, and his gray V-neck was snug against his tanned summer skin. Every time I looked at him, he was beaming, laughing, tapping his drumsticks on whatever surface was available, or sneaking looks right back at me.

Sean and Brian looked sharper than ever, too. Sean had his red hair tied back and wore a button-down shirt, probably for the first time in years. Brian wore his signature black vest with various, colorful patches sewn into it over a simple white tee and paired the look with black jeans which had several chains hanging from the belt loops.

The opening band went on right as Drew's parents, Emma, Emma's friend, Sean's mom, and Brian's parents arrived.

"Mom and Dad say break a leg," Drew read off the text from his phone with a growing smile. "Mom has discovered emojis." He rolled his eyes, and I bit my tongue to keep from howling with laughter.

"Let me guess—she sent a ton of hearts?" Sean asked with a cocked brow.

Drew groaned and nodded, but glanced at the screen with nothing but admiration in his eyes.

Sean stretched and then hopped up from the couch. "I'm gonna take this opportunity to take a quick smoke break."

Brian followed Sean to an outside area that was reserved for band members and staff. When I'd gone out there earlier for some air, I found the space too claustrophobic for my liking. There was a single, rusted-over table and two chairs pressed up against a slanted chain link fence. No, thanks.

After they left, I peeked over at Drew's phone from where we sat with our arms pressed against each other on the loveseat and grinned at the colorful heart emojis his mom sent. As I looked down, Drew opened a blank text on his phone, typed something, then handed it to me. We were all alone, but it was incredibly sexy that he wanted to type something for my eyes only.

Want to sneak into the dressing room to...practice?

Heat immediately crept into my neck up to my cheeks. Drew was such a flirt. I grabbed his phone from his palm and typed a message back to him.

What are you looking to practice? Percussion? Vocals?

He elbowed me in the rib cage and snatched his phone back. With a few furious taps on his phone's keyboard, he flashed the message to me.

Personally, I'd like to practice sticking my tongue down your throat. *face with tongue emoji*

I didn't write anything back because I realized we'd already wasted valuable time flirting over his phone when we could have been in the privacy of our dressing room. Without another word, we got up from the loveseat and practically ran to the dressing room.

Drew yanked the door closed behind us, then locked it in one swift motion. There was nothing but heat in his eyes as he pushed me roughly against the door, cupped my face in his hands, and bruised me with a torturously hard kiss.

I moaned into his mouth, and that small sound sent him further into his frenzy. He rubbed my aching cock through my jeans and my eyes rolled to the back of my head. His lips brushed against the tender spots along my neck, and his tongue flicked out and grazed me every so often. The songs from the opening band filled the room, and it was exhilarating to feel him growl against me as the bass thumped around us.

Drew came back up to meet my lips and stole quick, ardent kisses before his tongue plunged into my mouth and intertwined with mine. He skillfully undid my pants and slipped an excited hand underneath the waistband of my boxers. Drew gripped my shaft and worked my throbbing dick hard, fast, and to perfection.

Something about being all over each other behind a locked door with a ton of people nearby had me in a fit of ecstasy. His hand didn't stop pumping me, but his face pulled away from mine, and in seconds, we were tangled together on the floor. My knee throbbed from the impact, but that was the last thing on my mind.

"You're so goddamn sexy," Drew moaned into my ear.

He rubbed himself through his jeans from where he straddled me on the rug, bronze cheeks flushed and eyes molten. I had no idea what I'd deserved for *this* kind of treatment, but there was no way in hell I was going to complain about it, either.

"I'd say you're the sexy one," I breathed. "You most definitely started this."

He licked his lips. "How much time do you think we have before they come back?"

Even if Brian and Sean came back before we were done with whatever we were about to do, I doubted they'd think anything of our absence.

"Who cares?" I asked. "We're just rehearsing in here, after all."

Drew smirked, then he lunged for me. The music crescendoed around us as we replaced the need for oxygen with our desperation for one another. For several minutes, I forgot about the record labels and Green Day and everyone's family waiting for us to go on stage except for my own, and I got lost somewhere in between his ravenous kisses and electric touch.

No knock came on the door while we made out, and the opening band had two songs left from the count in my head. Mutually, wordlessly, we said *fuck it.*

I wanted to fuck him more than I wanted to go on stage and sing, but we didn't have the time for that. I'd only gotten the extreme pleasure of fucking and making love to Drew a few times over the past few months, and it was mind-blowing and life-altering each time. I'd have taken him more often, but it was my own fault that I usually bottomed—because in the heat of things in the darkness of his bedroom or in the confines of the basement, I begged him to take me as often as I could.

Drew tugged at my pants and pulled them and my boxers down to my knees, then he leaned back, balanced on the balls of his feet, and pulled down his own pants and boxers after a slight struggle. Skinny jeans were the worst to take off in the heat of the moment.

"I have an idea," Drew said in my ear as prowled forward and hovered above me in a plank. "We haven't done this yet..."

I was about to ask him what on earth he could be talking about when he hoisted himself up, turned around, and positioned himself so that his head was above my cock and his own throbbing member hung centimeters from my lips.

He lingered above me on his forearms, which gave me the most enticing view. My mouth watered, and I took his cockhead into my mouth greedily. His hips immediately jerked with the contact. I massaged his balls and delved deeper while a warm stream of Drew's spit spilled from his lips and traveled down my shaft. I moaned with him in my mouth, and then Drew wasted no time in swallowing me down as deep as he could, all the way to the back of his throat. It was hard to focus on pleasuring him while I fucked his mouth with tiny thrusts of my hips.

209

The end of the song came, and cheers from the audience sounded. Then, they began their last song, and we both picked up our paces. Maybe Drew had been counting, too. I didn't know. Didn't care.

He teased my hole with a wet finger and hit my G-spot with precision. He added a second finger, and I came apart at the seams embarrassingly fast. I loved how he fucked my mouth, sucked me off, and thrust into my ass all at once. Drew lapped me up as I spilled into his mouth, and though it was a struggle, I managed to keep sucking him as he did so. I tugged at his balls just right, then playfully took him out of my mouth and made him ache with the need for release before taking all of him into the back of my throat in one movement.

The crowd was going wild over something on the stage. Drew screamed out my name, and his cries were drowned out by the loud concert. Drew jerked his hips as he climaxed, and then he collapsed.

Unfortunately, there was no time to linger. We forced ourselves up and cleaned up our respective messes, then kissed one last time before going back to the loveseat behind the stage.

Brian and Sean weren't back yet, and that gave our mutual pink cheeks some time to fade.

That was much better than sneaking a simple kiss.

BY THE END of the night, we had meetings scheduled with both record labels.

Drew's mother cried and held onto both of us as soon as she met up with us after the show, and the ease of Drew's shoulders told me that a massive weight had been lifted off him. Even though he had his parents' support, it had to be entirely different to see how they felt after a show. Which was "fucking incredible" according to not only Drew's dad, but the entirety of Green Day.

Green Day thought we were fucking incredible.

The band had a lot to think about, but it could all wait. The four of us rejoiced as soon as we were back in the parking lot after loading up all our equipment. We came together in one giant group hug that was met with laughter and whoops of excitement, and in the middle of our embrace was the promise of the future we'd always longed for.

CHAPTER TWENTY-EIGHT

I wake up and immediately realize I'm with Ash. In his bed. I haven't gotten the luxury of waking up to him holding me in years. We're both in our dank clothing from the night before, and in desperate need of a shower. Still, I can't help but rejoice and allow a hopeful grin to spread across my face as I scooch my body closer to his.

Immediately, I'm welcomed by his morning wood. The sun isn't even up yet, but he's hard as a rock, and I can't control the gasp that breaks from my lips at the contact of his bursting cock and my ass, perfectly lined up. Ash moans softly in his sleep and grinds against me. My eyes flutter as he moans louder and places a hand on my hip.

Fuck. In my morning grogginess, I'm aware that we shouldn't be touching like this. Not before he follows through with his plans—which I pray are still in motion. But I'm in his bed. He didn't make me leave last night, and I think he means everything he told me this time. So, I don't resist grinding against him harder. I lose whatever sense of rationalization I had when I woke up.

It doesn't take long for Ash to become lucid. He stirs with a growl and he grabs my hips harder. He bites the back of my neck roughly, and I exhale through a hiss. He teases the elastic of my boxers and slips a warm hand underneath the thin fabric, and wastes no time in caressing me skillfully. I know he's fully awake now, so I turn and meet his lips with mine. Despite our mutual cases of morning breath, I delve deeper into his mouth with my tongue, opening him up like a flower in bloom, and taking what I can't stand not having.

Ash releases his hold on my dick and works my pants and boxers down my thighs one-handed as I rock into him. He forces me to turn toward him by flipping me onto my other side.

"Ash," I beg.

Ash pants against my throat. "Yes, baby?"

I'm not used to him calling me baby, but it's something I could certainly get used to. He'd only said it occasionally over the years, but now...now the word was different. Like a promise.

"This is wrong," I manage through gritted teeth. It's wrong and I want every second of it. "You're still engaged—and—"

His lips caress mine. "I know. I know."

Neither of us stops.

"You're done breaking promises?" I don't want to ask again, but I have to preserve my heart. Even if Ash tells me more lies or doesn't follow through.

Ash cups my chin and kisses one corner of my lips. "Yes, baby. Yes."

Regretfully, my last coherent thought before I allow Ash to throw me onto my back and plant his lips around my cockhead is that we've done this hundreds of times before, even with Lizette in the picture.

CHAPTER TWENTY-NINE

When the sun comes up and casts the hotel room in golden light, Drew stirs from where he passed out right after I blew him a couple of hours prior. I didn't take anything from him in return because he'd done more than enough giving over the years. I wouldn't think of doing that, even though Drew enjoys giving as much as he loves taking. It was my turn to make him, and only him, feel good for once.

He was right, though. What we'd done was wrong without me breaking it off with Lizette first. Hiding with Drew and keeping him to myself is as natural as breathing, and sometimes, so is the betrayal that comes with it. My shoulders ripple with tension as I look at my soulmate, cuddled up next to me on his pillow, breathing heavily and fully content despite smelling of old sweat and fresh sex.

He was right. I can't—*we* can't be together again until I tell Lizette and the band. I have to do this in as fragile a way as possible. I've made one hell of a mess over the past few years, and ensuring no one gets hurt any further is my top priority. Unfortunately, in order to do that, I have to cause Lizette's heart to break first, and that's going to be a tough pill to swallow.

After a few minutes of breathing exercises, I reach for my phone on the nightstand, which is still turned off from yesterday.

I turn it on. As soon as my home screen unlocks, the weight of my actions hits me like a bull ramming its horns into my gut.

Twenty-three missed calls from Lizette. Four missed calls from Drew. Five from Mike. Even one from Sean. Over one hundred text messages.

I open my messages and to no surprise, find that the majority of them are from Lizette, Drew, and the other band members. One sticks out to me, though. I put my plans to text Lizette on hold for a moment and click on the message string I have going with Drew's mother.

The last thing I texted her was the news of my engagement. It was cowardly to do so in a *text message* of all things, but that was the only way I'd been able to let her know before the press got a hold of the news.

The words from her newest text hit me hard, but they would've sent me to a worse place had I not come to my senses last night. In the light of the new day, I hadn't changed my mind about coming out, and I wouldn't.

Mama Dawson: Please do not continue hurting his heart. It is too big, and it aches for you, mijo.

Drew's mother has never explicitly talked with me about my relationship with her son. She's always been in the know—hell, I think she figured it out not long after the first time we kissed. Nothing gets past her. Admittedly, I've been absent more often than I ever wanted to be over the last few years—pretty much since I started dating Lizette.

The knife in my chest that I stabbed myself with slowly turned, making my chest ache and my stomach flip. It took a good ten minutes to write out a reply. I had so much to say to her, and a text message wasn't how I wanted to do it.

Me: Lo siento, Mama. I know I have a lot to make up for. I am making it up to him starting today. Te quiero.

Forgetting the time difference, I jump a little when my phone vibrates in my hand at her immediate response.

Mama Dawson: I knew you would make things right, mijo. In your own time. También te quiero. *kiss emoji*

And just like that, Drew's mother—my mother in many ways—believes in me again. Just from one text. I don't deserve her trust so fast, but I'm honored to have it.

I exit out of my conversation with Drew's mom and click on Lizzy's unread messages before I make up an excuse not to and avoid it altogether. There's no point in reading what she sent because it'll make everything about the situation worse. Still, I skim through the texts and shake my head as tears cloud my vision. Hurting her as I have—without her even knowing the totality of my actions yet —*God*.

Drew stirs beside me and exhales a peaceful sigh into my neck. I shift my eyes over to his profile and kiss him gently on the forehead before I return to my phone screen.

Lizette is set to meet us in San Francisco for the last show of our West Coast lineup before she heads back to Los Angeles in preparation for Fashion Week, which is only several weeks away. I hope that if I end things in San Francisco, that will give her some time to retreat into herself and heal before she's forced to be her bubbly, bright and shiny, model self.

Damn it all to hell.

It's still early, and in case she was up late, which she probably was on my behalf, I don't want to call her and wake her. That—and I don't want to lose my nerve.

Me: Lizzy, I'm so sorry. SO SORRY. I'm okay. I am so sorry I put you through that and I didn't think to have someone contact you about my phone. I'll see you in SF tonight. I don't want to leave you with something vague, but...we need to talk.

I hate the text message with every fiber of my being. Whenever I get the "we need to talk" texts or phone calls, I immediately grow severely nauseous and apprehensive. But I had to send it. Without the precursor of our impending talk, I may lose the small backbone I've grown in the past twelve hours.

"SEAN, I need you to sit down."

His eyes bug out with concern, but he leads me into his hotel room. We arrived in San Francisco about an hour ago, and I let him get settled with everyone else in our rooms before hunting him down.

Drew decided it was best if I did this on my own, and I agreed. Something about having him with me while I tell my dearest friend of fifteen years doesn't seem right. It's something I need to face alone.

I have no plan to tell Sean, Brian, or Mike about me and Drew yet, because as far as they know, I've been loyal to Lizzy, and I want them to sit with the whole "gay" thing first, but soon enough, I will tell them about us. However, I'll have to spit everything out to Lizette–all the lies, the affair, all of it–because I owe her that much and more.

All in all, I'm in for a very emotionally taxing day. There's no way around it. I roll my shoulders back and down and brace myself. Sean motions for me to sit at the desk in the corner of his room.

We sit down across from one another in the matching yellow

chairs by the desk. I sit back and look him in the eye. Sean worries his bottom lip and stares back at me.

"What's up, man?" Sean runs an anxious hand through his locks..

My whole body vibrates from the top of my head, all the way down to my toes with uncontrollable nervousness. The overwhelming urge to make up an excuse and run from the room hits me hard. Apparently, avoidance is a strong personality trait of mine.

So, naturally, I decide to blurt it out and get it over with. "Sean, I'm—I'm gay."

Sean's face pales, which I didn't think was a possibility given his stark white complexion. He rubs a hand down his face. Before he says anything, he rummages in his pocket and pulls out a vape. He takes a heavy pull and offers the small pen to me.

"What is it?" I mumble, unsure. The last thing I want to do is be high off my ass for the rest of the day.

Sean holds in the smoke, then exhales slowly. "It's a light blend, promise. A hybrid."

Fuck it. It's gonna be a rough day. Might as well.

I take the vape from Sean and take a small pull. After a little while, a faint sense of calm washes over me. I set the vape back on the table and lean back in the chair while I await Sean's response.

"You're...engaged, though. To a woman," Sean finally says.

I nod in confirmation. Sean stares at me like I've told him something in a foreign language.

"It's...complicated." I want to elaborate, but I'm at a loss. From his point of view, I probably seem like I've cracked or the engagement news has given me cold feet. "Sean—I've been lying. I love Lizzy. You know I do. But...not in *that* way."

He blinks at me, shakes his head, and takes another hit from the pen. "Then...why the fuck did you propose?"

"I was going to call it off, and then she found the ring."

"Why did you even *buy* the ring?" Sean snaps.

Sean and Lizette are friends. Not like me and Sean, but he's the band member she is closest with. When I was stressing over all the other possibilities of how Sean would react to my coming out, I neglected to consider how he would feel about my hurting Lizette in the process.

"Sean—it's hard to explain. I didn't even know I was gay until we graduated high school. By the time I figured it out, the band was taking off. And I was scared of what you all would think—not to mention our fans and the label. After that, I just kept making excuses like a coward," I spit the last part out, hatred for myself and my actions blossoming like a thorned rose in my chest.

Sean leans forward in his chair and places a hand on my knee. "Were you scared of us? What we'd think?"

I gulp down the knot in my throat and avert my gaze to look at the carpet.

Sean shakes his head and leans forward even more, then wraps his arms around me in a tight embrace.

"Dude," he sighs into me. "I love ya. Brain and Drew love ya. Even Trish loves ya at this point, I'm sure. Anyway, you know what I mean. We don't care about anything like that."

My parents would have cared. I cringe and think about the obscenities they used to scream at me before I even figured out I was gay. The thoughts won't go away, even as Sean hugs me tighter.

Tears stream down my cheeks. I thought I'd shed them all last night, but I guess not. Something about finally telling Sean who I really am after years of secrecy makes the back of my throat ache with raw emotion, because I've wanted him to know since I found out myself, and I've kept this part of myself from him for far too long.

"Are you afraid of what Mike will say?" Sean asks as he rubs my back.

I nod into him. "And our fans. And the label. It's been so long, and then I go and get engaged and—" I break off as my thoughts race.

Sean pulls back so he can look me in the eye, and then he places both his hands on my shoulders.

"Dude. Listen to me, like, *really* listen to me." It's always odd to listen when Sean gets serious because it happens so rarely, but I nod and hear him out, knowing he means whatever he's about to say. "We all love you. Our fans love *you*. I'm sure there will be some backlash from certain people, but fuck 'em, ya know? If they don't accept you for who you are, then that's on them."

"But what if it totally destroys the band and everything we've worked so hard for?" I choke out.

He shrugs. "What's the point in worrying about it before it happens? If it even happens at all, you know?"

My body trembles as I fight back a sob. My emotions ebb and flow, ranging from heartbreak to resolve to fear to a shocking newfound presence of peace. I'm nowhere close to explaining things to everyone, but starting out with Sean was the best move. I needed my friend to tell me that everything would be okay; to reassure me and accept me.

"You're right," I concede. I wipe my eyes with the sleeve of my shirt and exhale through my nose.

"Who else have you told?"

"You and Drew. That's it. But Drew has known for...awhile."

Sean crosses his arms and leans back in his chair. "Do you want me to come with you when you speak with Mike?"

"That would be amazing," I admit.

"What about Brian?" He pauses and his eyes widen. "Fuck. What about Lizzy?"

I chew on the inside of my cheek until I taste copper. "I was planning on telling Brian next, then Mike. Because I want to figure out a game plan for how to come out, you know, officially. As for Lizzy...I have to tell her. Tonight."

Sean groans a little and rubs both of his hands down his face. "That's rough."

A humorless laugh rattles through me. "Yeah. No shit."

I stay in Sean's room for a few more moments as we talk. He doesn't ask me too many questions, and for that, I'm grateful. We decide before he leaves that it might be better for my emotional state to rip off the Band-Aid and tell them together, so I don't have to keep repeating the same spiel. He shoots me a look that says *we will be talking about this more*, then leaves to fetch Brian and Mike.

In Sean's absence, I shoot off a text to Drew to let him know how things are going because even though he's not present while I spill my guts out to those nearest and dearest to me, I want to keep him in the loop. I want to prove to him that I'm capable of doing all the things he's ever asked of me.

There are still a couple of hours left before we head to the concert hall. I'm not sure how I'll feel before going on stage tonight—especially with the knowledge of the devastation I'm going to bring to Lizette afterward. But if it's one thing I know about my bouts of anxiety, and confronting things head-on when you'd rather jump off a bridge, is that it won't last forever. It can't.

After a few minutes of sitting alone with only my feelings to keep me company, the door unlocks, and the familiar voices of Sean and Brian joking around alongside Mike's flippant response fill the room.

Mike takes one look at me and his brows immediately furrow. Brian's face falls a little, and the smile spread across his face tightens.

"I have a feeling this is a serious meeting?" Mike asks Sean.

Sean shrugs and plops down on the edge of his bed alongside Brian, giving up the other yellow chair to our manager. Sean sends me a pointed look, giving me the go-ahead.

"Did you tell them anything?" I ask in a whisper.

Sean shakes his head.

I wipe my clammy hands on my jeans. I almost wish he would have briefed them in some way, but then this wouldn't be solely my responsibility. Just like with Sean, I manage to suck up my fears and blurt out everything I have to say as quickly as I can.

Their reaction is similar to Sean's. Brian asks several questions until Sean holds up a hand to stop him when I get overwhelmed and begin stuttering. Once things are okay with Brian, Sean leads him out of the room and onto the balcony so that Mike and I can talk in private.

Once the door is closed, Mike sighs and stares at me like he's clawing through my thoughts, trying to figure me out. Throughout the years, Mike has always had my back and been there with advice. I don't doubt that his support will change, but my knee still bounces in anticipation as I wait.

He loosens the tie around his neck and crosses one leg over a knee. "Well," he begins, "you're right about the fact that all of this might be a little crazy at first. Do you have any idea of how you'd like to do this?"

Mike's tone is all concern and understanding, and not that of a scolding parent like I half-expected. Instead, it was a voice resembling a parent or mentor trying to look out for their kid. I always think Mike will be hard on me, but to date, he's never been anything but an openly understanding support system.

I shake my head and look at my hands clenched together in my lap. "I want it to be straightforward. It's going to be confusing enough, you know?"

Mike nods and stares at the wall for a drawn-out moment, deep in thought, before he says, "It's Drew. Right?"

My head snaps up. "What?"

He shrugs nonchalantly, and I notice a small, secretive smile on his lips as he turns his head away to look outside and onto the balcony.

"I've been your manager pretty much from the beginning. I've always had my suspicions. Especially before Lizzy came into the picture," Mike says.

"H-how?"

He cocks a brow and looks back at me. "Well, you both have sneaky glances you give to one another when you think no one's looking. Not to mention you *always* disappear backstage before the encore." His eyes meet my own, and my cheeks and ears burn. "Drew also gave you the cold shoulder around the time you proposed."

Mike motions with his eyes to the balcony. "Those two are typically too stoned or busy pranking one another to see what's going on around them. But I've noticed."

"Wow." I stare dumbfounded at Mike, at a loss for words. Drew and I always thought we'd been so slick about our relationship in the past.

We sit in silence until I hear Mike let out a long exhale. He re-situates himself in his chair and leans forward. "I think I have a decent game plan. Want to hear it?"

No. I don't. I'm petrified of what's to come. So I say, "Sure."

"Like you said, the first thing you have to do is break things off with Lizette." He shakes his head glumly. Ever since I brought Lizzy around, the band and crew have always made her feel at home; she's been like an unofficial member. Breaking her heart will hurt my friends, too.

Mike pushes aside his feelings about it all and continues. "I figure we'll let the media freak out about it for a week or so, because lord knows it'll be several days before they move on from the gossip." We roll our eyes in unison. "Once that settles a bit, I think that would be the time for us to reach out to the label." I grind my teeth together and crack my knuckles. "Now, what're we going to do if the label doesn't agree with what you see happening after that?"

"You mean...coming out?"

Mike raises his brows and hums his confirmation.

I sigh. "I think if we don't get a positive answer, we should all regroup as a band and make that decision together."

He leans forward and squeezes my shoulder. "I think that's a good way to play this." A pause. "And what about Drew? Is he–on board with all of this?"

"We talked last night."

"So...I assume you will be telling the others about *that* very important part of the story at some point?" Mike asks.

"Yes. But again—that's on his terms and is dependent on all the other obstacles coming our way." I look up at him and smile, though I feel the gesture doesn't meet my eyes.

The others come in from the balcony. Mike and I stand up to leave. My legs feel weighed down and my head fogs with exhaustion.

"I do want you to know one thing, Ash," Mike murmurs in my ear as we make our way from the room. "I'm proud of you."

CHAPTER THIRTY

S ince last night, I feel like I've been stumbling through a dream.
A wonderful dream. The one downside is the toll it's already
taking on Ash.

We arrived at the concert hall a couple of hours ago, and now we
sit side-by-side in Ash's dressing room. It didn't take us long to do
our sound check and we left the rest up to our team, which was good
because near the end of our preparations, I could tell Ash was
becoming increasingly overwhelmed with the show about to begin
and the impending break up thereafter.

There hadn't been a chance for him to tell me what all had
happened with the others before we left the hotel, so after we made
our way backstage, I sat him down in the oversized bean-bag chair
provided, grabbed him some water, and listened as he told me everything at his own pace.

It was obvious he was mentally exhausted. Dark shadows are cast
underneath his eyes and his complexion is paler than normal. He's so
unlike himself, but I can't do anything to help him with it except
being his shoulder to cry on. He has to go through the rest by
himself.

Still, as he speaks, I feel my pride for him grow. He accomplished a huge step—telling Mike and the guys. Honestly, I'd lost hope that that day would ever come. But telling the guys was easier than it would be to tell Lizette, and I knew what was weighing him down.

Lizette was more than likely landing in San Francisco now. Luckily, we don't have a meet and greet tonight. If we did, I would be tempted to cancel it, even though canceling them is only something we do under extreme circumstances. I think the only time we canceled before was at the beginning of COVID-19 when we found out Brian and Ash had been exposed to the virus.

I move Ash so that his head can rest comfortably on my shoulder once I join him on the massive bean bag, which is undeniably comfortable. Even though Ash's pain has been a long time coming, it doesn't make his agony any easier to bear. After tonight, I hope he can relax a little, but knowing him, I doubt he'll be able to. Instead, he'll obsess over the media and Lizzy's well-being. I can't blame him for that.

We have some time before the show begins, so I stroke his scalp while he sips on his water and cuddles up next to me. After a couple of minutes, his breaths turn heavy, and I know he's fallen asleep. I grin against him as I press a light kiss to the top of his head. It feels wrong to smile given everything we've gone through, but I bask in the fact that Ash is finally taking all the proper steps so that we can come out of hiding and make a life together instead of being miserable apart.

"WHAT CAN I DO?" I ask.

Ash woke up a little while ago, and we've only got several minutes before we have to run out on stage. Despite his little catnap, he looks ill. His skin is peaked, and his hands tremble. It reminds me of the days when we first started performing and his stage fright was almost inconsolable.

I hold his head in my hands and kiss his temple.

"Tell me something good?" Ash whispers.

His hazel eyes bore into me. I pull him close and wrap my arms around him tightly, hoping that the physical contact will ease his nerves.

"After tonight, we're going to fly to D.C. and stay there for a little while. After a week there, that's when the press will really die down from the break up, and we'll fly back to New York and be hermits before the last show of the tour. We can stay in, and order whatever takeout we want. Maybe we'll lounge around naked." He chuckles faintly. "And when it gets late, we can have a few drinks, listen to records, and kiss a little. Or, kiss a lot."

"That sounds perfect."

I chuckle. "How about you don't find a new apartment?" I regret the words as soon as they leave my lips. The last thing he needs to freak out about right now is moving in with me. He's still engaged, for fuck's sake.

"And I can move in with you?" he asks. He pulls away from my stronghold to look at me.

I shrug. "I'm sorry. I got a little carried away."

"Is that what you want?" Ash cradles my head in his hands and kisses me tenderly before I can respond. After he pulls away, I manage a sheepish nod. My cheeks heat with a violent flush.

Ash gives me his first genuine smile in hours. "Yes. That sounds good. Amazing, actually."

The worry that was coiled around my ribs disappeared with his answer. That is, until his smile fades away and his brows scrunch up in concern.

He grazes a thumb over my cheekbone. "You know, I haven't asked *you* how you want to come out."

His words confuse me until I realize he's talking about my coming out to the public. But unlike Ash, that's never been a big concern of mine. I was only ever apprehensive about telling my father, but I told him years ago. My younger self always thought my parents were more critical of me than they actually are, and now I know that they support me no matter what. As long as I have them and Ash, I don't need the world's opinion of me.

"Mom knows about us, obviously. My sisters and father won't care. I think Amy will be jealous if nothing else. And when the world finds out that we're an item, I'll be relieved. I'll finally be able to show you off as mine." I chuckle. Ash rolls his eyes and looks away to hide the blush that creeps into his cheeks. "I'm not worried about it. Our fans have never seen me in a relationship, and I'm sure there's speculation about my sexuality because I've been asked about it during interviews more times than I can count." I sigh and shake my head. That question has always felt superficial to me. Who cares? Why do I have to explain myself and who I want to fuck? "You know I don't look at what the media says about me if I can help it. When you come out, I'll come out when *we're* ready to go public. Okay?"

Ash nods, and his smile returns. "Okay." He brushes a loose curl back from my forehead and tucks it behind my ear. "You're amazing."

I kiss him on the cheek. "Are you going to be okay on stage?"

He rakes his teeth over his plump bottom lip. "I think so. You know how I am. When I get on stage, most everything else falls away."

I do know because it's the very same for me.

With Mike's familiar knock on the door, I kiss him deeply before we break apart.

CHAPTER THIRTY-ONE

Every time thoughts of what awaits me once the show ends creep into my mind, I sing the lyrics louder and imagine what Drew's apartment will look like with both of our stuff in it. We always refer to it as an apartment, but it's really a gorgeous brownstone in Brooklyn, nestled on a rare side street that manages to remain quiet despite the city surrounding it.

As I sing, I imagine the life we will have, and when the song escalates, and I scream into the mic, I realize that moving in with Drew will be the best thing to happen in a long time. I know I can get through tonight so we can have our future together.

The show shoots by in a blur. Despite my aching spirit and the fatigue that's nestled down deep into my bone marrow, I use all the energy I can muster into the performance. I scream at the top of my lungs, playfully drum alongside Drew, play the air guitar with Brian, and mosh with Sean.

At the end of it all, I fling myself off the stage, into the crowd's arms and float above their supportive hands until I'm back on the ground.

No funny business happens before the encore. I'm too antsy

with the show about to end, and after having Drew in my bed last night, I owe Lizzy whatever respect I can salvage before I end our relationship.

Back at the hotel, I pace the span of my hotel room. Back and forth. Back and forth. Lizette rented a car after she flew to San Francisco, and she will drive directly to Los Angeles after. It's a lengthy drive, but she's not a fan of flying, and being on the road is more soothing to her than hiding from fans at the airport. I pray she's not too distracted after this evening to make the drive.

I type out a quick text to Drew and send it off. I'm not sure if I'll be up to see him after I'm finished talking with Lizette. Sometimes, it's better to be alone after things like this. If Lizzy wants to stay up all night talking things out, I won't say no, either. Despite how run-down I am, I will answer every question she has.

The mini bar has called to me since I came back to the hotel an hour ago, but it's not an appropriate time for alcoholic beverages. At least, not until after all is said and done.

A light rap sounds at the door, and I practically jump out of my skin. As I make my way to the door, I stop myself and look at myself in the mirror attached to the dresser. I point to my reflection and stare myself down.

You can do this. You have to. You've got this. It'll be okay. You're okay.

I take a few deep breaths and walk to the door.

IT WAS as awful as I could have imagined.

Actually, it's worse, because instead of getting so upset that Lizette screamed or threw things at me, she sat at the edge of the hotel bed, as far on the corner as possible without falling off the mattress, and stared at the walls behind me with vacant eyes. Silent tears fell down her cheeks which resulted in dark streaks of makeup from her eyelids all the way down to her neck.

Still, I told her everything. From the beginning to the end. I only left out the explicit details of the affair to protect her well-being.

The worst part was when I forced myself to tell her I'd been with Drew all along. She took my being gay in stride, but after I admitted to my affair, she wailed and curled over into herself. She covered her face with her delicate palms and shook her head, unable to grasp the reality of my words.

Then, the questions came.

Why did you even ask me out? Why did you flirt with me when we first met if you were with someone else? Why the hell would you propose? The *whys* didn't stop coming for a long time, and each question had been laced with absolute, unrelenting heartbreak.

She wasn't angry when she left, but I knew she would be eventually. She had to be. I expected it. Maybe not tonight, but soon.

When I asked her how she wanted to handle things—the media, the fans, all the interviews and photo-ops we had planned—she shook her head and nibbled on her trembling bottom lip. Eventually, we agreed that Mike and her agent would take care of all the interviews and appearances we had scheduled.

The only favor I asked was for us to break the news to the world in a neutral way, one where neither of us was to blame so that I could come out after the media calmed down about the broken-off engagement. I felt like even more of an asshole in asking her, considering all I'd put her through tonight and in the past, but she agreed without having to think about it.

The cherry on top of the shit sundae was when we had to draft our personal statements to share with the world. She typed on her phone as best she could through shaky sobs and uneven breaths. Whenever I tried to console her, it made matters worse. I tried to focus on my statement and give her space, but it took us over an hour to finish writing, and deafening silence had made the hour go by at a terribly long pace.

Lizzy gave me back the ring. I didn't know what to do—so I told her to keep it. After that, she practically threw it at me before running from the room.

Now, I sit on the edge of my bed, long after she hauled ass out of the hotel room. I stare down at the ring in between my fingertips, lost in the sight of the sparkling gem. My phone buzzes in my pocket occasionally, but I don't have the energy to take it out and look at it.

Instead, I pour all my hopes for Lizette into the ring. Because I do love Lizette in many ways, and I want what's best for her. She needs a person who will fall head over heels for her; someone who won't stop falling. She deserves someone who's as deeply in love with her as I am with Drew. I clutch onto the ring and pray that someday she gets everything she wants, everything she deserves, and more.

After a while, my bones begin to ache from sitting for so long. I force myself up and to the bathroom. Once there, I take my phone out and strip down while the shower turns scalding hot. I take a look at my notifications.

There are a few texts from Drew checking in on me, and another from Mike with my boarding pass for our flight to D.C. tomorrow. During past tours, I'd always enjoyed our shows in California. Now, I was eager to get back to the East Coast and be close to home.

Before I hop into the shower, I reply to Drew and let him know things are as okay as they can be, and that I'll see him tomorrow. Tonight, I need to be alone. I don't feel like being in his presence. Finding comfort in his arms doesn't feel right after shattering Lizette's heart.

CHAPTER THIRTY-TWO

As much as I'd like to go and be there for Ash after his hellish night, I respect his request for space. Still, sleeping next to him last night and waking up to him this morning had been like something from a fairytale, and I miss his presence as soon as I get into bed.

I'm proud of Ash. When he made more promises last night, I didn't believe him at first. Why would I? But after he illustrated his need to talk with Mike and the others, then his plans of breaking things off with Lizette, I knew something inside of him had changed. The fact that he broke things off with Lizzy shows me that I can learn to trust him again.

I reach over to turn off the lamp on the bedside table when I hear a knock at the door. The clock on my phone says it's past one in the morning. I hop out of bed and move to open the door. Maybe Ash changed his mind, after all.

When I open the door, Lizette stares back at me, and I stop breathing. I flinch as she shoves me aside and storms into the room.

She paces in between the bed and balcony. A steady flow of tears falls from her eyes. Smudges of damp, black makeup crowd her temples from where she's rubbed her tears away, and her eyes are glossy and pink. I've never seen her look anything except perfect, and I feel bad for her–I do. It's not her fault this happened. Anyone in her position would be confused and torn apart. Ash is mostly to blame, but it's not like I stopped messing around with him when he was with her, either. My heart strains in my chest.

The fact that she's here and pacing around my room tells me that Ash was completely honest and told her about us. I'm glad he did because I wasn't sure he'd follow through with that part of the story.

I try to say something, *anything*, but each time, I choke on air, and the words refuse to come out.

"I can't fucking believe this," Lizette mutters to herself after a few minutes.

"Lizette–" I walk toward her, but she holds up a hand and signals for me not to come any closer.

"Ash said–he said that *you*–that it's been going on this whole time?"

It's like she's registering his words as she speaks. I watch in horror as her eyes transform from sadness to fury.

"I cut things off as soon as you started dating." It's a shitty excuse, but it's true.

She laughs and shakes her head before she stomps over to where I stand and shoves me. Lizette is strong from her workout regimen, and the contact of her hands on my chest makes me stumble backward.

"Seriously?" I bark.

"Yes, Drew, *seriously.*" She gets in my face. "How could you? For *two years* you fuck my boyfriend? For *two years* you act like you're just best buddies in front of me?"

I don't point out that we've been pretending in front of everyone for much longer than that because I have a feeling she might punch me–or worse–if I do so.

"Lizette, I'm sorry for that. Truly. Like I said, I tried to stay away. I did. But it takes two–" She looks away from me like I've slapped her. "I'm not going to defend Ash, but I'm also not going to take a beating for this. I'm sorry, Lizette. I begged him to break things off with you from the beginning because I knew things would end up this way."

"End up how? With you getting your way?"

I stare at her, totally dumbfounded. Does she not understand that he's gay? That he wasn't in love with her?

"You're upset and taking it out on me. That's all this is." I motion in between us.

She scoffs and wipes at fresh tears with a wrist. "Ash could have loved me if it wasn't for *you*. You don't know him like I do, Drew."

Well, now I'm pissed. The sour bite of rage hits the back of my throat, and without thinking, I lash out. "Is that so, Lizette? You know him better than me?" I shake my head and get in her face this time, my anger untamable. "Were you the one to save him from his shitty parents ten years ago?" She clenches her jaw and takes a step back. "Do you even *know* about his abusive, good for nothing parents?" I'm seething as I spit the words out.

There's no going back now. Jealousy from the last two years rises up and blends with my anger, and creates a venomous concoction of words on my tongue. "I was his first, Lizette. His first *everything*. Did he tell you that?" She doesn't answer. She looks down at the floor. I know I should stop, but I can't. "I was the first person he sang for. The first person to believe in him. I was his first blow job, his first French kiss, his first fuck. The first time he ever made love to someone, it was *my name* on his lips. Not yours. The first time he said 'I love you' was to *me*. Not you. Do you want me to keep going?"

My hands are curled into tight fists by my side. Lizette sobs and shuffles around me toward the door.

Fuck. I went too far. I didn't want it to come to this, but Lizette has to get it through her head that Ash isn't hers. He's *mine*. He's finally mine.

"I *am* sorry, Lizette. He shouldn't have gotten involved with you. That wasn't my decision. I never wanted to see you hurt, but you can't place the blame on me. I know you want to, but you can't." She pauses in front of the door. "It's a shitty situation, and that's an understatement. But the sooner you understand that Ash is in love with me, the better." I huff out a breath. "Be mad, Lizzy. Get drunk, throw shit, light the fucking world on fire. You deserve to–but the sooner you understand that this is real, the sooner you can move on and find someone who worships the ground you fucking walk on. Okay?"

Lizette turns her face toward mine. Her lips tremble, and her shoulders quake with the sob she's keeping back from me. She spares me a single glance, and then she's gone.

WE BOARDED our flight to D.C. a few minutes ago, right as the news about Ash and Lizzy went live. With all the commotion, Mike pulled a lot of strings last night and found a way to fly us back to the East Coast on a private jet for Ash's sake. If there was any day to avoid the paparazzi and our fans, it's today.

Unfortunately, the first thing I had to tell Ash this morning was about the confrontation I had with Lizette. I texted her when I woke up to check in and apologize, even though I'm sure I am the last person she wants to hear from. She hasn't texted back, and I don't expect her to. Ash wanted to reach out, too, but at that point, I told him that maybe he should back off so that she can process everything. That's what I would want if our roles were reversed.

I'm no longer mad at Lizette, because what happened to her was horrible, and she was a victim in all of it. All she did was fall in love with the wrong person. I still feel awful about what I said to her last night, but at the time, I didn't know what else to say or do. As she lashed out, the feelings that I'd shoved down for years came to the surface and I lost control.

Trish had been left in the dark accidentally—along with our

bodyguards and sound crew. Spilling the beans to Sean and then Mike and Brian had taken enough of a toll on Ash, and we all forgot to keep the others in the loop amidst the pandemonium of our last Cali show and Lizette's visit.

After we all get buckled into our respective seats, Trish's eyes dart from her phone screen over to where Ash and I sit across from her.

"What the fuck?" Trish asks under her breath.

Ash blows out a nervous sigh and leans over to put his head in his hands. I pat his back sympathetically and wordlessly motion for Brian, who's sitting next to Trish, to update her on everything because he's closest to her, and there's no way I'm leaving Ash's side.

Sean makes a hilarious facial expression of regret as Brian leads Trish as far away from where we're seated as possible. It isn't long before we hear Trish exclaim, "What?!" into the space surrounding us. Mike, who sits next to our two bodyguards nearby, rubs his temples with meaty fingers. If our guards, Jim and Evan, know anything, they don't make a big deal out of it. Jim's already asleep, and Evan reads something on his tablet, unconcerned.

Though I want to respect Ash's space, I can't help but ask him what it is they wrote in their breakup posts. Less than a minute after the posts went live, my mom texted me several of the dancing girl emojis and then the gif of Jennifer Aniston and Lisa Kudrow from *Friends* bouncing up and down excitedly. I rolled my eyes at her texts, but on the inside, I was all sunshine and rainbows about it.

"I don't care if you look at it," Ash groans.

Despite my best efforts, I cave and look at Lizette's post on Twitter and Ash's post on Instagram before we lift off. Both announcements are cordial but come across as cold from the lack of emotion on both ends. It's like someone instructed them on exactly what to say, how to write it out, and to keep it professional. It makes sense given their situation, but I know it will leave a lot of fans speculating.

There's no getting around the fact that the internet is blowing up with the news. I don't bother looking into what's being said about them after I read their respective posts. Instead, I put my phone on airplane mode.

It's killing me not to touch Ash more intimately, but for now, I keep a hand on his sweaty back and hope it grounds him. I want to pull him onto my lap, but eyes are watching, and no one knows about us yet. Except for Mike, I guess. When Ash told me that Mike had his suspicions all along, I wasn't remotely surprised. If anyone was to figure us out, it'd be him. Like my mother, not much goes on without Mike knowing about it.

Trish and Brian take their seats before the jet starts moving. Trish leans down over Ash and gives him an awkward half-hug. I can't help but notice a hint of disappointment in her eyes. Is it because he's gay? Probably. I've seen the way she ogles him when we're rehearsing and hanging around together in between shows. I can't really blame her. Ash is undeniably attractive and talented as hell. And he's all mine. *Finally*.

It's a nice, long flight to Washington. At some point, I'm the only one awake. The lights are off in the cabin, and I sneak a light kiss to Ash's temple from where he snoozes next to me, thankful that he's able to escape the confines of his consciousness for a bit.

When we land on the East Coast, it's dark, and I'm grateful for it. I think the emotional rollercoaster we've been riding on is starting to take a toll on me, too. All I want is a chance to lay in bed with Ash on my chest, in a private space away from everyone online and their unsolicited opinions.

The great thing about playing in D.C. is that we get to stay in Mike's Tudor-style house in the city. When we aren't on tour, Mike is home in Alabama with his wife. He rents out real estate all over the country as a side gig, mostly for fun. He was raised by a realtor and an architect, and his passion for houses is nice when we've all been on the road a little too long, and we need the sense of a home away from home.

From the airport, we (the main band members, along with Mike, Evan, and Jim) get into a couple of SUVs that escort us through the city of crazy drivers to the house, which is in a side neighborhood somewhere off of H Street. For the next two days, we will leave the outside world at the door as much as possible while we rest and recharge.

As soon as the SUVs pull up on the side of the house, the outside light by the front door comes to life. Mike, who sits next to me, shoots out of the car and bounds up to the door like his life depends on it, and as soon as we get out behind him, I understand why.

Miranda, Mike's wife, opens the door. Mike hauls her off her feet and engulfs her in a giant bear hug. We lean against the cars, snickering to ourselves as we let them have their moment. Even though they saw each other a few weeks ago, being on the road more often than not can take its toll on the strongest relationships.

From the road, I can hear them laughing in between kisses.

"Alright!" Miranda calls after a long, passionate kiss. "Come on, you heathens! Dinner and fresh cookies await!"

God, I've missed Miranda.

We rush up to the house—well, most of us do. Trish hangs back with her thumbs hooked around the belt loops of her jeans. I realize that she's never been here or met Miranda before. Wanting to give Brian a chance to help her out, I meet his gaze and nod behind me to Trish as nonchalantly as possible. It takes him a moment to get the hint, but by the time we're halfway to the door, he's explained who Miranda is and what to expect. By the time we make our way inside, Trish is beaming at Brian and has her arm looped through his.

Miranda beams at each one of us as we walk through the threshold. She kisses Sean's cheek and holds onto Brian as tight as she can. When she releases Brian, she takes Trish's hands in her own and beams at her. Trish devours the attention and whatever tension she had when we arrived disappears. Miranda makes Jim spin in a circle so she can get a full view of him, as he's gained a lot of muscle since the last time we were here. She exclaims how gorgeous Evan's girlfriend is—because we're all friends on our secretive social media accounts, of course. And when she reaches Ash, she runs her fingers through his hair in the most maternal way, then hangs on to him. She whispers something in his ear before diverting her attention to me.

Miranda is a little younger than Mike, with bright blue eyes, a pale complexion that makes her light dusting of freckles stick out, and long, natural, red hair that reaches the top of her butt. She's only ten years older than us, but she acts like we're all her kids.

The rest of the crew walks through the foyer and into the kitchen, where the savory smell of homemade chicken Alfredo and garlic bread wafts through the open doorway.

I wrap my arms around Miranda and force myself to bend down a little bit to accommodate our height difference.

"Andrew!" Miranda squeals into my ear, her voice laced with a thick Alabama accent. My name is pronounced more like *Ayin-drew* when she says it. I grin as her hair brushes against my face. "Is our Ash gonna be okay, darlin'? I sure hope so. I didn't want to pry, but I was awful worried when I saw the news this mornin'."

I squeeze Miranda in a tight hug until she protests and swats playfully at my arm.

"He's not okay right now," I say. "But he will be."

We walk into the dining room where Miranda has the long table set up with everything we'll need for our home-cooked meal. I could cry at the cloth napkins she folded, the baskets of warm bread bundled up in towels to keep warm, and the vase of fresh flowers in the center.

After we're all seated, Mike comes in wearing oven mitts, holding a giant dish of Alfredo.

"Dinnertime!" Mike cheers.

FORTUNATELY, neither one of us has to sneak into the other's room. Though the house is large, it isn't large enough for eight people to have their own rooms, so Ash and I bunk together.

Ash and I always stay in this room when we're in town, but it's been years since we've been here. Next time, I hope we don't have to hide the fact that we will be sleeping in the same bed.

We take a shower in the adjoined bathroom, and though we no longer have the guilt of screwing around on Lizette hanging over our heads, we simply bathe, hold onto each other, and stand in the hot stream of water until Ash's tension-filled shoulders fall a few inches from his ears.

In bed, the plush mattress and lush comforter threaten to take me out before my head hits the pillow, but I force my eyes open and pull Ash into my side.

Despite the largeness of the house, we can hear Brian laughing down the hall, a snore coming from one of the other rooms, and the faint sound of a headboard metronomically hitting a wall somewhere above us.

"I'm glad to hear Mike and Miranda are enjoying themselves," I say with a grin.

One corner of Ash's lips tugs up. "It's good to be here," he says after a moment.

It really is.

Ash left his phone off and in his backpack, and I turned mine off not long after I called my parents after dinner to let them know we arrived safely.

"Are you holding up okay?" I whisper.

Ash lays his damp head on my bare chest and breathes in. He trails warm fingertips over my stomach, making goosebumps erupt in their wake.

"I'm better now that we're here. Now that yesterday is over."

"You did it, Ash," I murmur into his ear.

He looks up at me with an agitated scowl. "Would have been a lot better if I'd done this years ago. I don't know how you put up with me."

I rub his chin with my thumb and shake my head. "What's the saying? Better late than never?" Ash rolls his eyes. Sometimes my eternal optimism annoys him, but I don't care because he's mine and we're in bed together, and in the morning when I open my eyes, he'll be curled up next to me.

We kiss and touch for a long time until we both drift off into dreamland.

CHAPTER THIRTY-THREE

It's been a week since we left D.C., and sometimes I wish we were still at Mike and Miranda's. Somehow, their little slice of the city seemed to be out in the middle of nowhere, and the sleep I got for those couple of nights was the best I'd gotten in years.

The D.C. show had been stressful. Some people in the audience had to be hauled away by security because they kept shouting about Lizette and I. Thankfully, I couldn't hear most of the screams thanks to the music, but each time I gathered bits of what they said, the more overwhelmed I became.

For the most part, the tabloids have calmed down over the broken engagement. It's liberating to be able to go on my phone and not be bombarded by notifications. But now it's time to meet with Pete from our label.

In five minutes, to be exact.

Unfortunately, that means that Mike and I are back in L.A. Drew is with his family in Virginia for the weekend, and I'm glad for it, albeit a bit jealous. As we sit in the waiting area of P.G.B. Records, Drew and I text back and forth.

When my phone vibrates, I open Drew's text to see a picture of him, his mother, and his father sitting together in the well-loved dining room. His mom holds up one of their most recent rescue dogs, a small chihuahua in the process of re-growing its hair after being in a hoarding situation. His dad holds up their overweight Russian Blue, better known as Thunderbolt, and my boyfriend is as handsome as ever with his untamed curls peeking out from underneath a baseball cap and his signature, crooked smile spread across his face.

I save the picture to my photos right as Pete's assistant calls us back. It feels like an eternity has passed by the time we make our way across the massive expanse of the room and into the hallway beyond.

The slacks I wear feel a little tight around the waist, and the buttons of my shirt feel suffocating as well, like they're digging into my flesh. I swallow down the giant knot in my throat as Pete's assistant opens the door to his office.

In the eight and a half years since we met Pete at the show we played at The Antidote, he's hardly changed. His hair is shorter, now reaching above his shoulders rather than falling down his back, but other than that, time has been good to him. Pete walks around from the side of his standing desk and greets us with open arms as soon as we walk in.

"Mike! Ash!" He beams. "So good to see you. Drink?"

The assistant looks at us with a well-rehearsed smile on her glossy lips.

"Water, please. Thank you," Mike says.

"Make that two. Thanks."

Pete motions for us to sit down on the couches he has set up in front of his desk. I plop down on one of the red sofas and cross my ankles, forcing myself not to bounce a foot while we speak. Mike takes a seat next to me while Pete perches on the couch next to us. As we exchange pleasantries, Pete's assistant comes back with a pitcher of water and three pristine glasses. She pours us all a cup and then takes her leave.

As soon as we're alone, Pete takes a sip of his water and asks, "So, what brings two of my favorite men here today? It's a long way from New York." He chuckles. "I figured you'd want to meet via Zoom or FaceTime as usual, so this is a delightful surprise."

Mike shakes his head. "Some things are better done in person, don't you think?"

Pete nods. "I suppose so."

Mike looks at me, and I know that's my sign to open my mouth and talk, but as soon as my lips part, I freeze up like maybe they'll forget I'm here if I sit still long enough.

"Are you okay, Ash?" Pete asks, leaning in. "Whatever it is, we're all friends here. Though I must admit, I was a bit taken aback by the news of your broken engagement." His lips turn down and his brow furrows.

"Well," I choke. Immediately, I lunge for the water in front of me and take a long sip. Before I continue, I think about the picture Drew just sent me; the happiness that's written all over his face. It might suck to be me right now, but it'll suck much, much more if I don't come out with it already. I look down at my shoes and blurt out, "I had to break things off with Lizzy. Because. Well, because I'm—gay."

Pete stares at me and Mike pats my knee in encouragement. Even the Xanax I took ahead of time to get me through this meeting has lost its effect now that we're here.

"Gay?" Pete sounds out the word like it's something he's never heard of.

"Gay," Mike and I confirm.

Pete blinks rapidly, like he's trying to clear something from his line of vision. He opens his mouth to speak, then snaps it shut like a snapping turtle. "I'm not sure I know what to say about that." He holds up his hands defensively. "Not because I'm against it, or anything—"

"But I was with a woman. Publicly," I finish his train of thought. It's what everyone else has said, too. Freddie Mercury was with Mary for a long while before that ended, too. People also seem to forget all about Elton John's ex-wife. The list of gay men who were in heterosexual relationships before coming out could go on for miles. Maybe it's shocking that people are still closeted in the twenty-first century, but I'd be willing to bet there are more closeted people in heterosexual marriages and partnerships than anyone cares to admit. Maybe one day it won't be like that anymore.

At the end of the day, it's terrifying to come out after I've made an image and a name for myself. The idea that everything I've worked so hard for could shatter overnight is what kept me back from coming out and admitting the truth to myself for so long, despite my love for Drew.

I've always feared that if I came out and our fans didn't approve, maybe I'd go back in time and wind up in the trailer with my parents again, where they'd throw ashtrays and beer bottles at me while calling me all the horrible homophobic slurs they could think of.

It had never stopped them before, and that was long before I knew I liked men.

The thumping in my heart speeds up. I close my eyes tightly and picture Drew's smile as I force the memories of my childhood out of my mind.

"I know it's a little shocking, to say the least. But it's not uncommon, either, when you look at the music industry just in the last few decades." My voice shakes, but I continue. "We're here today because —well, I don't want to live a lie anymore, Pete. It's been a decade of hiding who I am. I realize it would have been easier if I'd been upfront from the very beginning." I pause and look at my hands which are tightly clenched in my lap. "Truthfully, I was too scared ten years ago. Shit, I'm *still* scared. But I don't want to live a lie anymore."

Mike leans over to me and squeezes my shoulder. His act of affection eases my tension a little, even when Pete says nothing. My internal organs tighten up more and more as the seconds tick by in silence.

Mike must feel the awkwardness in the air, too. After he removes his hand from my shoulder, he leans over to face Pete. "What are you thinking?"

Pete runs a hand through his hair and shakes his head. "I'm shocked, I guess. I wondered why you two would be flying out for a meeting, but I thought it had to do with the engagement or a new project—this—this wasn't on my radar at all." Pete chuckles and shifts in his seat. "So, you want to come out, and you want to know where to go from here?"

Mike and I nod in unison.

Pete blows out a long breath. "We can figure something out. It's been a little while since the break up now. I haven't been paying attention to it online. Has it died down for the most part?"

"Yes," Mike says. "The tabloids have moved on to another Kardashian scandal or something." He throws his hands in the air, making it seem like he has no idea about it, but I know damn well that he watches the Kardashian shows on longer flights.

Pete nods. "Okay. What are you thinking, Ash?"

"I'd like to do an interview."

Pete arches a brow, and Mike looks at me in surprise. I haven't mentioned to him that I've been in contact with a few journalists in the past week.

"An interview with whom?" Pete asks.

"*Rolling Stone* or perhaps *Mojo*. I'm also currently in contact with a journalist at *GQ*. Obviously, I'd like both of your opinions before I move forward."

Before Pete can intercept, Mike looks at me and asks, "Which would *you* be most comfortable with?"

I consider his question carefully. I'm grateful that he gave me the space to think about it before Pete told me his thoughts, because I know he'd probably prefer *Rolling Stone*.

"I think I'd feel most comfortable with the journalist from *GQ*. They would want to do an extensive photoshoot as well, but I'm okay with that."

Mike nods. "*GQ* it is. Sound good, Pete?"

247

Pete stares at Mike, dumbfounded. I have a feeling Pete isn't used to being talked to so casually anymore. Ever since his father retired, Pete has unfortunately grown a large head.

"When would the interview be?"

"Soon. Their original cover story slot fell through a few days ago. That's why I was approached by the journalist in the first place." I never would have considered reaching out to *GQ* on my own, and when the journalist, Jason Ambrose, hit me up, I was shocked.

Pete nods again. "Okay. Well, I guess that's what we'll do. The only thing I will say is this—and it's just to err on the side of caution." Pete takes a sip of water and wipes at his forehead. "If this goes south after the interview, we might have to... reevaluate."

Reevaluate. I mull the word over in my head.

After an awkward silence, Mike crosses a leg over a knee and asks, "Are you saying you'll drop the band if there's backlash?"

My breathing hitches. *Seriously?* I knew it was a possibility, but I didn't think Pete would consider not renewing our contract almost immediately.

Pete holds his hands up in the air, as if in surrender. "Let's not jump to any conclusions. You both know how near and dear April Renegade is to me." He places a hand over his heart, and I'm overcome with the sudden urge to punch him. "But we need to see how this goes over with fans. I would never in my wildest dreams *want* to not renew the contract, but if this doesn't go over well, we'll have to meet again and talk logistics."

There isn't much more to discuss after that. Mike and I say our goodbyes and are led out of his office.

"Is it me, or did his 'not wanting to renew the contract' sound a whole lot like he *already* made that decision?" I ask Mike as soon as we get into the car.

Now that the meeting is over, we're hauling ass back to the East Coast, more than ready to get out of California.

Mike runs his hands down his face. "What a *fucker.*"

CHAPTER THIRTY-FOUR

Despite how the meeting went with Mike and Pete, the band unanimously told Ash to do the interview with *GQ*. Pete didn't exactly say no, but from what I'd heard about the whole thing, he wasn't exactly cheering Ash on, either. Honestly, I'd noticed he'd become more self-absorbed and less understanding several years back. Still, I didn't think he'd be so black and white about our situation.

Now, a little over a week later, I stare at the brand-new copy of March's *GQ* with Ash on the cover. It was a giant, stressful rush to get the photos and interview finished on time, but they'd managed. Ash brought the magazine home with him several minutes ago, threw it down on the coffee table, and then hopped in the shower without a word. I knew he needed time to be alone, so I didn't ask him how he was feeling. Not yet.

I bite down on the inside of my cheek as complete lust overtakes me as I stare at my man on the cover. I know he was nervous as all hell throughout the shoot and interview, but I can't help ogling his tall frame in the photo as he poses in front of the camera dressed in a coral suit. The giant "GQ" letters are printed above the top of his head. He doesn't wear an undershirt, and you can see every defining line of his torso. His loafers are glitzed out and rainbow—because *of course* they are. Though, I must admit, the shoes go really well with the suit. There's no denying it. Ash is decked out in several rings alongside a statement necklace. They slicked his short hair back, somehow, and I'm impressed at how well the style suits him. I don't know how long I stare at the cover, but I vow to get it framed as soon as possible.

With a shake of my head and a steady drum roll in my heart, I flip through the pages until I reach the interview. I'm anxious as anything to read the extensive interview, but first, I want to look at the pictures beside it, because I obviously have no self-control.

Damn, they did good. In one picture, he's posed on a barstool and dressed up in something he'd wear on stage—he might not typically go for a yellow beanie, but it suits his complexion. In another, he's holding up a sign that says, "Say Gay!" above his head. The only article of clothing is a pair of sinfully tight, ripped jeans that probably cost more than my mortgage payment. Nonetheless, pride courses through me. After thinking he'd never come to terms with who he truly is, he did it. We still have a long way to go—announcing our relationship to everyone and dealing with whatever backlash he might receive after people get a hold of the magazine—but my heart flutters as all my love for the man taking a shower in the next room wells up inside my chest.

Finally, I turn my attention to the interview.

I asked Ash Lancing to do an interview with me regarding the recent break in his engagement with American model, Lizette Carol. What I didn't expect was for him to reply to me and provide me with the opportunity of a lifetime.

Ash and I met somewhere quiet—in fact, it was just at my office in New York City. He came in wearing a white t-shirt, skinny jeans, and shades. A lot of times, meeting with

rock 'n roll stars makes me nervous, but as soon as Ash sat down across from me in my seating area, I felt I'd known him for a long time. (No, I'm not just saying that!)

I decided to address the proverbial elephant in the room after we exchanged pleasantries. Ash was a little nervous. He tapped his booted foot up and down on the bohemian rug below us, so I blurted it out: "You're gay."

To my delight, my comment made him laugh. He nodded and leaned forward in his seat, eyes ablaze with a newfound freedom that only manifests when a person comes to terms with their true identity.

"I'm gay."

Over the next two hours, several cups of coffee, two bath-room breaks, and getting off the topic more than I care to admit, I asked Ash how he knew. When he knew. You know—the kind of things you'd want to ask a dear friend who's just come out to you.

Ash blew out a long breath and leaned back on the sofa. He looked out the window, down to the raging city below us and began. "Jason, I'm going to tell you something that a lot of people don't know about me." He took a long pause, almost like he was purposely letting the suspense build around us. I tapped my pen silently on my thigh and watched as the seconds from my recording app ticked up.

"I had a really shitty childhood. Like, really bad. My parents destroyed my stuff if I played music too loud. They were addicts–pills, alcohol, cocaine–pretty much anything they could get their hands on. They're probably still addicts; I don't know. Anyway, they called me horrible things. Typically homophobic, awful slurs, even though I didn't even *know* I was gay then." Ash paused for a moment and ran a hand through his hair, deep in contemplation. "I left at eighteen and never looked back. It took a great friend to make me realize what a true family looks like." He talked more about his parents for a while, but after a little back and forth, I agreed with Ash to focus on the here and now, and not his past.

Eventually, he got around to answering my original questions.

"I wasn't attracted to anyone until I was almost out of my teenage years. Sexually, I mean." The last part was said after a low chuckle. "I thought I was asexual, but in reality, it took a certain person for my sexual awakening to come. I don't know if it's because of the rough past or what, but being intimate with anyone, kissing, sex, all that? It wasn't on my priority list."

Ash shrugged and leaned forward, placing his elbows on his knees. "For too many years, I've hidden a very large part of what makes me, me. I locked it in a small box, buried it somewhere deep inside of me, and tried to ignore it. I thought it would be better that way. Honestly? I was scared. Hell, I'm still terrified out of my fucking mind to be sitting here with you, discussing this. But I have to. In order to be honest with my fans, and to be honest to myself, I have to come out to the world."

I realize that I'm crying, and I don't want to get my tears on the magazine, so I rub my eyes with my long-sleeve thermal and read on.

When I brought up his ex-model fiancée, he frowned.

He looked up at me and shook his head. "Lizzy deserves the world. For the rest of my life, the consequences of my actions and all that I've put Lizzy through will haunt me." Ash struggled to go on. He chewed on his bottom lip for a while, but finally resumed after a long sip of water.

"The thing is, I thought I could 'get over' being gay. Now I know, that's *not* how this goes. I dragged Lizette down with me in those delusions. Even after everything, after I told her I was gay, she allowed us to break off our engagement publicly in a civil manner. She didn't have to do that. Truly, she is one of the greatest people I've ever known. I hope you don't mind me saying during this interview how sorry I am. To Lizette, to her fans, and to my own. An apology doesn't count for much unless you back it up with your actions moving forward. I've learned that through a ton of trial and error. But I mean it."

Though it wasn't an easy topic to speak about, Ash and I continued on for a while after that. Finally, I asked him if he was seeing anyone now.

Ash raised a pointed brow in my direction and smirked. "That's a question that I'd better leave off as 'To Be Continued'..."

There are several more paragraphs to read, but as soon as I hear Ash turn off the shower, I place the magazine down on the couch where I was seated and rush to him.

Steam rolls out and into the hall as soon as I whip the door open. Ash is naked, placing the towel around his waist after using it to dry his hair. I pull him into me and cling to him. We end up on the bathroom floor cradling one another and crying. The magazine marks the end of a decade of secrecy and heartache, and in return, holds the promise of an entirely new beginning for us.

We stay on the floor until we're ready to emerge into our brand-new world.

CHAPTER THIRTY-FIVE

T he interview with Jason Ambrose had somehow felt like meeting up for coffee with a long-lost friend. I couldn't explain why I had a connection with him, but he was the kind of person who made me feel at home the second we shook hands. His office was comfortable and quaint, and I breathed easily through the topics he brought up.

After the interview, he told me that he was gay, too, and though he had been out for a long time, it was an honor to help me tell my story. It felt like too much respect after all I'd done to those around me—but I tried to accept his kind words.

That's something I'm trying to learn more each day: how to accept myself, accept the things I did that led me to the present, and to forgive myself. The forgiveness will take longer, but I'm trying.

After my issue of *GQ* was released, everyone went wild. People who didn't like or follow our music had a newfound interest in April Renegade. I was overwhelmed with the outpouring of love from other celebrities (Sir Elton John included). Most April Renegade fans seemed to support me, though a handful were taken aback by the news. Each day, I get more tweets, DMs, and letters encouraging me and thanking me for being brave. A few people messaged me and told me I'd given them the courage to come out to their friends and family. Those are the only messages I respond to, because I want those individuals to know that I see them, hear them, and support them.

Some fans dropped us without a second thought. It was expected. I'd done my best to brace for it—but, despite it being 2022 and all the progress that's been made to treat LGBTQ+ individuals with the acceptance we deserve, some people can't get behind it. It's been a hard pill to swallow. Instead of wallowing in the hate messages, I try to focus my attention and energy on those who do support me and the band.

Before the magazine was released, I texted Lizette and gave her a heads up. She didn't respond, but she did send me a message after reading the article. Despite everything I'd put her through, and the things Drew had told her, she told me she hoped I was happy; hoped that being out in the open gave me everything I always wanted. After that, it took me two hours to respond–I didn't know how to reply to her kindhearted well-wishes. I ended up sending her a long text of all my hopes and dreams for her, and ended it with how sorry I was, again.

I didn't get a reply. I didn't expect one, but I hope that she read it and knew I meant every word.

My parents evidently saw or heard my mention of them in *GQ*. They tried to reach out to me about it, and threatened to appoint legal counsel. "I'd like to see them fucking try," is all Drew said about that. I couldn't agree more.

As for Pete—well, we hadn't heard much from him, which either meant he was handling it okay, or that he was conspiring to break the news to us that our contract would not renew next year.

The magazine has been out for a little less than a week, and tonight we are set to have our final show of the tour at Madison

Square Garden. It's been ages since I've suffered such sickening stage fright. As I dress in my massive dressing room, it's hard to ignore the butterflies, moths, birds, and whatever other winged creatures flap around restlessly in my gut. I'm too afraid to take a shot or a Xanax or a puff off Sean's vape for fear of fucking up on stage, so I deal with it as best I can. My breathing exercises don't bring me much relief, so I try to focus on the fact that soon, this tour will be over, we will have some time to rest before we begin making new music in the studio, and tonight, after we exit the stage, Drew and I get to leave together and go home. To our home.

Tonight, I will wear something a little out of my comfort zone. The decision to do so isn't helping my nerves, but I'm going to stick with it. I was allowed to keep the blinged out rainbow loafers from my *GQ* shoot, so I said *fuck it* and brought them with me in the bag that housed all of my stage clothes. I paired the shoes with black skinny jeans with tears in the knees so severe that they almost ripped apart completely, along with a simple, white muscle tee covered. Over the tee, I threw on a black button-down. To top off the look, I put on one of Drew's beanies that I grabbed from his drawer before we left. It's worn in, and less of a vibrant orange in color than when he first bought it, but I think having a piece of him on my body tonight will help with my nerves—like a security blanket.

There's a knock on the door. "Come in!"

Drew comes in, looking hotter then ever, like pure sin. I wag a finger at him and turn back to look at myself in the mirror, adjusting the beanie on my head. "Don't come in here looking at me like that. I'm trying to stay calm, cool, and collected."

He stalks toward where I stand in front of the mirror, then brushes up behind me. Drew wraps his arms around my waist and kisses my neck. My body immediately responds; it has a mind of its own when it comes to my partner. Drew wears cut-off shorts stained with blue and white spatter paint, bright yellow Vans, and a long sleeve black t-shirt that I know will end up somewhere on the stage halfway through the show, if not before. My man gets hot when he's drumming. For once, he's not wearing a baseball cap or beanie, and I like it. His curls frame his face wildly, which makes him look like a devilish angel sent here to torture me with his good looks.

Drew's cocky grin fades as he turns me around to face him. "Are you ready, babe?"

He's been calling me babe, sweetheart, lover, and a string of other endearments since I broke up with Lizzy and officially become his, and *only* his. I love it—especially when we're in bed.

"As ready as I can be."

He spins me around and pulls me into his broad chest. We stay like that for a couple of minutes until we agree that it's time we get our asses to the stage.

Before we leave, Drew turns to me from where he has a firm grip on the door handle, and motions for me to come closer. I inch into him, and he kisses me tenderly. "You've got this. And I love you. Don't forget that."

I laugh against his lips. "I will never forget that, Drew. Ever."

He kisses me a little bit deeper before releasing me, then we leave the room, go through our "Before Show Checklist" with the rest of the gang, and run onto the stage like it's any other show.

The bass matches the vibrations dancing throughout my nerve-ridden body, but I force myself to focus on Drew's drumming, and that eases me into what I do best: I sing harder than ever before. I release all the pent-up, anxious energy from the past month into my performance. At one point during the climax of one of our faster songs, I stare up at the lights above us, and I think how lucky I am to be on this stage, right here, right now, with the love of my life behind me.

It's at that moment that I make one more bold decision.

There's no funny business during our break before our encore. Instead, I take the time to thank Mike, Drew, Sean, Brian, Trish, and everyone else nearby for supporting me. We hug and cry a little. Well,

Sean is the one who cries the most, but I swear I see Mike tear up at one point, too.

The encore goes harder than ever before. All members of the band and the audience sing alongside me. It's like all of our overlapping lifelines have interwoven and tied together, and it replaces my lingering doubts with a strong, energetic feeling of hope.

Once I'm in the crowd and surfing, I get a better look at the signs that surround me in the sea of people. *We love that you love freely, Ash! Say GAY! LGBTQ+ and PROUD! Stop the hate, love the gays!* The list goes on, and I can't help the tears that stream down my face. I cry alongside many in the audience and try my best to hold onto and squeeze each hand that I can reach while I'm among them. I blow kisses and fist pump, and they send them back to me.

When my feet are back on stage, my friends come stand next to me at center stage, right before our final bow. The crowd is screaming at the top of their lungs; I can hardly hear a thing. Confetti and smoke surround us in a cloud, and the music bumps and blares throughout the square.

Now's the time.

As the others bow, I keep Drew from doing so. I turn him toward me and take his face in my hands. I look him straight in his wide, shocked eyes and I devour him in a heated kiss more appropriate for the bedroom than on a stage in front of thousands of people. The crowd is silent for a millisecond, and then they go ape-shit crazy with cheers and screams that fill up the venue, almost overpowering the music. When Brian, Trish, and Sean come up from their bow, they jump all around us, hooting and hollering. Drew deepens our kiss and slides his tongue in, obviously incredibly fine with–and turned on by–my *very* public display of affection.

We break apart and beam at each other like it's the first night we met on that chilly April evening when his laughter changed my life forever.

Sean's face is littered with tears. He and Brian hug onto Drew while Trish clutches at my midsection. I reach for the mic that I'd abandoned before crowd surfing and bring it up to meet my lips.

"My name is Ash Lancing!" I scream into the mic. "I'm in love with Drew Dawson, and we love every person standing on this stage tonight! We're April Renegade! Good night, and rock on!"

THREE YEARS LATER

ASH

"I've never been so exhausted in my entire life," Drew groans.

One thing I've learned since adopting the twins is that Drew *does not* do well without his eight hours of sleep every night. For a rockstar, I'd expected more from him. I roll my eyes and take Amelia from his arms.

I cradle our baby girl in my right arm so that she's foot to foot with her brother, Averie. Our three-week-old infants are simultaneously the greatest things that have ever happened to us– as well as most tiring. We'd lucked out and found the perfect young couple to adopt from. The birth mother is Puerto Rican and white like Drew, and the father is fully Puerto Rican. We didn't care about ethnicity or gender (we *did* think there would only be one baby, but surprises happen), and the fact that the twins will learn about their culture by growing up in a part Puerto Rican family sat well with the biological parents–and with us.

As the due date crept up, we decided to ditch our brownstone in the city and move closer to Drew's parents—a decision we couldn't be happier with. Drew's mother was desperate to be closer with the kiddos coming, and it made sense for us to be in a more suburban area, which has granted us more peace and quiet away from most paparazzi.

We still live far enough away from Drew's parents to have some breathing room, but they're conveniently close by when we need them.

Like now.

Amelia refuses to sleep and Averie is suffering from tummy troubles. We're still trying to figure out—well—*everything* when it comes to parenting, but I hear it takes a while to adjust.

Drew leans back in the baby glider, closes his tired eyes, and moans.

My husband can be so dramatic.

As if on cue, there's a knock on our bedroom door, and Drew's mom tiptoes in, two burp cloths thrown over each of her shoulders. She's all rainbows and sunshine these days, basking in her new grandmotherly role. She's ecstatic that her son and son-in-law live so close after years on the road. Still, she respects our distance and is never overbearing. As always, she seems to know us better than we know ourselves. She can tell when we need a break, knows what to say and when to say it, and is forever our biggest supporter.

Drew and I got married a year after our big show at Madison Square Garden—my favorite show of all time. We got hitched at The Antidote, Leah and Jeff's venue.

Jeff was more than happy to let us have the wedding there and brought out his very special liquor stash for the occasion. Only our closest friends and family were in attendance. Brian and Trisha performed a gorgeous set of acoustic songs throughout the evening. Now that they're an item, I can't help but wonder when they'll bless us with gorgeous, talented kids one of these days—if they choose to, that is.

Our wedding was perfect and then some. Though I'd been a part of Drew's family for a long time, becoming part of the Dawsons officially on paper hit me in a way I wasn't expecting.

Out in the open with Drew, showing our love for one another to the world and no longer hiding, well, I was finally *home*.

We adopted the twins at the end of our fourth tour. Unsurprisingly, Pete wouldn't renew our contract once it ended. At that point, we all said good riddance. Laura Rose from Tidal Wave Records contacted us not long after, and even though we'd signed with Pete initially, she didn't hold it against us. When it came down to the two record labels, Pete was the right choice at the time, but now that Tidal Wave is more established, they extended their offer again. We signed without hesitation.

Drew's mother gently takes the babies from my arms, but I don't let her leave the room before giving my babies a peck on each of their little foreheads. Averie squirms and crinkles his squishy red face at my kiss while Amelia coos and sticks her tongue out. Their personalities shine through more and more as time goes on, and I love every second of our exhausting days and nights together.

I don't know how I deserve this life after everything, but I thank the universe that I have it every night before I allow myself to close my eyes and enter dreamland.

"Get some rest, *mijos*. I'm going to put them down for a nap and start on supper."

I grin as my mother-in-law leaves, always in awe of the love she gives.

"Come on, baby. Let's take a shower," I tell Drew.

Drew groans and peeks at me through eyes that are barely open. *"Nnnngh."*

I grab his hand and pull him up and out of the glider. I hold him tightly against me and nuzzle my face into his neck. I'm just as sleepy as he is, but he sure knows how to put on a show. "We both smell like spit up, and I can't even remember the last time we had a shower. Come on, we'll take one together."

Drew makes another unenthused, guttural sound before sluggishly moving with me into our large bathroom. He flops down on the toilet seat while I get the shower running.

"Has anyone ever told you how dramatic you are?" I tease as I take off my crusty t-shirt and slip my sweatpants off.

He nods. "You. Every day."

I snort and help him take his shirt off. With a heavy eye roll, he stands up and shimmies out of his pajama bottoms. I think he's worn them for three days straight, but I don't dare mention that.

Once we're in the shower, Drew immediately drops down onto the built-in bench and leans his head back once more, inhaling the steam. I swear his body improves with each year that passes—he's still muscular and defined, but with a little more weight on him in all the right places. He has a few more tattoos now–the most recent ones are of our children's names in a well-defined script, one adorned on each wrist.

I sit down next to him and kiss him deeply, turning his body to face my own. He moans, deep with arousal despite the exhaustion.

"What are you doing?" Drew mumbles.

"We have to find *some* time to get it on," I tease.

He laughs, which sends glorious tingles down my spine. "Don't we have the rest of our life for that?"

I nod. "But think how good our nap will be if I get you off first."

Drew's eyes come back to life. He bites at the corner of his bottom lip, right where his lip is. "I suppose you may be onto something there. But only if you top." He winks at me.

"You're too tired to top, aren't you?" I snort.

He leans into me and nibbles on my neck. "Absolutely."

"Whatever you want, baby."

I pull him onto my lap to straddle me. I kiss him deeply and feel him up for several long moments before moving to do anything else. The water envelops us, making our position almost uncomfortable, but we don't care about that–because we have each other, our babies, our family, and the rest of our lives ahead of us.

WANT MORE OF ASH AND DREW?

Click here to read Ash and Drew's steamy bonus scene.

ABOUT THE AUTHOR

B. G. constantly has several fictitious storylines playing out in her head. She aims to write diverse characters and storylines, with emphasis on those in the LGBTQ+ community and those who struggle with their mental health like she does. B. G. can typically be found chasing after her toddler while desperate for (more) coffee.

Look out for *A Mare's Nest* by B. G. Thomas, releasing October 1st, 2022.

f facebook.com/bgwolfeauthor

twitter.com/bgwolfe_author

instagram.com/author_bgwolfe

Made in the USA
Middletown, DE
31 January 2026

27795439R00165